FIRST
TIME IN
PRINT

LUCINDA, DANGEROUSLY

THE *demon* PRINCESS *chronicles*

NATIONAL BESTSELLING AUTHOR OF *LUCINDA, DARKLY*

SUNNY

"Fans of Laurell K. Hamilton
will love Sunny."
—*New York Times* bestselling
author Lori Foster

BERKLEY

$7.99 U.S.
$9.99 CAN

San Leandro Public Library
300 Estudillo Ave.
San Leandro, Ca. 94577

ISBN 978-0-425-22898-2

5 0 7 9 9

EAN

PRAISE FOR

LUCINDA, DARKLY

**2007 *Romantic Times* Reviewers' Choice Award Nominee
for Best Paranormal/Fantasy/Sci-Fi Erotic Romance**

**2008 Golden Quill Award Finalist in
Fantasy/Science Fiction/Futuristic**

"Once again Sunny has created an awesome story popu-
lated with endearing and sexy characters. This unabash-
edly sensual gothic story will feed your need for something
new and fresh."　　　　　　　　—*Romantic Times* (top pick)

"Lucinda and her men are scorching hot, and you don't
want to miss them."　　　　　　　　—*Joyfully Reviewed*

"*Lucinda, Darkly* has it all. Write on, Sunny, write on!
Don't miss any of this author's books, especially this one.
A very, very good read."　　　　　　　　—*Fresh Fiction*

"An emotionally intense, sexually charged, gothic romance . . .
Phenomenal! I would love to tell you about it—but I can't
and I won't. If you're in the mood for a different kind of
paranormal read that is superbly written, marvelously told,
and extremely sensuous, look no farther. *Lucinda, Darkly*
is the book for you!"　　　　　　　　—*Romance Reader at Heart*

"Exotic, erotic, and full of adventure and gripping action
scenes. What a powerful beginning to a new series. Talk
about coming out with a bang! Immensely addictive . . .
Sunny is an amazingly gifted author who knows exactly
how to grab her readers and bring them along for the ride."
　　　　　　　　—*Romance Junkies*

continued . . .

"[A] superb fast-paced urban fantasy in the tradition of Laurell K. Hamilton."　　　　　*—Midwest Book Review*

"One of those books that grabs you and won't let go! Such an incredible start to a series, *Lucinda, Darkly* simply has it all. Each turn of the page will take you step-by-step into this intricately fascinating world. Sunny's ingenious imagination captivates . . . Both erotica and paranormal readers alike will be engrossed by the story as Sunny introduces a place where pain brings pleasure and blood is an aphrodisiac."　　　　　*—Two Lips Reviews*

"*Lucinda, Darkly* is . . . spellbinding. Sunny tells a wonderful story that is very intense, emotional, and sexually charged about a demon dead princess who finds romance and a part of herself that she was missing."

　　　　　—Night Owl Romance

"Full of paranormal passion, Sunny's fast-paced first in a new erotic fantasy series, the Demon Princess Chronicles, introduces Lucinda, a six-hundred-year-old demon princess who's getting bored with her long unlife."

　　　　　—Publishers Weekly

"Sunny is a wonderful writer who has created characters that readers will demand to learn more about and who they will enjoy reading as the characters find their way to happiness . . . A captivating series."　　　　　*—A Romance Review*

PRAISE FOR

SUNNY AND THE MONA LISA NOVELS

"Tantalizingly erotic . . . seduces readers into the powerfully imaginative world of the Monère." —L. A. Banks

"A terrific debut sure to appeal to fans of Anne Bishop or Laurell K. Hamilton." —Patricia Briggs

"Darkly erotic." —Bertrice Small

"A seductive tale of magic and romance . . . Suspenseful twists . . . Heart-throbbing surprises . . . A haunting erotic fantasy series." —*Publishers Weekly*

"A pulse-pounding erotic adventure . . . Sunny creates a fascinating world that's violent and sexual."
—*Romantic Times*

"Oh my, Sunny, why have you addicted me? You awakened me to the world of the Monère and Mona Lisa, made a love for these characters bloom within me, and now you have me craving more and more of Mona Lisa and her extended family . . . A truly excellent read." —*Fresh Fiction*

"I have been impressed with the complexity of the series from the beginning and am amazed at the new threads that were woven into the whole in this installment. I cried myself silly when I read this and see that as a mark of a great writer, one who makes you feel for the people they have created." —*Fallen Angel Reviews*

"Wow! . . . Scorchingly hot and so incredibly touching."
—*Two Lips Reviews*

"[An] erotic fantasy saga." —*Midwest Book Review*

LUCINDA, DANGEROUSLY

SUNNY

BERKLEY BOOKS, NEW YORK

THE BERKLEY PUBLISHING GROUP
Published by the Penguin Group
Penguin Group (USA) Inc.
375 Hudson Street, New York, New York 10014, USA
Penguin Group (Canada), 90 Eglinton Avenue East, Suite 700, Toronto, Ontario M4P 2Y3, Canada
(a division of Pearson Penguin Canada Inc.)
Penguin Books Ltd., 80 Strand, London WC2R 0RL, England
Penguin Group Ireland, 25 St. Stephen's Green, Dublin 2, Ireland (a division of Penguin Books Ltd.)
Penguin Group (Australia), 250 Camberwell Road, Camberwell, Victoria 3124, Australia
(a division of Pearson Australia Group Pty. Ltd.)
Penguin Books India Pvt. Ltd., 11 Community Centre, Panchsheel Park, New Delhi—110 017, India
Penguin Group (NZ), 67 Apollo Drive, Rosedale, North Shore 0632, New Zealand
(a division of Pearson New Zealand Ltd.)
Penguin Books (South Africa) (Pty.) Ltd., 24 Sturdee Avenue, Rosebank, Johannesburg 2196,
South Africa

Penguin Books Ltd., Registered Offices: 80 Strand, London WC2R 0RL, England

This is a work of fiction. Names, characters, places, and incidents either are the product of the author's imagination or are used fictitiously, and any resemblance to actual persons, living or dead, business establishments, events, or locales is entirely coincidental. The publisher does not have any control over and does not assume any responsibility for author or third-party websites or their content.

LUCINDA, DANGEROUSLY

A Berkley Book / published by arrangement with DS Studios, Inc.

PRINTING HISTORY
Berkley edition / October 2009

Copyright © 2009 by DS Studios, Inc.
Excerpt from *Demon Forged* by Meljean Brook copyright © Meljean Brook.
Cover art: *Photo of Woman* by Phillippe Regard / Getty Images.
Cover design by Monica Benalcazar.
Interior text design by Kristin del Rosario.

All rights reserved.
No part of this book may be reproduced, scanned, or distributed in any printed or electronic form without permission. Please do not participate in or encourage piracy of copyrighted materials in violation of the author's rights. Purchase only authorized editions.
For information, address: The Berkley Publishing Group,
a division of Penguin Group (USA) Inc.,
375 Hudson Street, New York, New York 10014.

ISBN: 978-0-425-22898-2

BERKLEY®
Berkley Books are published by The Berkley Publishing Group,
a division of Penguin Group (USA) Inc.,
375 Hudson Street, New York, New York 10014.
BERKLEY® is a registered trademark of Penguin Group (USA) Inc.
The "B" design is a trademark of Penguin Group (USA) Inc.

PRINTED IN THE UNITED STATES OF AMERICA

10 9 8 7 6 5 4 3 2 1

If you purchased this book without a cover, you should be aware that this book is stolen property. It was reported as "unsold and destroyed" to the publisher, and neither the author nor the publisher has received any payment for this "stripped book."

To Jacky Sach,
brilliant copyeditor and talented wordsmith,
who has saved my ass many a time.

A true pleasure working with you on these two series.

ONE

THEY SAY YOU get wiser as you get older. I don't know about that. In my opinion, sometimes you just get dumber.

A Queen saw us and screamed. A Monère Queen garbed in the usual long black gown denoting her status. Like you couldn't tell by the feel of her presence alone. She took one look at the seven of us and let loose a wail of terror as if the Wild Hunt had spit itself out of Hell and come to hunt her.

It wasn't really her fault. But she was old enough to know better: close to three-quarters of a century, as far as I could tell. Then again, you could argue that I should know better also. I was over six hundred years old. Over seven hundred if you counted my other life before this, my Monère life— what I had been before I died and became demon dead. I lived in Hell now. Or at least I had before I was booted out due to circumstances entirely of my own making.

Those circumstances stood beside me now, cringing as
the young Queen screamed her silly head off—the two I
had bonded with. One was a demon creature as black as
night. No, I take that back, he was even darker. The entirety
of him was a charcoal shimmer of hair, skin, and eyes. No
whites in those eyes, just darkness against darkness. Talon.
My Floradëur, which literally meant flower of darkness.
A poetic name that aptly described his tall, willow-wand
slenderness, and the delicate features that edged over into
feminine prettiness.

On the other side of me stood my other bondmate, Nico,
the Monère warrior who had been intimately sheathed
inside my body when Talon had forged the bond between
us. The supernatural tie had accidentally linked all three of
us together. It had been like, *Oops, didn't know* that *could
happen*. Not just the three-way bonding, but that something dead could be tied to something living. We were
bound together now, the three of us, two creatures from
Hell and a living Monère. And not just a living Monère,
but a former Monère rogue—former because Nico was
mine now. Officially recognized as such by High Court,
where we presently were. Bringing us back to the screaming ninny at hand.

It wasn't so much Nico and I who upset her. Demon
dead that I was, I was a petite woman. Not too threatening in appearance, unless I wanted to be, which, trust
me, I wasn't trying to be at present. Nor was it Stefan—
beautiful Stefan, the Monère warrior who I loved—or his
human/Monère Mixed Blood ward, Jonnie, a young man
of eighteen. Nope. It was the last two of our group that
struck unholy terror into the Queen's heart and made her
raise up such a ruckus—Ruric and Hari. My royal demon
bodyguards.

Yup, royal. I was a princess, daughter of the High Lord of Hell, and sister of its current ruler, Prince Halcyon. I was Princess Lucinda. But it was an empty title really. The only thing I ruled over was the occasional wayward demon I had caught over the last few centuries while roaming this earthly realm. As a guardian, it had been my job to find them and drag them back to Hell before they wreaked more havoc.

Another problem—a big one—had been that my paternity had been called into question. But no longer. I had proven that I was the High Lord's daughter in a most indisputable way. And Daddy dearest had in turn sicced his two oldest demon guards on me. They were supposed to watch over me and keep me out of trouble. Hah!

Whatever my father's intentions may have been, they seemed to have backfired. One look at Ruric, and your instant gut reaction was to scream in terror.

Ruric meant *rock* in the old language, and that was exactly what he happened to look like—one great big pile of hardness. Massive not so much in height—he stood only an inch or two over six feet—but more in width and depth. A great hulking mass of muscles. His impressive physique alone would have made him intimidating, but it was the startling ugliness of his face that took your breath away—and not in a good way. His coarse, heavyset features were rough and brutal, his eyes deep-set and slightly uneven. He was ugly as none of the Monère were. Even the plainest child of the moon caught a human's eyes, and we had all been that once—Monère, supernatural creatures descended from the moon, blessed with her gifts. Ergo, those lucky enough to become demon dead afterward were usually blessed with pleasing looks. Not so, Ruric. He was exquisitely, revoltingly uncomely. He was also one of the last two existing demons, outside of my family, who carried the blood of the *drakon*. The dragon clan.

The other last existing demon of that almost extinct line stood next to him. Hari, who was handsome in a bad-boy, slithering-snake kind of way. Lean and mean, arrogant and abrasive, as dangerously mesmerizing as Ruric was ugly. The color of their skin was a lightly shadowed bronze, darker than even my golden hue because they had existed longer than I had in Hell. The only one cooked darker was my father, Blaec, whose skin shone a darkly burnished bronze after existing for over a millennium in our realm. Which put Ruric and Hari's age at greater than my six hundred years, and less than the High Lord's one thousand years of being.

Hari literally meant *clever like a monkey*. But if that was so, it was in a spoiled, infantile manner. He stood as tall as his clan mate, his sharp-bladed features curled into a snarling sneer. Not too handsome at the moment with that look of distaste distorting his face and casting it, well, more demonically.

We were an odd, assorted lot. But of everyone there, it was probably Hari, Ruric, and Talon who inspired such pure gut panic in the Queen. Hari and Ruric because they were exactly what they looked like—big, bad, demon predators. Talon because he was something she had never seen before—a creature of absolute darkness, as if he had been distilled from the very bowels of Hell. Of course, only someone who didn't know Hell very well would think that. There were much worse things than the lovely flowers of darkness.

"Shut up," I snapped. *My* instant gut reaction. Because the loud noise was not only embarrassing me but hurting my ears. She shut up. Not because she wanted to but because she had no choice. My verbal command, for the benefit of her guards who had all drawn their swords, and my even stronger mental one, had left her unable to do anything but obey me—one of the reasons why we demons were so feared. Not only for our greater physical strength but for the frightening psychic power we wielded. But, hey, you had to have some compensation for dying.

"Leave us," I told her, waving my hand. "Go away." It wasn't so much my shooing motions but the unheard mental command I issued again that had her and her men leaving us in great haste.

Running toward us, in their place, was a whole slew of other guards—official ones belonging to High Court.

We hadn't poofed out of thin air to appear in front of everyone, although their extreme reaction made it seem so. Nope. We'd arrived the usual way via the portal in the woods behind Halcyon's little cottage here at High Queen's Court. We had stopped at Halcyon's quarters, happily reunited with Stefan and Jonnie, and then all of us had walked like calm, civilized beings onto the walkway where our paths had crossed with that dim-witted Queen, who acted as if she had never seen a demon before.

To give her the benefit of the doubt, she probably hadn't. Most Monère didn't unless they came to the bi-monthly Council sessions and caught a glimpse of my brother, Halcyon. He was like me, not that intimidating to look at. Unfortunately, that couldn't be said of Ruric and Hari, who were intimidating even to other demons. And add to that the startlement factor of a midnight-black Floradëur.

But, come on. Most of the guards knew me. Or at least knew *of* me. I'd walked here quite tamely among them only a few days ago, and they had seen Talon then. But—memory kicking in belatedly—he had been a short, stunted thing at that time. Now he was as tall as Ruric and strikingly lovely, with his head in proportion to his body. I guess the change in him *was* rather startling. And one look at my two new demon bodyguards, with the Queen's terrified screams on top of that, which had to have really harried their nerves . . . and you had guards approaching us with drawn swords.

Exactly what I had wanted to prevent. A situation.

I tamped down my urge to command them all mentally as I had the Queen: *Put away your silly swords.*

I didn't, out of respect for the Queen Mother; these guards belonged to her. But my teeth ground together in irritation, and my fingers curled into half-claws at being treated like the dangerous predator that I was. How very impolite.

A voice called out that I recognized. "Hold, men! Sheath your swords. It's Princess Lucinda." Captain Gilbert coming to the rescue. Not of me, but of his men. The well-trained guards obeyed their captain and put away their swords.

Captain Gilbert strode forward, and if his eyes were a bit wary as they swept over Ruric and Hari, they warmed up quite nicely as they came to rest upon me.

"Princess Lucinda," he said. Bowing, he pressed a kiss to the back of my hand, his mustache lightly brushing my skin. He was one of the few men I allowed to touch me in such a manner because of a genuine liking for the man. And, okay, because he had been my willing and eager blood donor the last few times I'd been here.

"Welcome, Princess. We weren't expecting you back so soon," Captain Gilbert said. For good reason. I hardly ever came here. Maybe only once or twice a century, if even that. Now I'd put in three closely spaced appearances, the last one only days before. Days that seemed to have wrought quite a change at High Queen's Court. It had been quietly tranquil then. Now it was overflowing with people.

"Is Council in session?" I asked in surprise.

"A short, perfunctory one, yes," Captain Gilbert said. "Is that not why you are here?"

I had taken Halcyon's seat on the Council a short while ago when they had called that special session to question Mona Lisa over the death of another Queen. Halcyon had been too weak to do so. He had still been recovering from the violation that dead Queen had dared inflict on him. I had gone in his stead because the only other person who could have substituted was the High Lord himself. But my father had been the one who had actually killed the Monère Queen after she had broken one of our greatest taboos, and was recovering himself from his recent trip to the living realm exacting his revenge. I'd gone because there had been no one else to go. Otherwise I stayed far away from Monère politics. I was the least civic-minded demon in my family. Halcyon had been raised up in that tradition and swam the political waters well in both realms. I didn't. I didn't give a damn. I'd had no ties, no interest. Now I was loaded abundantly with them—five people who suddenly belonged to me now, for different reasons. Why I was here.

"No," I said in answer to his question. "I've come to see the Queen Mother on another matter. A personal one."

The captain's gaze flicked past me, and polite demon that I was—while at High Court anyway—I made the introductions. "Captain Gilbert. You've already met my other men: Talon, Nico, Jonnie, and Stefan."

The captain inclined his head and they politely nodded back.

"The two new demons are Ruric and Hari, royal body-guards my father has assigned to me."

"Are you in danger, Princess?" Captain Gilbert asked, his gaze becoming even more sharp and alert.

"There is a rogue demon at large—one of the things I have to speak to the Queen Mother about. Until he is captured, Ruric and Hari will be at my side."

"A rogue demon?"

"Yes. Derek, a former guardian."

Even greater worry filled the captain's eyes now. A rogue demon was reason enough to be anxious. They targeted humans—much more plentiful and easier prey. But nothing was as sweet and powerful as Monère blood. There had been slaughters in the past, entire territories wiped out when wayward demons found their way into this other realm and glutted their thirst on Monère blood; incidences almost unheard of now due to the presence of demon guardians.

A rogue demon was easy enough for a guardian to deal with. But a former guardian going rogue . . . Well, Captain Gilbert had good reason to be alarmed.

He was in a pickle, the good captain was. Common sense dictated that he report this immediately to the Queen Mother, who ruled High Court and was the ultimate authority over all the Monère on this continent. Common sense also dictated that he not let me or any of the other demons out of his sight. Nor could he risk bringing me and my new demon bodyguards into the Queen Mother's presence, not when the captain's whole purpose was to protect her. What to do? And who to dispatch with carefully worded news of our arrival?

Captain Gilbert was saved by the arrival of Lord Thorane. The Council Speaker's familiar authoritative presence and warm smile was a relief to both the captain and me.

Lord Thorane greeted me with a low bow. His eyes took note of the two new demons looming beside me, but he didn't seem overtly alarmed. "Princess Lucinda. Your return is most welcome. But the timing could have been better."

"When the Council is not in session, you mean?"

"It's the Lunar New Year," he said, shedding much light and great dismay over me. Oh! So that's why so many people. Of all the days to return, this had to be one of the absolute worst: when High Court was packed with thousands of Monère gathered to attend the holiday festivities.

"So much for trying to see the High Queen," I muttered. The presence of not just one but three demons here at High Court—two of them highly threatening, unknown entities—would send all the Monère into a panic.

I glanced surreptitiously at the two demons by my side to see if there might be any way to part them from me. Ruric returned my look with a slight frown while Hari looked amused. The mocking laughter in Hari's eyes, however, did nothing to hide the steely message in them. *Don't even think of it, Princess. Wherever you go, we go.* Ruric *looked* like the greatest threat, but appearances, as I quite well knew, could be deceiving. Hari, to me, was the one to watch out for, the less predictable one.

Nope. Separating me from them here was not going to happen, which left me with the idea of trying to soften their appearance. Ruffles and lace popped to mind for some ridiculous reason, and my lips curved in sly amusement. Which wiped the smirk off Hari's face and replaced it with a wariness I was much more comfortable with.

Lord Thorane cleared his throat. "The Queen Mother

has put her private jet on standby, in case you should happen to return during this busy time." No need to say where to. I had no other place to go to other than my small territory. And no need to say when. It would be now, of course.

"We'll be happy to escort you there now," he graciously offered, confirming what I already knew: that the sooner we were gone, the better. Our presence here in the midst of the New Year celebration could only cause disruption, if not outright panic. Not the sort of demon diplomacy my father would have encouraged.

"Our luggage?" I asked, though in truth it was only just what Jonnie and Stefan, and Hari and Ruric had brought. We had left their things at my brother's cottage. Talon, Nico, and I had nothing other than what we wore.

"My men will transport your luggage down to the plane," Lord Thorane assured me, and led us discreetly away to a back lot where two vans were waiting for us.

"Three demons, one black Floradëur, two Monère rogues, and a Mixed Blood whisked away from sight in under two minutes. Now that's true magick," I said dryly once we were seated and on our way to the private air-strip. Hari sat in the back, while Nico, Talon, and I took the middle row. Lord Thorane was seated in the front passenger seat beside the driver. Ruric, Stefan, and Jonnie followed behind in the second van.

"The Queen Mother holds you in great esteem and the highest regard," Lord Thorane carefully returned. "Indeed, she looks upon you with deep fondness. And those feelings, and respect, extend to your men as well. She does not see you as mere categories," he said, softly chiding.

"I know. I'm sorry," I said, apologizing. "I just wish I could have seen her. But I can tell you everything just as easily." And I proceeded to relate to him how my father and brother had hunted for Derek down in Hell, but hadn't been able to find and apprehend the rogue demon. Derek had tried to end my afterlife, and had almost succeeded in doing so. "We've already spread the word to the other guardians," I told him, "and they'll be on heightened alert until he is caught."

"As will we. So that's why your father assigned you bodyguards," Lord Thorane said thoughtfully, glancing back curiously at Hari.

Belatedly, I introduced Hari to him.

Lord Thorane's eyes lit up. "A true pleasure to meet you," he said to Hari. "Is Ruric the other demon guard?"

"You know of them," I said with surprise.

He nodded, looking quite delighted. "Yes, I have indeed heard of the last two great warriors of the dragon clan. The Queen Mother's regret at missing you will be even keener with this news."

"We'll be around. I'm sure we'll have a chance to see her later." I was certainly going to be spending a lot more time topside in this realm.

The jet's engines were already primed when we arrived. And our luggage arrived three minutes after we did. In a surprising short order of time, we were in the air, hurtling toward Arizona, our new home.

Two

Sitting in an airplane was an uncomfortable dichotomy. You both accomplished something with great speed, and at the same time had nothing to do while all this vast distance was being covered. It gave me time to be nervous, and not enough time to do anything about it. No time to call ahead like I had planned, to arrange cleaning of the house.

Welcome home. To cobwebs and Goddess knows what else.

I'd intended to keep my little group at High Court for a couple of days while I had everything cleaned and freshened up. Well, that plan had been nixed, and we were traveling faster than I wanted, or was ready for, to my tiny province in Arizona.

With nothing else to do, I made my way to the cockpit and had the pilot place a call through to Donald MacPherson, a human who had unknowingly been in Hell's employ for—what was it now?—almost twelve years. He took the news that I would be arriving in Arizona in a few short hours and expecting to stay at the house with a calmly murmured, "I'll try to have the power and telephone turned on before you arrive, and arrange for housecleaning the next day."

I rattled off the last known location of my car and asked him to arrange to have it delivered to me. Then I asked him to do the same for Stefan's car. Silence greeted him after I gave him the make, model, license plate number, and airport parking location—details I had committed to memory. I almost smiled, picturing the precise little Scotsman frowning and wondering how to ask his next question.

My voice smoothed into a lazy purr of amusement. "Don't worry. I'm not stealing the car. The car's owner will be staying with me at the Arizona property. Just have it towed there," I told him, and ended the call.

"That was very kind, arranging the delivery of my car," Stefan said when I sank back into the cabin seat across from him. We were speeding toward our new home in padded leather and gleaming burlwood luxury. Which kind of sucked because the contrast between this moneyed plushness and the barren home that awaited us was going to be real stark. The thought was enough to make me almost bite my razor-sharp nails. "But I would have made my own arrangements when we arrived. When I knew the address," he went on to say.

"My fault you had to abandon your car." The thought of all that he had been willing to give up and leave behind for me softened my eyes and muffled the anxiety for a moment. "Only right that I take care of recovering it for you." It surprised me, as it always did, that this beautiful, living, breathing creature would want me . . . desire me.

Dark liquid eyes stared back at me without any of the fear I usually inspired in other Monère—what dead demons usually inspired in the living. I'd been a little fearful of Stefan's reaction, returning with two demon males in tow, but all I'd seen had been relief in his eyes at my safe return. He hadn't known if he'd ever see me again; if we would even survive the trip.

"You're nervous," Stefan said. "There's no need to be."

"You haven't seen the house yet," I warned. "It's been a couple of years since I've stayed there." The recent hop in and out of my province to snag Nico, who at the time had been a rogue warrior I'd been sent to catch and then ended up keeping, didn't really count. "It's not going to be a pretty sight without any time to get it cleaned up beforehand."

"A couple of years? I thought it was your home here."

I hitched one shoulder in a shrug. "It's just a small province carved out between two territories that High Queen's Court awarded to me thirty years ago for my long centuries of services." I had spent almost five hundred years roaming this realm, guarding both demon and Monère interests—although the latter was more of a happy afterthought that coincided with my messy cleanup of bad and naughty wandering demons. "It's not so much a home as a neutral area where I can land occasionally without making people nervous. Don't get me wrong. I'm as territorial as any Queen. No Monère comes into my province without my permission." I'd made that crystal clear by dismembering the first two offenders and sending them back to their respective Queens when they had unwisely infringed across my borders. "But it's usually years between my visits."

"Then you must have other places you stay."

"Each Queen maintains a place, by Council rule, for passing guardians. Usually a small apartment on the fringe of their territory."

Unlatching his seat belt, Stefan stood and crossed over to me. "Come on," he said, pulling me to my feet.

"Where are we going?" I asked, bemusedly following him. The private jet was roomier than most, but still there was only so much space in a plane.

"We're switching seats," Stefan announced, and stopped in front of where Jonnie, his ward, was sprawled out across a long couch, capable of sitting three across, watching a movie on a small handheld machine. Across the aisle from him, Talon and Nico sat facing each other in the same coupled arrangement as the rest of the plane.

"Sure, no problem," Jonnie said, rising to his feet with careful movement, reminding me that he was still recovering from a bullet wound. He winked at me and made his way to the seat Stefan had vacated.

Unbelievably, I blushed.

Stefan sat and pulled me down beside him. We ended up looking straight at what should have been Talon's and Nico's profiles, only their faces were turned, watching us. Everyone in the cabin was.

"You're nervous, tense, and tired," murmured Stefan. "Close your eyes, and lay your head down on my shoulder. Try to rest."

Surprisingly, I followed his gentle orders, savoring the closeness—his arm around my shoulder, my feminine softness resting against his masculine hardness. For the first time in days, I relaxed. No questions. No answers I had to give.

He offered me peace, a brief respite in the mad and unbelievable complexity my existence had suddenly taken on—a chance to rest. And so I did with a soft sigh.

All else could wait. I was exactly where I wanted to be.

THREE

H ARI COULD SCARCE believe his eyes. But he could not discount his senses, and all of them told him that Lucinda, his Princess, his dragon queen, slept. Her body was soft and relaxed, trusting against the Monère warrior who held her so tenderly. They should not have fit so easily—so comfortably—together, a demon dead and living Monère. But they did.

The way she looked at him and the way he looked at her. The way he held her . . .

She cared for the two who were bonded to her. But this man she cared for in a deeper, different way. In this man's arms she could sleep peacefully. Allow herself to be gently ordered by him. With this man she was docile. Even sweet.

As necessary as Nico and Talon were to her well-being, this man was even more essential to her. Just because a

demon's heart did not beat, didn't mean he did not have one.
Demons were by nature more callous, hardened, and cruel.
It took something unusual to touch their hearts. But then
this man was far from usual. He was a warrior, Hari could
tell by the weapons he carried, by the fluid way he moved
and saw everything. Another ex-rogue, by Lucinda's comment to Lord Thorane. And he was beautiful, like a bright,
glittering star cast against the black canvas of the sky, his
skin pale perfection, his hair as raven dark as the shadows that framed the moon's luminous glow. With quietly
intelligent eyes, dark winged brows, and a lover's sensuous
mouth, he was lovely, exquisite, even among the beautiful
Monère. But it was the strong character in that handsome
face that made him truly special: the quiet confidence, the
gentle command, the *goodness* that radiated out from him
like a core of light, evidenced by his caring, considerate
actions. He made softness and gentleness strengths instead
of weaknesses. Even more curiously, he did not act like a
normal Monère warrior, subservient and submissive to his
Queen, fearful of her. He acted like an equal. And Lucinda
treated him as such.

There was an . . . affection among this group that
stretched to include even the young Mixed Blood, one
much lesser in strength than all the rest.

Hari wondered how Ruric was faring in this new strange
environment. Wondered if his brother demon felt as awkward and coarse and ill-fitting as Hari did among these
people. Like a clumsy, rough brute set down to play with
fine china. It wasn't so much the disparity in strength, but
the friendly and nice way they treated each other.

The last things demons were was nice!

He and Ruric had spent their entire afterlife existence in the High Lord's service, living in rough service

barracks filled with the fiercest, toughest warriors Hell had to offer, and being the most feared and most dangerous among them. Now they were thrown into the living realm to guard the Princess, her two living—and therefore fragile—Monère lovers, a soft and gentle Floradëur, and a weak Mixed Blood boy.

Hari had signed up willingly for this. He really, unbelievably, had. But he hadn't known what he was getting into. Hadn't known that the greatest, most immediate threat to those he was supposed to protect would be himself—his vicious temper and equally vicious mouth. Not just the deadly fangs but the rough words that came readily spilling out all the time without thought. He was a dangerous demon bastard who liked to fight, wench, and drink. A loner. Not even Ruric was his friend—he didn't have friends.

He had only served two things in his afterlife—the High Lord and himself. And not always in that order.

He remembered the exact moment when that easy, unthinking rhythm of his selfish existence had changed and his priorities had reordered themselves. It was when he had seen the impossible happen. When Lucinda had magickally transformed into a dragon.

All the lies Hari had believed—that she was not of the High Lord's blood but a bastard child foisted on him; that she was not truly *drakon* . . . the only other thing in this existence that meant anything to him, other than himself— all these lies were proven false.

Hari had treated Lucinda as he did any others not of dragon blood, with sneering disrespect. He flushed, remembering the way he had crudely propositioned her, and how furiously angry he had been when she had spurned him, and how, only by Ruric's intervention, he had not damned himself further. Only now did he feel the bite of shame. Before, she had been just another female piece of meat to him, and one too hoity-toity for her bastard blood. Now she was not only the proven High Lord's true daughter, she was the last precious female dragon of their kind.

Why had she allowed him to be one of her guards?

Hari pondered that frequently. He knew she didn't fully trust him; rightfully so. Even Ruric, with his hulkish, brutal ugliness, fit in better than he. Ruric was fiercely loyal to the High Lord, whereas Hari had served the High Lord because he had been the most powerful, most deadly demon; and because he had been the last full-blooded *drakon*.

Hari's musing came to an abrupt halt as Stefan's eyes intercepted his from across the cabin, with Lucinda's sleeping form softly draped against him. As their gazes locked, Hari wondered what the Monère saw on his face. Threat? Challenge? Or safety and protection?

A polite acknowledging nod from the former rogue, and their eyes broke apart. Despite himself, Hari felt grudging respect rise up in him for the other warrior. An ingratiating smile, any gesture of eager friendliness on the Monère's part, would have lowered the other man in the demon's esteem. The slight nod had been a gesture of respect from one equal to another. And he had broken eye contact before it could turn into a dominance challenge. Lucinda had entrusted her heart to a smart man.

Had Hari been a better man—a better demon—he would have been happy for her. But he wasn't. Because being with Lucinda, being with *them*, somehow made him want to be more. To be better.

It was something either to laugh at . . . or weep over.

FOUR

THE HOMECOMING WASN'T as bad as I thought it would be. It was worse. As the two taxis that had brought us here drove away, I tried to see the place like someone seeing it for the first time might view it. Unfortunately, I had a very easy time doing so. It looked dismal and depressing. Abandoned, uncared for.

The house was a nondescript brown composed of tan vinyl siding, some shutters hanging crookedly, and a brown tile roof. A simple rectangular box like most of the properties in the area, ranch-style, single level. Not as butt-ugly as some in the area, but no real beauty either.

Only the scattered green of a few juniper and piñon trees broke up the drab landscape. During the day, the vivid blue sky would add dramatic color, but now at night there was not much to brighten the sparseness of the land.

Making my way to the nearest tree, I sprang onto the

highest branch and retrieved the key I had hidden in a notch. Opening the front door, I flipped the light switch— that was something at least. MacPherson had gotten the electricity turned on. Not that it made it any better. Maybe worse.

A quarter-inch of dust covered everything. And the smell of stale air was mixed with the dank, musty scent of fur. I released a pulse of energy, unseen but clearly felt by all the insect and animal inhabitants that suddenly skittered noisily away, abandoning the building. A trick that made Jonnie gasp as they scuttled past him outside. Old droppings and new remained behind, evidence of their long residence here. Gee, I should have dropped by more often just to keep the place vermin free, if nothing else.

Sound and movement swung my gaze back around to see Jonnie and Stefan step inside, with Nico and Talon peering in curiously behind them. Ruric and Hari were nowhere in sight, but I felt their demon presence; one outside on the porch, the other making a wide sweep around the property.

I remembered the warm and comfortable feel of the apartment Jonnie and Stefan had left behind, and how sharply it contrasted with this derelict place. I didn't have to ask them how they felt about it. I knew.

"It's awful," I said, with a flat press of lips. "Nothing like the comfortable home you had to leave. I'm sorry."

"No need to apologize," said Stefan, slipping his hand into mine. It still surprised me how easily and comfortably he did that—held my hand like it was the most natural thing in the world. "You are opening up your house to us, giving us a place to stay." He squeezed my hand. "We can help you make it more cozy and comfortable."

"I'd like that," I said, wriggling my long, sharp nails. "I have lousy domestic skills."

"No problem," he responded easily, "I'm pretty handy in that area."

"And in quite a few other areas, too," I murmured, igniting a dark blaze in his eyes. Naughty me.

We spent the next four hours cleaning up the place and settling in, despite my telling them that a cleaning crew would be in the next day.

"Cancel it," Stefan said. "We'll be sleeping by then."

With a sigh, I did, waking MacPherson up at six A.M. to have him cancel the cleaning arrangements he had made. Dawn was breaking softly across the horizon by then. Windows that had been thrown wide open to air out the staleness were closed and locked back up, and heavy curtains drawn to block out the encroaching daylight. If nothing else, the house was well equipped in that regard. Every bedroom, not just the one I used, had the same heavy, lined curtains that threw the rooms into complete darkness.

Sunlight burned Monère skin, not instantaneously—it took time, several hours. It was also harmful to demons, only there was no pain for us. We could walk outside without feeling the burning discomfort Monères felt, but after several hours under the sun's rays, we cooked, too. Not the red-blisters-and-boils way they did, but in a more dangerous softening of our flesh, to the point where the barest press of a fingernail could split open our skin. There was also a dangerous leeching of our power, which was finite here in this realm. We had a limited amount, like batteries that carried only so much charge in them. Demons had to return to Hell to juice back up before their power got too low to make the return trip home. Sunlight was a definite drain on our power that we didn't need. Hence we slept during the day.

Four bedrooms had seemed too big for one demon. Now it seemed too small for the seven of us. Crap. How had we grown from one into seven in less than a week's time?

I had the master bedroom, which seemed a large waste of space for my small self when everyone else had to double up. But they refused to let me take one of the smaller bedrooms. The way it was set up, the master bedroom sat at one end of the house, and the other three bedrooms at the other end. The six of them would have to share one bathroom between them, while I had the master bathroom entirely, wastefully, to myself.

"Okay, decide how you guys want to double up," I said, leading them to where they would be sleeping.

Jonnie and Stefan chose the bedroom nearest the front entrance, while Ruric and Hari claimed the private corner bedroom. By default, Talon and Nico ended up in the bedroom next to Jonnie and Stefan. The bathroom separated their two rooms. Unfortunately, there was only one twin bed in each of the three bedrooms.

"One person is going to have to sleep on the floor in each room until I can get some more beds in," I said in apology.

"Don't worry," Nico said. "We have a roof over our head, a clean floor, now that it has been swept, and protection from sunlight. We'll be fine."

"Easy for you to say," I snorted. "You'll probably take the bed and make Talon sleep on the floor."

Nico winked and grinned. "You know me so well." At five nine, he was the shortest among my men and more stocky. Blond hair fell in a tousled wave over heather-gray eyes, his most stunning feature. The rest of his face was square-jawed and masculine. With a bold beak of a nose and cocky confidence, he was roguishly attractive in a rough and charming sort of way.

"I do not mind sleeping on the floor, Mistress," Talon said softly.

"Call me Lucinda," I said, reminding him gently yet again. Patience was not normally one of my virtues, but it was hard to snap at Talon. He had a delicateness to him not just of face and body but also of emotions.

"I'm sorry," he said with soft chagrin. "I forgot."

"That's okay, Talon. It'll take a while for all of us to adjust to things." Including me, I thought. *Especially* me.

"Yes, Lucinda." He said my name shyly.

I rewarded him with a smile, and left to hunt up bedding for everyone, my two bodyguards trailing like bronze shadows behind me.

There were enough sheets and blankets to go around but we were short two pillows, I discovered after a quick inventory.

"We'll have to go shopping for things later," I said, handing out what I had.

Talon took the sheets and blanket but declined a pillow, as did Hari.

"I understand Talon passing up a pillow, but why you?" I asked Hari.

The dark demon had been unusually quiet since we had arrived. I expected a smart, glib remark tossed back at me, something like him being too macho to need one. Instead he said, "It will be easier for me to go without than you."

Implying what? That he'd passed on a pillow because I would have ended up without one had he taken one? True, but not something I thought he would have been sharp enough to observe, much less care about.

"Okay," I said, only halfway teasing, "where did you bury the real Hari?"

The look he gave me was hard to decipher. No sneering arrogance in his manner, no crude joke. Just a somber and serious look that was almost unsure—which was something I was totally not used to from this quick-mouthed, foul-tempered demon. His voice, when he finally spoke, was bland without any inflection. "As you said, it will take a while for us all to adjust to things."

His careful words only confused me more.

He disappeared into his bedroom and I was left pondering the odd puzzle that Hari had suddenly become.

Stefan stepped out of his bedroom, his pillow tucked beneath one arm. "Are you going to your room?" he asked.

With all the others, I could be my usual insouciant self, but not with Stefan. His presence pulled out something soft and strangely womanly in me so that I almost melted in his presence. "I was going to turn in for the day," I said.

"May I join you?"

His request filled me with vivid yearning, but only for a moment. "The others . . . I can't erect a cone of silence," I blurted out, blushing yet again. Erecting the sound barrier for privacy would sever the bond between Nico and I, and he did not do well being cut off from me like that.

"I just wish to be with you," Stefan said. "Hold you and reassure myself that you are truly returned and safely here, and not something I just desperately dreamed up."

I held out my hand to him, and he came to me without hesitation. He seemed to have perfected the art of holding hands with a demon.

He sighed, and within my soul so did I, with happy, nervous contentment.

FIVE

LUCINDA WAS LIKE a dream come true to him. A dream Stefan had not even known existed. He had not lied when he said he wanted to touch her to convince himself that she was real.

She was dazzling to the eyes with her startling and striking face, voluptuous form, honey skin, and metallic gold shining hair—gossamer strands of unearthly beauty that spilled down her back in soft waves.

She was exquisite. Not in a soft way but a rather hard one, her eyes cool and glittering with dark sardonic knowledge, her smile thrillingly seductive and a little cruel, except when she was with them . . . with *him*. Then her hunter's cool, stealthy grace, and calm assurance faltered, disappeared, and in its place was a glimpse of woman's softness and vulnerability that few saw.

She was *his*, first.

Stefan shared her now with two others in a bonding he was excluded from. He didn't mind that—well, in truth, he only minded it a little. Stefan could share her as long as she loved him most. A rueful snort in his mind. Okay, as long as she just cared about him and wanted him. He was hers, anyway she wished to have him.

Color warmed her cheeks as they entered her bedroom. It delighted Stefan, that gentle blush. Chased away his uncertainty.

Yes, he thought with joy and relief, *she still wants me!* And the warmth of that knowledge filled him with giddy comfort.

"You must be tired," he said.

"Exhausted." But she just stood there in awkward silence, eyes dropped shyly to the floor.

The thought came to Stefan that perhaps he should give his lady some privacy to allow her to prepare for sleep. With her permission, he retreated into the bathroom and peered curiously around. But there was little to be learned of her.

Small liquid containers of natural, unscented soap sat on the sink and in the shower-bath, full and unused, like the kind you saw in hotels. A hairbrush, toothbrush, and tiny tube of toothpaste were laid neatly out in a drawer, everything new; the small trash can nearby held the discarded packaging. The storage compartment underneath the sink held a small supply of everything he had just seen, along with several rolls of toilet paper.

It was bland, functional, and impersonal. No strands of hair left on an old brush. Nothing to give away anything of the woman who stayed here on occasion. This was her property but it held nothing of her essence, nothing to indicate that it was a home to her. And that perhaps was the most revealing observation of all.

It was what she had said—a place she came to rarely. And everything she used was disposed of after she left, leaving behind no evidence of her stay. It had not been a home to her; just another anonymous stopping point at which she occasionally landed. This was the most permanent thing she had here in this realm, this small province of hers, and she had touched upon it lightly and infrequently.

But that was before, Stefan thought, taking a deep, calming breath. Before him. Before them, her new family. And as he had told her, he was blessed with handy domestic skills, something he had learned from taking care of Jonnie. They would help make this a true home for her.

Using a new toothbrush and small tube of toothpaste he found under the sink, he quickly brushed his teeth and washed his hands and face.

He returned to find her sitting on the bed, her clothes unchanged.

"I'll have to add pajamas to the list of things to buy later," she said, slightly embarrassed.

He opened his mouth to ask what she normally wore to sleep, then closed it as the answer occurred to him. Nothing. Just raw, bare skin.

He swallowed. Cleared his throat. "I have an old, comfortable T-shirt you can wear to bed if you like."

"That sounds nice," she said as she slipped past him into the bathroom.

Jonnie was lying in bed, eyes closed but not yet asleep.

"You sleeping here tonight?" he inquired drowsily, pushing himself up on an elbow as Stefan slipped back into the room.

"Nah, just grabbing some clothes." Not only for her but himself, too. He usually slept in the raw also. It looked like both of their sleeping habits were about to change. "Can I borrow two of your boxers?"

"Sure," Jonnie said, looking curious but asking no questions.

Stefan changed outside in the living room, and happily found that Jonnie's loose boxers were not as bad a fit as he feared. He hoped they would be as comfortable for Lucinda.

She was waiting for him when he returned, seated once more on the bed. The picture she made, a mix of fierce demon and shy, vulnerable woman, stole Stefan's breath away, as did the look in her eyes, as they traveled slowly, appreciatively, over the bare skin that his new T-shirt and boxers revealed. He had thought they covered him rather modestly, but the sudden flare of heat in her eyes made him feel as if he were walking toward her naked. His body reacted and he turned away, closing his eyes. "I'm sorry," he muttered, trying to impose rule over his suddenly unruly body. "Just give me a moment."

"Are the clothes on top for me?" She was there suddenly, standing in front him, even though he hadn't heard her move. Hadn't sensed her come near him.

He caught the twitch of her lips.

"Pleased, are you?" he asked.

She grinned openly then, showing that yes, she was pleased indeed as she took his offering of clothes.

"You're going to pay for that another night," he warned. And she laughed, a soft musical sound, her awkwardness gone now as if it had never been as she transformed into the sly and sultry seductress that she could slip so easily in and out of like a second skin. "Promises, promises," she purred. It was an enchanting sound, her laughter—her sudden relaxation.

"You are a witch," he said with a smile. "Go and change."

When she returned, it was his turn to run his eyes over her. My God, what she did to his old T-shirt! He had thought it would be too big on her, and it was in some ways: the shoulder seams fell halfway down her arms, and the hem reached down to her knees, so long that it hid the boxers underneath and made it appear as if that was all she was wearing. But dear blessed Lady, in other ways the fit was just perfect. The round, generous swells of her breasts were faithfully molded by the soft, stretched cotton, and he could see every quiver and bounce as she swayed her way over to him. Could see the mouth-watering outline of her nipples growing pebble hard beneath his avid gaze. His body roared with such a hot, aching blaze of need that he had to flop back onto the bed, gritting his teeth, as he tried to think of something else. Anything but how deliciously appealing she looked wearing his shirt.

The bed dipped down, and the mattress shifted as she crawled underneath the covers.

"You need another minute?" Her voice was not as innocent or as bland as it should have been.

He turned slowly to find, to his relief, that it was safe to look at her now. Her sinfully curved body was hidden beneath the bed covers. Only her stunning face, the gentle slope of her shoulders, and uncovered arms could be seen. Temptation enough. But much easier to bear.

"You're enjoying this, aren't you?" he said as he joined her under the covers.

She made a sound that was perilously close to a giggle. "I have to confess. It's hugely flattering."

"Nothing different than how any other male looking at you would react."

"But it's not any other male. It's you looking at me, reacting that way, that pleases me so."

"Lucinda." Her name came out a low groan. "Are you sure we can't . . ."

She bit her lip. "I'm sorry . . . the others. They would be able to hear us."

"Let them! The only one whose sensibilities I care to protect is Jonnie; he won't be able to hear us. The others should have more manners than to listen in."

"It's not so easy to tune things out when everyone is so close and no other sounds are being made," she said with soft regret. "Are you in much discomfort?"

"Come here." He pulled her into his arms.

"Won't that make it worse for you?"

"Not as bad as *not* touching you would be."

She lay curled against his chest. Her body, though, didn't relax.

"Does it bother you? Being this close to me?"

"A little. But like you said, it's not as bad as *not* touching you would be." She snuggled close, tried to find a more comfortable spot against his shoulder.

"I can go back to my room if it bothers you," he valiantly offered.

"Why?"

"My beating heart. Being so near my blood."

"Oh. That."

"Yes, *that*. Being so near your food. Are you hungry?" he asked. "Do you need to feed?"

She leaned back, leveled him a reproving glance beneath her lashes. "You are not my food; I don't think of you that way. And no, it doesn't bother me. Does it bother you, having my nails and teeth so near you?"

"Don't be silly," he said, and then grimaced. "I guess that applies to me also." Sighing, he pressed a gentle kiss to the top of her head, and pulled her back to rest against him. "I like being here, holding you like this. You feel so warm."

"You feel cool. And no," she said before he could ask, "it doesn't bother me. It feels good."

A few more heartbeats passed.

"Are you tired?" asked Stefan.

"Yes, but I don't think I can sleep right away. Can we talk for a little bit?"

"Only if you don't mind doing most of the talking. I thought you were going to return Talon to his people. What happened down in Hell?"

She explained while she lay there nestled against him, the complicated story of how they had tried to deliver Talon back to his kind, and had been violently surrounded and captured by the distrustful Floradëurs. How the bond had gifted her with the new ability to transform into dragon, and fly with the others on her back to safety.

Stefan's heart was pounding hard and fast by the end of the tale.

"What's wrong?" Lucinda said.

"Nothing. Only that you almost perished, and that I almost lost you." His hand buried itself in her long, abundant hair. Clenched into a trembling fist. "I thought the only danger to you was from Derek. Are the Floradëurs a threat to you also?"

"No, they live rather far away. Highly unlikely for them to leave their territory and try to attempt the portals on demon land. It's just Derek we have to worry about here. But we should be safe enough with Hari and Ruric. They are my father's best men."

"The last two great warriors of the dragon clan, Lord Thorane said."

"They are last of our line, other than my father, brother, and myself," she said sadly.

"Are they enough to keep you safe?"

"Yes. They'll be able to sense another demon's presence long before he gets close to us. As will I."

"Derek had an easy time getting close to you last time," Stefan said darkly.

"Last time I was quite distracted and wasn't expecting him." She had been dying actually, the second and final time. "Now we're warned and much better prepared."

"How will they get the blood they need, your two demon guards?"

Lucinda shifted against his shoulder, sighed. "One of the many things I have to take care of when we wake up. We'll go into town, I guess, to a place where humans gather. Probably the bar."

"How often will they need to feed?"

"I don't know. It varies here. For myself, it's usually just once a night."

"Here? As opposed to back in Hell?"

He felt her nod. "Our metabolism slows down once we cross into this realm. Back home, we don't just drink blood, we also eat two meals a day."

"Food?"

"Yes, silly, we eat food. But blood is still our primary sustenance. While we're in this realm, we only need our most basic blood requirement."

"How long can you stay in this realm before you need to return?"

"Five days usually for me. Probably close to the same for Hari and Ruric, I'd guess; maybe a little longer. They're older than I am. I was thinking of staying here for three days to get everyone settled, then returning with Hari, Nico, and Talon, while Ruric stays here with you and Jonnie. Hari can switch off with Ruric when we return a couple of days later."

"You don't need to leave Ruric behind," Stefan protested.

"I won't leave you and Jonnie unprotected here. Not while Derek is still roaming free."

"Then you need more guards. One demon isn't enough to guard the three of you."

"You forgot to count me. It's not one demon guarding three. Its two demons guarding two others."

Understanding came to Stefan then. "That's why Ruric and Hari are here, from your point of view. To guard us. Not you."

"I would not have allowed my father to shackle them to me otherwise."

"Gently," he admonished. "Remember. Long ears."

"Those long ears should be giving us the courtesy of not listening in on our conversation."

"Like you said. It'll take a period of adjustment." Odd finding himself in the role of trying to protect the feelings of two fierce demons. "I'm pretty sure, though, that's not how Hari and Ruric see their duty, which is you, first and foremost, then Talon and Nico. Not me or Jonnie."

"Everyone here is of equal priority," she said. "I'll make sure they understand that."

He prudently changed the topic. "So you'll take them out to hunt up some blood. What about you?"

"What about me?"

"You do not need to seek out strangers," he said, "not when you have Nico and me."

"I told you. I don't think of you as my food."

"I am your lover." He said the words with relish. "And I enjoy seeing to your needs. But since the lover part is put on hold for the moment, all that is left to me is the pleasure of feeding you. Drink my blood," he urged. "Take what you need from me. The thought of you with other men that way . . ." He took a deep, steadying breath. "I do not like thinking of you drinking from other men, not when you can drink from me."

Hunger, blood hunger, was always there for Lucinda—for any demon. She would have to feed tonight. But why wait when waiting would only torment one who had come to mean so much to her.

"Stefan," she murmured as her body changed subtly against him. It was natural to slip into seductress mode when blood presented itself, even when it was knowingly offered and the prey before her willing. It was hard to stop her body's natural instinct to beguile, to entice. She tried to restrain that part of her nature as much as she could, but could not completely cut off what was innate in her. She looked at him with hooded lids, the dark draw of her eyes more intense, the smile on her lips both lazier and sharper—mesmerizing, enthralling temptation.

"You don't need to seduce me," Stefan murmured.

"I know," she whispered. "It's just a natural reaction for me." She shushed him when he started to say more. "Hush. Let me enjoy this."

He was amused and more than a bit seduced as he did as

she bid him do—stay quiet and let her enjoy it. There was a more noticeably feline quality to her now, he thought. Then reconsidered. Knowing what her other form, what her other nature was—dragon—he could see it now in the sinuously elegant grace of her movements, the hypnotic allure of her eyes and body.

Her mouth ghosted up his chest, slid to the curve of his neck, and his heart quickened, thrilling, despite himself. Her nostrils delicately flared as she scented him, scented the blood flowing so near the surface just beneath the skin.

Without any other inducement, his body tightened, readying itself for her strike, her touch, her caress.

A thrilling touch, the tiniest brush of her sharp fang against his skin, and a groan almost escaped him. He hadn't foreseen how it would affect him, this building tension, the torturously pleasurable anticipation. And she was behaving herself, being good—restraining herself. Holding back the psychic powers she could have unleashed on him. But even without a single shot fired from that formidable arsenal, he was seduced by her—her closeness, her nearness. The potent focus of her desire on him, and what he could give her.

Yes, he thought, *drink from me.*

Another teasing brush of her fangs over the beat of his pulse. A gentle glide of her knuckles to turn his head to the side, stretch out the long smooth line of his neck. He felt anticipation tighten his body. Felt blood surge powerfully through him, filling him with throbbing tumescent need, the beat in his stiff organ echoing the frantic one hammering against his throat. It was terrible, wonderful, unbearable, this willing/unwilling rapture, the utterly carnal sensuality of her light graze over his sensitive skin like a threatening caress.

"Bite me! Drink from me!" he urged hoarsely, his voice scraping thick and raw. His eyes closed against the overwhelming inundation of his senses from the light skim of her teeth, the press of her full breasts against his chest, the heat of her silky thighs smooth against his hair-roughened legs.

With slow, savoring delight, her fangs slid in with sharp, clean precision, burying deep in his flesh, cutting neatly into his vein. He gave a strangled cry, unable to hold it back, powerless to stop the strong grip of his hands holding her to him as she drank from him in strong, sucking gulps that cut pleasure into him sharp as a knife, hot and sizzling. Filling him up, filling him up so hard that he felt as if he would explode with just a touch. But nothing touched him down there, nothing but air. He throbbed, he ached, he almost groaned, suspended on a stretched rack of aching desire and painful pleasure as he fed his lady. Fed her with his blood, with who he was, with all that his heart and body could offer her. *Mine!* he screamed inside. *You're mine. Just as I am yours.*

When he thought he could stand it no longer, when the pull of her lips against his throat made him dizzy with love and lust, aching pain, deep pleasure . . . she touched him, her palm against his turgid hardness. The slow press and grind of her opened hand against his throbbing erection . . . and he erupted. With light, with love, with everything that he was. He came in a dizzying onslaught of blurred emotion and sharp sensation, of spiking pleasure and shuddering ecstasy, all in a strangled, choked silence filled with the fast pounding of his heart, the harsh gusts of his breath, the fading light of his being.

One final sweet sip of his blood and she released him.

He breathed out a shaky imprecation. "That was even

better than the first time you drank from me. You should restrain yourself more often," he said with a very weak but pleased smile.

"That didn't hurt you too much, did it?" she asked, her face flushed with hectic color, her lips a fuller, darker red now.

"Hardly at all. And that tiny bit only in a very good and delicious way." He pressed a gentle kiss against her lips. "My thanks for drinking from me and not using any of your other powers while doing so." If she had, their session would have been much noisier.

Stefan cleaned up and slid back into bed, making a note to bring an extra pair of boxers for himself next time. Gathering Lucinda back into his arms, he saw with satisfaction that her face was soft and slumberous. His lady dragon was sated and replete.

He gave a brief thought to the other men in the house. Wondered if they had listened, and the state they were in if they had.

"Good night," Stefan murmured. To her and any others that might be listening.

"Good night," she murmured in return, and tumbled sweetly into sleep in less time than it took for him to feel two of his slow heartbeats.

SIX

IT WAS ODD waking up to sound in the house. Heart-beats—two slow, one faster. The sound of breathing, of movement when usually all was still and silent here. Beneath that was an electrical hum. The refrigerator was plugged in and running.

Overlaying all that was the new sensing of others. Not only of like to like, of demonkind—that I was used to—but also the new constant rub of Monère presence. That I was not used to. Odd that it didn't flare up my hunger, those tantalizing beats of life and the even more tantalizing feel of their presence. Not just Monère but Floradëur. Then I remembered this morning. Remembered Stefan. He was already up, gone from the bed. I grimaced. How hungry the other demons must be, teased by my earlier feeding.

Not nice. But better than the sounds of sex would have been.

I rolled out of bed and dressed quickly, suddenly aware that I was responsible for feeding six other mouths, all of them with different needs. And there was nothing in the refrigerator, nothing in the house. Why should there be? Demons only drank blood, which was the only thing we were in current supply of here—walking, talking, pulsing founts of blood. I became more anxious at that thought.

Hari and Ruric were among the oldest of our kind, presumably with the greatest control. Among my father's men, the two of them had hardly glanced at Talon and his tempting Floradëur blood—one of the reasons why I had not fought my father too hard when he assigned them to me. But still, that control had to be a tentative thing when a demon was as hungry as they must be now.

I rushed into the breakfast area and stopped short. Everyone else was there. Jonnie and Stefan sat at the small breakfast table, while Talon and Nico were perched on stools around the raised kitchen bar. Hari and Ruric stood outside on the covered porch.

"Good eventide, Princess," Nico greeted, and the others echoed him, even my stoic demon guards outside.

My brows slanted up. "Are we being all polite and formal this evening?"

"Nope," answered Nico, giving me his trademark grin. "That was it. All the politeness for tonight. Did you sleep well, Princess?" He wagged his eyebrows, the look in his eyes suggestive and knowing. To my mortification, I felt warmth steal across my face. I was blushing more in these past few days than I'd ever blushed in my life and entire afterlife combined.

"Like a rock. And you?"

"Also like a rock," he said with a leering twinkle in his eyes.

My gaze almost dipped down to check out his statement. But I controlled myself, and was saved by the sound of a deep, powerful engine turning into the driveway. A long auto transport truck pulled up in front of the house a few moments later.

My car and Stefan's had arrived. Perfect timing.

It took less than ten minutes to unload both cars and sign a receipt for mine. I had dashed back into the bedroom to grab a pair of gloves with hidden titanium cup shields secured at each fingertip. They made my fingers appear half an inch longer than they actually were, but kept my sharp nails from slicing through the leather. Manipulating a pen with the gloves on wasn't even awkward for me anymore; I'd had plenty of practice. I made a note to have some gloves made up for Hari and Ruric.

It was almost six when the transport truck left. Removing my gloves, I turned to Ruric and asked him to hold out his hands. He did so without question, displaying nails that were thicker and longer than normal humans, curved lightly at the tip into sharp talon points. Those, distinctly above all our other features, declared us as Other. With the glide of my hand just above his fingertips, I smoothed away that telling feature, leaving behind normal human-looking fingernails in their place.

"Is that real," Jonnie asked, "what you just did?"

"No, only illusion. His sharp nails are still there. Just not seen."

I called Talon next, and he peeled out of the dark shadows into which he had seamlessly merged and came to me. With a pass of my hand above his skin, I lightened his face, neck, hands, and wrists from pitch-black to a much lighter shade of brown. Another smooth pass over his eyes, and white sclera formed into definition. I left behind tingling energy upon his flesh, but he was not frightened or surprised. I had camouflaged him like this once before.

Hari came next, but he did not obey blindly as the others had. "You expend valuable energy on illusion that will only last several fleeting hours," he admonished.

"Then we had better hurry up before it wears out," I said with a dry smile. "Spread your hands, Hari."

He did so reluctantly. "Will you waste your energy like this every night?"

"Until I can get some special gloves like mine made up for you and Ruric, yes."

"The gloves will take care of our demon nails, but what of the Floradëur?"

"The Floradëur has a name, and I would prefer that you use it. Talon, I will continue to camouflage as often as needed."

Hari's lips curled into a silent snarl, a frightening sight had the others been able to see it.

I returned his look in silent challenge.

Grudgingly he lowered his stormy eyes.

With a simple, smooth gesture, I coated his nails with illusion. "We can go into town now if you wish to feed," I said to Hari. "But if you can wait a few more hours, more humans will have gathered."

"There is ready blood here," Hari said. "Why must we wait?" He sounded angry and surly from the silent battle of wills he had just lost. Others who didn't know him would think his question rude. For Hari, however, it was being remarkably civilized and restrained. He hadn't just reached out and grabbed someone and started sucking on someone's neck. He was asking a legitimate question. In his own way, asking for the rules.

I laid them out for him. "No one's blood here is to be taken against their will."

"Stefan and Nico are for the Princess," Ruric said in his low bass rumble.

"And Jonnie is off limits," Stefan declared, calmly stating fact much the way I had.

No one asked why the demons could not drink Talon's blood. Talon had been a blood slave to Derek for over twenty-six years, stolen from Hell and hidden in this realm. I'd like to say compassion was the reason why no one asked, but it was for a more practical reason why none of the demons considered him a viable food source. Drinking a Floradëur's blood garnered a demon great strength, an abundant flooding of it, like gulping down a slurry of raw adrenaline. But you paid a price for it. After the power high ended, you crashed into unconsciousness and stayed knocked out from several hours to an entire day, the same length of time that you usually soared under its power. Being taken out of commission like that was not something my two demon bodyguards were going to allow to happen to them. So in a way, Talon was the safest one among us. Still . . . it was wise not to strain the limits of hungry control.

"We'll go into town first," I decided.

"No, Princess," Hari snapped. "I can wait several more hours."

I looked at the lean, angry demon and wanted to ask him if he was sure, but didn't dare do so. Compared to Hari's usually obnoxious self, he was being remarkably contained. I didn't want to set him off by questioning either his pride or control in front of the others.

"You need not worry," he said, an irritated frown darkening his sharp-bladed face. "I won't let pride interfere with my duty to protect you. If my hunger becomes too great, I will let you know."

From him, that was sheer politesse.

"Hari, are you okay?" I asked again. "You aren't acting like your usual yourself."

Ruric guffawed, with great booming gusto. Hari, however, didn't seem to find my question or Ruric's laughing response at all funny. With a loud, angry snarl, Hari launched himself at the bigger demon and they rolled on the ground in a quick blur of movement that none but I could follow.

Then it was over, hardly before it had begun. The two of them stood, dusting themselves off, no visible injury to either of them, though they had exchanged blows hard enough to hurt. But not enough to inflict any real damage to themselves or spill demon blood. As violent as it had seemed, they had been very careful in that quick and vicious tussle.

"I'm good," Hari snarled, his eyes flashing a scary bloodred. Then more calmly, "I'm fine for now, Princess."

Oddly enough, his quick flash of temper and sudden outlet of violence reassured me. *That* was more like the Hari I knew.

"Okay, then," I said, feeling more sure of him. "Let's go grocery shopping."

SEVEN

SITTING IN THE cramped quarters of a car was a new and unpleasant experience for Ruric. Riding in the large van back at High Queen's Court had been bad enough. This was much worse.

He sat in the front passenger seat next to Stefan, who was driving. Jonnie sat in back. It was a bigger car than what Lucinda drove ahead of them. And Stefan had even slid the front seat back to make more room, but still Ruric felt like a big fish that had been stuffed into a small bag. His extra-wide shoulders encroached beyond his boundary, almost bumping against Stefan, and his head hit the roof if he sat up straight. He had to hunch in on himself to try to make himself as small as possible—not an easy feat for someone with his wide and solid frame.

Trying to put on what Stefan called a seat belt had been humbling in the extreme, even after Stefan demonstrated how to latch the harness. But what was simple for Stefan was far from simple for Ruric. When Ruric had gently pulled on the belt strap, it had slid out a foot then jerked to a sudden halt. Stefan explained how to unjam the thing by sliding it back a few inches then pulling it forward again with slow and easy motion, but the delicate maneuver was not as simple for Ruric, who gravely feared breaking the thing with a too-hard pull, or severing it with the accidental graze of his nails.

When Ruric asked simply not to wear the device, Stefan explained that it was human law to wear such a thing when sitting in the front seat. Law officers would stop them if Ruric did not wear this confounded contraption. Stefan finally had to secure the cursed thing for him, making Ruric feel like a big, clumsy, awkward child.

"This is all new to you?" Jonnie inquired.

"Yes, very new and very strange," Ruric answered. "It has been at least five centuries since I last came to this realm. Much had changed since then."

"Five hundred years." Jonnie whistled. So did Stefan silently.

"You were last here in the sixteen century," Jonnie said, his eyes lighting up as he did the calculation. "Wow! You've missed everything—the invention of the telephone, radio, TV, Hollywood movies . . . the Internet. You are really going to be surprised by how things are now."

"I already am," Ruric replied. A great understatement. The air-flying metal object that they called an airplane had flipped Ruric's stomach inside out and wrung it into twisting knots. There had been even more wonders on the ground he had glimpsed through the window. He had seen and marveled at all the lights and houses and vast buildings and structures that the humans had built. Seen the numerous auto-cars that crawled along orderly, paved roads like busy little colored ants. But that had all been from a nullifying distance. Experiencing it now, up close and personal, was an entirely different experience.

They pulled onto a bigger road and soon were crowded alarmingly close by many other cars, all speeding along at a fast pace. Lucinda, driving the auto-car ahead of them, handled her vehicle with easy deftness, as did the quiet Monère sitting beside Ruric.

When Stefan assured Ruric that they would not lose Lucinda among all the many other cars, Ruric ventured a question that had been puzzling him greatly. "This auto-car. You signed receipt of it. Does it belong to you?"

"Yes," Stefan answered.

When Ruric asked how one was able to own such a thing, he was flooded with information about the currency here, what they called money, and the complicated and many varied ways of both the earning of it, and the spending of it.

"Don't you have something similar in Hell?" asked Stefan.

His question brought forth a far more easier explanation from Ruric about the barter trade common among demons. Of how land was owned by titled lords and ladies and granted out in leaseholds to be worked by peasants and laborers, and how craft skills were learned by apprenticeship.

"That's really feudal," Jonnie said. "In this modern age, we own things. Not just small things like our clothes, but bigger ticket items like land, buildings, and cars."

It was a fascinating concept. But further pursuit of this new knowledge was halted as Lucinda's car, and then their own, peeled off onto a smaller road, and pulled up a short distance later in front of an enormous building.

Setting foot in a grocery store was another extraordinary experience. Only here, there was room—a plentitude of it housing the space of what an entire outdoor market square in their capital city would comprise. It was an interesting system these humans had established. You didn't have to pay for each item, going from different vendor to different vendor. You simply pushed a cart, as Stefan was doing, and put all the food items you desired into it. It was amazing the vast number and sheer variety of food that humans ate and drank. Equally amazing and more disturbing was the large amount of humans gathered into this indoor market-place. None, however, wore any weapons or acted aggressively against each other. Like the cars, they all seemed to operate harmoniously, following unseen rules. Many of them, in fact, gave Ruric a wide berth—none of the others, just himself.

It wasn't surprising that people avoided him; he expected no other reaction. Even the other elite guards down in Hell had been wary and uncomfortable around him, his disquietingly uneven features bearing mute testimony to the horrible trauma that should have ended his existence. He had literally been torn apart by their enemies.

Blaec—not the High Lord then, not even a challenger yet for the throne—had miraculously healed him. The final put-together product was not a pretty sight. But that he still existed and functioned wholly intact and unimpaired was nothing short of a bloody miracle. A few unsymmetrical features were nothing to complain about, as far as Ruric was concerned.

It surprised him then, when a human girl not much older than Jonnie's age walked by their group. Not that she walked by them; many humans had. But that she didn't seem to follow the unseen rules that governed the actions of the others. She obviously saw Stefan and Jonnie because she moved to the left to avoid them. Ruric thought she would do the same with him, and keep moving farther out left, but she didn't. She adjusted her course as if he weren't there, and walked straight into him. It took both of them completely by surprise.

She bounced off him, and Ruric couldn't even reach out to keep her from falling. His demon nails might not be visible, but they were still a very real and hazardous presence. If he grabbed for her, he might inadvertently cut or damage her without meaning to; humans were so fragile.

He could only watch as the young woman hit the floor in a hard, backward sprawl. Could only catch the falling basket she had carried, saving all the contents contained within from spilling out in a loud and messy clamor that would have drawn even more unwanted attention to them. But he could not save the human herself.

Her fall, painful though it was to watch, occurred in near silence. There was only the clatter of her glasses as they flew off her face and hit the floor; the sound of thick lenses cracking at hard impact with the ground.

"Oh," she said, blinking large eyes in his general direction but higher up, as if he still stood instead of where he was, crouched down in front of her. "I'm so sorry," she said. "I didn't see you. Please forgive me."

It was hard to believe that she was apologizing to him! "Are you harmed?" he asked with concern.

At the sound of his voice, she adjusted her eyes lower down, aimed vaguely in the direction of his face. She blinked a few times, puzzled, clearly mortified. "Oh, no, I'm fine. Are you? I didn't hurt you, did I?"

His weren't the only eyebrows that raised at her question. Looking at the two of them, the slight human girl and the massive demon more than thrice her weight, it was an almost ludicrous question.

When he assured her that he was unharmed, she scrambled to her feet. He assisted her then, a light touch of his big hand beneath her arm, very careful to end the contact as soon as she was on her feet and apparently stable.

She took the basket when he offered it to her with a flustered, "Thanks for saving my basket. What great reflexes you have." Words that made Ruric cringe for not saving *her* from the fall instead of her bloody basket. Even more guilt flooded him when he handed her the broken glasses.

"Oh!" she said in great dismay as she ran her fingers over the cracked, uneven surfaces of her lenses, after slipping them on her face. There was a single crack in the left lens, and a jagged three-part fracture on the right.

"We will, of course, pay for the damage to your glasses," Lucinda said, drawing the girl's startled gaze her way, giving Ruric the odd impression that she hadn't been aware of Lucinda until the Princess had spoken. Pulling out her wallet, Lucinda withdrew three bills and passed them to Nico, who pressed them with a charming smile into the girl's hand.

"Oh, no! I couldn't," she protested, trying to give the money back.

"We insist, on behalf of our companion," Nico smoothly said. "He feels quite awful for breaking your glasses."

"But it's not his fault, it was mine. I bumped into him. I have very poor vision, as you probably guessed."

"I was at fault for not getting out of your way," Ruric said in a quiet rumble, drawing the girl's eyes—distorted behind her fractured lens—back to him.

"Don't be silly. You couldn't have known that I'm half

blind. Please take your money back," she said, holding out the folded bills. When he didn't take them, she blindly touched his solid chest, slid her way down his arm, and tried to push the money into his hand.

He was stunned for a moment at the touch, so innocently fearless, only then truly realizing how impaired her vision must be. She could not have seen him *at all* to touch him in so casual a manner! He pulled his hand away before she encountered his nails, and stepped back, leaving her still holding the money.

"My friend is correct," Ruric said. "I feel quite badly. I should have caught you instead of your basket. If I had done so, your glasses would not have broken. Please allow this recompense of money"—he hoped he said that correctly—"and accept my apologies."

She became even more flustered as she heard the clear misery in Ruric's voice.

"All right, thank you," she said, her face flushing a dull red. "I'll, ah, let you finish up your shopping then and be on my way."

They watched as she made her way easily down the aisle, veered neatly around a small display stand, and turned the corner. Watching her, you could not tell that her vision was impaired in any way.

"How much money did you give her?" asked Ruric.

"Three hundred dollars," Lucinda answered. "That should hopefully be enough to repair her glasses."

They completed the rest of their grocery selection and pushed their loaded cart to a line where they paid for their items. The total came to ninety-seven dollars and seven cents, which Stefan paid for.

"My food, my money," he said when Lucinda pulled out her wallet.

"Nico's going to be eating some of that," she pointed out.

"Allow me to contribute in this small way. You can pay the next time. We could switch off in this manner," he said with a smile.

Amazingly, the Princess allowed Stefan to pay for the groceries, even though she didn't look too pleased with him doing so. The blind girl was nowhere in sight. In the parking lot, Ruric caught a trace of her scent, a clean fragrance mixed with the soap and floral shampoo she used. But it ended there. He wondered who had driven her away. Wondered if she had family. If so, why had they let her venture alone without escort? Then he wondered how he was going to repay Lucinda the money she had given the human on his behalf—three times what Stefan had paid for the six bags of grocery they had purchased.

Ruric wondered why he even felt the need to. As one of the Princess's men, she was responsible for providing for them. And yet, it seemed the human rules were dissimilar—a divergence that she had allowed Stefan, who clearly belonged to the Princess as surely as Ruric did.

Things were different in the living realm, the Princess had told Hari and Ruric. They were to walk lightly among humans here, to do their best to blend in.

"This is going to be my home," she told them. Implicit in her words was the silent command not to mess this up for her.

Guarding the Princess was going to be easy.

It was the other objective, blending in, that Ruric was going to have a real problem with.

EIGHT

M ARY SUCKED DOWN club soda through a straw, and
dryly told her sister, "You know, it's pretty ridiculous to pay six dollars for two glasses of carbonated water.
Seven dollars if you include the tip you probably gave to
the bartender."

"Ugh, this stuff *is* pretty nasty," Julia said. "I'll order
Sprite next time. You're legal. You could have ordered a
real drink." No doubt this was said with a pretty pout.

"With your fake ID, you're legal, too," Mary returned.
"You could have imbibed wicked liquor if you wished to."

"Imbibe? Wicked liquor?" Julia snorted. An unseen roll
of eyes here. "Nobody talks like that in real life, Mare,
only in books."

"Of which I read a lot in Braille."

This time the pause was uncomfortable—no eye roll or
pout. It was always that way when Mary mentioned the big

white elephant in the room—her blindness. Not complete
blindness; she could see motion and flashes of color—
green, blue, and brown. The rest, though, was a very vague
and mysterious darkness. A darkness that her sister—her
pretty and silly but sweet, adopted sister—minded more
on her behalf than Mary did herself. It was all she'd known
her whole life, since her earliest memories. Not that of a
newborn thrown into a trash bin, whose pitiful cries had
alerted the workmen as she was roughly dumped into the
garbage truck along with the refuse. The driver had fortu-
nately shut down the compacter before she was crushed.
But the trauma of the fall and the rough jostling during the
brief moments of compacting had broken three of her ribs,
her left arm, and partially detached both of her retinas.

She was lucky. The doctors had been able to laser down
the remaining parts of her retina, allowing her limited,
precious vision instead of complete blindness. A little bit
of something, in her opinion, was much better than nothing at all.

No. Mary had no memories of that early traumatic time.
She remembered only the soothing hugs and kisses lavished
upon her by Mr. and Mrs. Jack Carroll, a warm and loving
couple who had failed to have children after ten years of
trying, and had adopted her. Two years later, as if in reward
for their good deed, Samantha Carroll became pregnant
and Mary was blessed with a little sister—although who
was little and who was big sometimes got confused in the
issue of Mary's blindness.

"You know Mom would *kill* me if she smelled liquor
on my breath," Julia said. "You, though, now live on your
own. You could drink alcohol if you wanted to."

"But I don't want to," Mary said. "If I'm complaining
about paying three dollars for seltzer water, how do you

think I'd feel about paying eight dollars for fermented brew that will mess up what little senses I have left? Besides," Mary said dryly, "you're supposed to be checking up on me, not encouraging me to drink."

"I'm not checking up on you," protested Julia. "I'm having *you* check out a guy I met in the supermarket. Pierre Dumont. Isn't that a beautiful name? So French. He's supposed to be singing here tonight with his band. Seriously, Mare. I want to know what you think about him. You have great intuition."

"Great intuition that you don't always listen to."

"Well," Julia said, giggling, "some things I just have to find out for myself. Oh, Mare, this guy is so hot! I just about combusted when I bumped into him."

A small smile. "You bump into a man who invites a nineteen-year-old girl to a bar—"

"I told him I was legal."

"—and I run into a guy who feels so guilty about my clumsiness that I get three hundred dollars stuffed into my hand for damage he did not cause."

"Maybe I should frequent grocery stores more, and you should avoid them." Another giggle.

Affection for her sweet and pretty sister warmed Mary. "Even if you did come to check up on me, it's good to see you. Although, without my glasses, I guess that's a really poor choice of words."

"I, for one, am glad that man felt bad enough to insist you take the three hundred dollars. It's going to cost at least that much to replace your lenses."

"Two hundred," Mary corrected. "I called and found out it'll only cost me two hundred dollars. I wish I could return the extra hundred."

"Oh, pooh. So what if he overcompensated a bit. Being

without glasses and having to wait for the new lenses to be made up makes it much worse for you. Doesn't it?"

"My glasses sharpen up what I can see. Now things are, I don't know—even more blurry, I guess. Although that's not really correct. It's more like I can only see half of what I could see with glasses on." Which was hardly anything at all.

"Oh, Mare." Just those two words like a warm hand squeeze. Then the sound of the door, a sense of her sister turning her head. An excited whisper. "Pierre's here with his band. Oh, look, he sees me. He's coming this way."

Then a masculine voice with an admittedly sexy French accent. "Hey, it's Julia, right?" He chatted amicably with them for a minute before excusing himself to help his band set up, after getting her sister's assurance that she would be staying for a while.

"So what do you think?" Julia asked after he left.

"I think that he's very good looking, like you said," Mary said slowly. You could hear it in his voice, the same ease and assurance her sister had. "And that he's used to girls, *lots* of American girls, being attracted to him."

"And . . ."

"He finds you attractive and would like to spend more time with you."

"Come on, Mare."

"And there's nothing really objectionable that I sense about him," she said, letting out a breath. "Other than he's a confident, good-looking guy who invited you to a bar, and is likely just looking for a good time rather than someone to share the rest of his life with."

"In other words, he's perfect for me."

"Julia . . ."

"Ma-ry," she sang back. "So. Nothing objectionable, right?"

"Nothing that I sensed in that one brief minute of conversation that was mostly between you and him," Mary clarified. "I'm not infallible, you know. Just because there was nothing disturbing I got in that first impression doesn't mean he's not an asshole like any other guy."

"Oh, Mare." A tinkling, short laugh. "Such rose-colored spectacles you view the world through."

To tease her, Mary slipped her broken glasses back on. "You mean these spectacles?"

"Take them off," Julia said horrified. "Oh, God. I hope Pierre didn't see you. It makes you look like you were in a train wreck!"

Not an inaccurate description, Mary thought, putting her poor broken glasses back into her pocket. Despite her limited vision, her senses usually guided her accurately around objects and people. She could function amazingly well for someone with her severe degree of visual impairment. But her infallible senses had faltered completely with him—that man. For some reason, he hadn't show up on her radar at all. Running into him, into that hard, solid mass, had indeed felt like a train crash.

There was another stir at the door. A sudden change in the atmosphere.

"Oh . . . my . . . God."

"What?" Mary asked.

"You know how I said that Pierre was good looking?"

"Yeah?"

"Well, in just walked a bunch of people that make Pierre look as homely as mud pie."

"They're good looking?"

"No. They're beautiful. One woman and six guys. And
if I'm not mistaken, that boy with them isn't one day older
than I am. But the woman . . ." A soft groan from Julia. "If
the guys make Pierre look homely, that woman makes me
look like cow manure."

The dramatic way she said that made Mary smile. It was
not often that someone outshone her pretty sister. "Is she
blond, like you?"

"No, her hair is *gold*. And she has a body that puts
Angelina Jolie to shame. She looks, I don't know . . . like
a goddess."

"What, like Venus?" Mary asked, amused at the mix of
awe and angst in Julia's voice.

"Body and face, maybe. But not the attitude. The attitude is more dangerous. Like she could irresistibly lure a
guy into bed. Then not only shred the skin off his back, but
have him enjoy it, and come crawling back for more!"

"I can't believe you're going on about the woman instead
of the men. What about the guys you mentioned. Are they
all handsome in a drool-worthy sort of way?"

"Three of them are," her sister immediately said. "One
guy's black or Hispanic or maybe from India, I can't tell.
He's tall, thin, and beautiful in this metrosexual kind of
way. The guy next to him has like, wow, movie-star looks.
The third guy is the complete opposite, good-looking in a
villainous, dangerous, sexy kind of way."

The last guy sounded like someone Mary wanted Julia
to stay far, far away from.

"The other three guys include the boy my age I mentioned earlier, and a shorter man who isn't as beautiful as
the others but still ruggedly attractive, very manly. The last
man . . . now *that* is one very scary, lethal-looking brute.
He's the size of two men put together and looks like hired

muscle. His face is battered-looking, like he spent a lot of time in a boxing ring. Oh, God!" Julia's voice choked down into a hiss. "He's looking at us! He couldn't have heard me, could he? Oh shit. He's coming this way!"

She was mildly alarmed by the panic in Julia's voice. But that was nothing compared to the shock Mary felt when she heard him speak . . . and recognized that deep, gravel-pit voice.

"I caused you to fall earlier this evening. I hope I did not cause you any physical harm other than what was done to your glasses."

"Oh, it's you," Mary said, surprised—no, actually shocked. She was having a really hard time lining up her sister's description with the man she had stumbled into. The kind and gentle man who had seemed so miserable over the accident. A trace of that guilt still colored his voice.

"No, I'm fine," she was quick to assure him. "Nothing broken in the fall other than my glasses. Speaking of which . . ." Mary pulled out the extra hundred-dollar bill from her pocket. "I didn't know how much you'd given me. It seems that I only need two hundred dollars to fix my glasses. Please give this back to your lady friend with my thanks." Mary didn't bother waiting for him to take it. He never would, she knew. Reaching out like before, feeling truly blind since not only could she not see him, she couldn't sense him, she patted her way down his hard stomach to his left hip pocket, and tucked the hundred-dollar bill in there. He stood very still while she did this. Her sister, on the other hand, was making odd, squeaking sounds.

"Forgive me if my hands were a bit free over your body—it seems to be a very nice body, by the way," Mary murmured with a quirked smile, eliciting more choking sounds from her sister, "but I knew you wouldn't take it if I just held it out to you. And then I'd end up not only looking like a blind fool but an idiot as well. This saves us—well, saves me, at least—from an embarrassing experience."

No reply. Just a blank and empty silence.

"Are you still there?" Mary asked uncertainly.

"Yes," that low voice confirmed.

Mary didn't know if she had offended the man, embarrassed him, or possibly even angered him. No clue whatsoever. He was just an odd emptiness to her. "I hope I haven't offended you," she ventured tentatively.

"You haven't," came the gruff reply.

"Good, well . . . thank you for coming over to check on me. You needn't feel bad. Nothing broken from our encounter that can't be fixed."

"Good evening then." He bowed, if Mary interpreted the lowered position of his voice correctly. Other than the rough physical looks Julia had described to her, excepting that, everything else about him seemed to be courtly and mannered, old world. A gentleman in the true meaning of the word. A gentle man.

"Is he gone?" Mary asked after a time.

"Yes," whispered Julia.

A pity, Mary thought, as she bid a silent good-bye to her phantom mystery man. He'd been a brief dash of something different in her simple, contained life. Now it would return once more to its steady, constant mundaneness like the carbonated water that had lost its pop and fizzle, she noted as she took a sip. For one brief moment, Mary almost wished she'd done as her sister had suggested and ordered something stronger. A brief moment of discontent, then it drifted away.

Carbonated water was enough. Anything more potent

would threaten to wash away what little remaining senses she had left, and her ability to function along with them.

A pity, Mary thought again.

A pity that anything more intoxicating in life was beyond her reach.

NINE

EVEN AFTER RURIC walked into the room where
the others had gone, he could still hear them talking.
Could still hear clearly the shocked and appalled voice of
the other girl taking the blind girl to task.

*Are you crazy, Mare, touching him like that? Stuffing
money into his pocket like he was some kind of stripper in
a nightclub! You're lucky he didn't take your hand off, or
think you were coming on to him!*

A frown furrowed Ruric's brow. The blind girl's name
was Mare? Humans were even more peculiar than he
thought if they named themselves after animals. He wondered what a stripper was.

A large, green, velvet-clothed table took up the center
of the small room Ruric stepped into, onto which Jonnie
and Stefan were gathering round, colored balls, loading
them into an empty triangular frame. The fresh scent of

human prey was mixed in with the acrid stench of lingering smoke. But whatever humans had been here had obviously vacated the room when the others had entered. Most
humans' instinct for danger was still intact; just not the girl
he had just left. *Her* sense of danger, of self-preservation,
was sadly lacking, he thought sourly as he continued listening to the two girls—the worried, blistering chastise-
ment of the blond girl, and the meek, soothing agreement
of Mare in turn.

Maybe we should leave now, Mare.

Yes, Ruric thought, you should leave.

Even though Lucinda described humans as peaceful
creatures, for the most part, there were still violent elements among them. He found himself greatly discomforted
by the thought of the two women sitting there unprotected
in this bar with so many males present. Peaceful or not,
men were by nature more aggressive and powerful than
females.

*And miss Pierre sing, sis? My guy must be even more
dangerous looking than you described to make you suggest that.*

Ruric's frown deepened. Pierre? Who in blasted hellfire
was Pierre? Even more disturbing was the possessive Mare
had used for him—my guy.

The blond girl was apparently Mare's sister. *My guy?*
she intoned ominously. He could hear the sound of her
teeth clenching.

*Don't have a heart attack, Julia. It's just an expression.
Of course a man as big and tough looking as what you
described could never be my guy.* And then more softly,
*I know someone like him is beyond my reach. He's not
attracted to me—he pities me. I know that. Nothing for you
to worry about.*

Ruric tuned out their next words, too disturbed by what he had heard, and discovered Hari and Lucinda looking curiously at him. It reminded him of what had been stuffed into his pocket, the extra hundred-dollar bill. Had he been able to, he would have returned it to Mare, but he had been hampered again by his cursed nails.

"Here." Ruric returned the money to Lucinda without an explanation. She had no doubt heard the exchange.

Jarring music came from the central room, along with the husky rasp of a male voice singing to loud, abrasive music.

"Ah. That must be Pierre," Lucinda said with a tiny smile.

"You should be concentrating on protecting the Princess," Hari said, reprimanding Ruric, "not concerning yourself with a human."

Ruric wanted to snarl at him, because he was right. An odd reversal of their roles.

"There's nothing to worry about," Lucinda said, amused. "We're the most dangerous ones here. Relax, Hari. Go hunt up some food. You, too, Ruric. Here . . ." She handed them some bills. "Ten dollars to buy a drink at the bar to help you blend in. You can even try drinking what you order. Leave one dollar as compensation to the barkeep on the counter."

"And the other rules here?" Hari asked warily. "Are we to take no one's blood unless they give it willingly?"

Lucinda looked at him curiously, unsure if he was asking that in jest. "Of course not. That rule applies only to those of us here in this room. But I do ask for discretion, and no killing. No harm to those you drink from. The humans here reside within my province." And, as such, belonged to her.

"I understand, Princess," Hari said, gliding from the room. Ruric followed him, half his attention back with the Princess, the other half focused on the dangerous demon in front him.

To Ruric's relief, Hari steered clear of the two girls by the front entrance and made his way instead to the far corner of the bar. Women's eyes were drawn to the dark saturnine demon, and he returned their stares with a slow, wicked smile of enticement. Eyes stared at Ruric also, but with repellent fear rather than tempted fascination. So it was since his healing, so it always would be . . . except for the veiled innocence of a blind girl.

He remembered the feel of that small hand running lightly over him. Remembered her smile as she had said, "A very nice body, by the way." As if she didn't quite believe herself that she dared tease him, touch him like that.

With Hari safely hunting on the other side of the room, Ruric glanced toward the front and found the table empty where she had sat. A hollow sensation of disappointment filled him, no matter that he told himself it was better they had left. A clear lie when he caught a glimpse of blond hair making its way back to the table and a familiar darker head following behind her.

"Oh, drat. I forgot my purse in the bathroom," he heard Mare say. "You go on, save our table. I'll go back and get it. I know my way now."

He watched with disbelief as Julia returned to the table and let Mare return by herself to the bathroom. She walked as if she were fully sighted, pausing when a couple crossed her path, then continued unerringly to the end of the room, disappearing down a back corridor. He positioned himself so he could see her. Watched her walk past a man talking on a telephone, and push open a door labeled "Ladies."

The area back there was empty but for Mare and the man. The fume of fermented brew clung to the disreputable-looking male. She clearly was unaware of the appraising look he had cast at her, since she didn't react with wariness or distaste. The other man seemed to take that for invitation, and his lazy interest in Mare sharpened.

When she came out a moment later, the man had ended his phone call and was lounging against the wall, waiting for her. He stepped into her path, blocking her. "Hey, pretty lady. You looking for some company?"

Her voice was cool, distantly polite. "No, thanks, my sister is waiting for me, if you'll excuse me."

"Aw, come on." He ran an appreciative leer up and down her body, which made Ruric want to tear his throat out. Again, Mare didn't react, and again the scruffy male took that as encouragement. "Two young and pretty gals in a bar. Course you came looking for some company. Well, look no further. I'm more than willing to provide all the action you need tonight, honey."

"We came to hear the band play," Mare said with cool frost. Surely the dolt heard that. "Step aside," she said in a tight voice.

"Aw, darling. You don't want a young, inexperienced boy. You should be looking for a real man like me, who knows what he's doing. Trust me, I'll have you purring in no time," he promised with a leer and reached for her.

Belatedly, alarm spiked through Mare, and her heart began to race.

Ruric moved then with inhuman speed, so that none of the other humans in the room saw him. He was there

then suddenly gone, reappearing in the back corridor with
his large hand wrapped around that reaching male arm,
though he hadn't really needed to touch him; he held the
man's will under his tight control.

"Stay here," Ruric snarled to Mare, and saw relief cross
her face as she recognized Ruric's voice. Viciously he yanked
the unresisting male into the empty men's bathroom.

Ruric was not gentle in his feeding. He took the man's
blood roughly, savagely, drinking down the human's pain
along with his lifeblood as the man screamed silently in terror, locked inside his body by Ruric's strong mental will.
And well he *should* be afraid. Were it not for Lucinda's clear
injunction not to harm the humans here, Ruric would have
taken the man outside and ripped out his tongue, his eyes, and
torn off his offending arm for daring to try to touch Mare!

*You will not remember me or this encounter. And you
will avoid the girl outside—who is blind by the way, you
fool—and her blond-haired sister. You will feel anxious
and uncomfortable anytime you come upon them and wish
to immediately leave their presence.*

Ruric took one final, deep pull of blood and grudgingly
released healing agent into the wound, watching as the torn
skin of the neck knit back together. Not all demons could
heal bite wounds, but that was one of Ruric's gifts, and
he grudgingly used it, watching the traumatic redness fade
away, leaving behind no evidence of the less than gentle
feeding that had just taken place. He left the man slumped
against the wall with the command to sit there for the next
five minutes, and stepped out of the men's bathroom no
more than twelve seconds after entering it.

Mare was still there. Ruric had been acutely aware of
her presence just outside the door while he had taken that
quick moment to feed, and to punish.

"Your sister should not have let you wander off by your-self," Ruric said tersely, and watched her eyes turn his way.

Mary felt a deep wave of heat rise up her neck and flush her face as the fear she had felt—fear that had turned to profound relief—now switched to an anger so intense, so blistering hot, that she lifted her hands and for the first time in her life deliberately pushed another person. Shoved him hard.

He felt like a rock, a boulder, and didn't move a damn inch. Which infuriated her even more.

"Oh!" She smacked his hard chest, so hard her hand stung. And this, of course, only added to her ire. "I am *not* a stray dog! And I do not *wander*."

Another smack that landed across a broad and heavy shoulder.

"I'm legally blind, not a child! What independence I have earned has been hard fought for and well earned by me."

He just stood there and let her pound on him, and Mary suddenly felt like an idiot, stunned by what she had just done—hit another person. Beat on him. Misery hit her in a swamping wave, but not quite remorse, not yet anyhow. Body trembling, breath coming fast and hard, she swayed in bewildered anger and shock, wondering what shrewish creature had suddenly possessed her usual calm and serene self.

She felt the fleeting touch of his palm against her back as he steadied her. Heard the concern in his voice as he asked, "Are you all right?"

She laughed. An abrupt, unhappy sound. "No, I'm frightened and scared, and so *angry* at you."

A brief, stilted silence.

"It was not my desire to frighten you. I would leave

you," he said, quietly distant, as if he had walled himself up. "But I cannot leave you here alone. You must be the one to depart."

"Oh!" she exclaimed, exasperated. "I'm not frightened of *you*. The other man . . . *he* scared me. You, I am totally, completely angry at. What did you do to him, by the way?"

"I warned him to stay away from you. He will not come near you again," he said, his voice suddenly hard and brutal sounding.

"Did you beat him up?" she asked in a smaller, quieter voice.

"No."

"Did you . . . you didn't kill him, did you?"

"No, although I was tempted to," he confessed to her.

She felt relief at his words and then wondered at herself, at him, that she could so easily ask if he had killed another man, and believe him capable of such a thing, and yet not be afraid of him. Mary shook her head, more at herself than at him. If she were wise, she would do as he said and walk away from him, but . . . she couldn't. Some foolish, imprudent part of herself didn't want to sever that tenuous connection—a moment filled with violence, danger, and a strange intimacy.

"Did you injure your hands?" he asked.

She laughed abruptly. "Yes. You're as hard as a blasted rock."

"That is what my name means." A slight hesitation. "Ruric. What is your name?"

"Mary," she answered.

And suddenly what her sister called her made better sense to Ruric. She was not named after a horse. Mare was simply a shortening of her name, Mary.

"Can you see me?" he asked quietly.

"No. No, I cannot see you at all."

"What about other people? Can you see them?"

Mary shook her head. "No one else either. I see movement mostly, sometimes color. It's been that way all my life."

"But you walk so assuredly. Seem so aware of other people and objects that cross your path."

"Movement again, and I can sense them somehow—people, objects."

"But not me," he said puzzled.

"No. You, I seem to be truly blind to. I can't sense you at all for some reason. I didn't hurt you, did I? I . . . shouldn't have hit you like that."

A low sound rumbled up from his chest—a sound Mary belatedly realized was a chuckle.

"Next time you wish to hit me, little one, use something other than your hand. You injured yourself unnecessarily."

Mary sniffed, then smiled slightly, her humor getting the better of her. "You, sir, are arrogant. Conceited."

Her accusation surprised Ruric. He had viewed Hari as being that way, not himself. Then again, many things were in disorder tonight. It had been he who had found Lucinda's restraining injunctive necessary, not Hari.

"But," she added softly, "you are also kind. Thanks for helping me. I'd better go. Before my sister starts to worry."

Ruric watched her leave. Watched her return safely to her sister. Then he moved with quick, blurring speed back to where he belonged. To the room filled with other dangerous demons like himself.

TEN

Nico noted Ruric's silent return, as with a smooth thrust of the cue he sent a four ball into the right corner pocket. The faint scent of blood told him that Ruric had fed, much more quickly than Nico had expected.

Being here in this place felt almost like home—what it had been to Nico for several weeks after he had fled his Queen. As if Nico's thoughts had conjured him, the owner of this quaint bar-restaurant stepped into the room.

Jim Banion, the proprietor of Smoky Jim's, took in the billiard room's mixed occupants with a single, shrewd, encompassing glance.

"Nicky," Jim exclaimed, his eyes lighting up with pleasure as they landed upon Nico. Striding over, he gripped Nico's arms in warm embrace. "You just up and left with a pretty lady one night, and never returned. Some of us were worried. Others, though, were real envious of you," he said, winking.

Nico threw back his head and laughed. "Let me introduce you to that pretty lady. My Lucy," he said, presenting her to his friend. Lucinda's brow creased dangerously at the casual shortening of her name. "This is Jim Banion, the owner of this fine establishment, and my good friend."

"Thank you, *Nicky*," Lucinda said with dry, subtle emphasis on his own nickname. "It's a pleasure to meet you, sir," she said, greeting the proprietor.

"Believe me, ma'am, the pleasure is all mine. I'm surprised all the males here in this establishment haven't swamped you yet. Then again . . ." His glance flicked to Ruric. "Maybe the dumb louts are smarter than I gave 'em credit for."

Lucinda laughed as Nico continued the introductions. Ruric became Ralph—the big demon didn't even blink at that—Stefan was altered to Steven, and Talon became Allen. Jonnie's name remained unchanged.

"I'm living with Lucy now," Nico told his friend.

"Are you, lad?" Jim sighed. He was a man in his late forties, not much taller than Nico, shrewd and tough, but honest and fair. "A loss for me. I was hoping you'd come back—I still have your stuff. But I'm happy for you," he said, slapping Nico on the back.

"Thanks, Jim, for everything you did, taking me in like that. Giving me a place to stay."

Jim waved it away. "You kept my place trouble-free. There's been two brawls since you've been gone. And your, ah, friends." The subtle change in Jim's voice told Nico he was speaking about the three beautiful human women he had kept very pleasurable company with. "They've missed you sorely, lad. Been moping around, asking if I've seen you or heard from you."

"You can tell them that I'm back in the area but no longer free to spend time with them."

"Will do." Jim nodded—message received. "Well. You probably want to collect your stuff then."

"Sure." He caught the keys to the car Lucinda tossed to him. "I'll come with you now and take it off your hands."

Exiting out the kitchen, the two of them made their way up the back flight of stairs that led to the small attic space that had been converted into living quarters.

"Your buddies," Jim said, opening the door to a small studio apartment, "an odd group of friends you found yourself there."

"They certainly are," Nico said, grinning. Even more than Jim knew.

"Two of those fellows I wouldn't want to tangle with."

"You have nothing to worry about, Jim. If anything, they're like me, more apt to keep the peace than stir up trouble."

"That's good to hear. That big brute especially, I'd hate to come up against."

"Who, Ralph?"

"Yeah. I was keeping an eye on him from behind the bar. I see him one moment. In the next blink, he's gone. He moves real fast for a fella that big."

You have no idea, Nico thought. His words to Jim, though, were much more reassuring. "Ralph might look big and scary, but he's an honorable man." Well, an honorable demon, at least, he hoped. "You don't have to worry about any trouble from him."

"We lost a lot of the lady customers after you left," Jim said regretfully.

"Ah, so it isn't really the peacekeeping I did for you that you miss, but the increased female clientele I drew in."

"Both talents were good for business. But seriously, lad, you've always got a room here should you ever need it."

"Thanks, Jim," Nico said, touched by the kind offer. "But I've got a home now, people I belong with."

"I'm glad for you, then," Jim sincerely said. "Well, be sure to lock up when you're done. At least you're back in the area. Feel free to drop by anytime, you and your pretty friends. See if we can't draw back some of those ladies."

Nico grinned widely. "You can count on it."

Jim left. A moment later Nico felt Lucinda behind him, a soundless demon, but one he felt now. Was totally aware of the silent beat of a second heart.

"There's no need to give up your lady friends," she said in a soft murmur.

Grabbing an empty garbage bag, Nico began stuffing the few things he had into it—some shirts, pants, a few sweaters, a jacket. Gifts, mostly, from the same lady friends currently under discussion.

"You are my lady now," he replied diplomatically.

"You sound quite happy about that."

"I am," Nico said, turning to look at her.

"It wasn't your choice, what happened. Our binding. It was an accident. You just happened to be in the wrong place at the wrong time."

"Inside you, you mean?" Nico asked with a wicked smile. He'd been buried deep inside her luscious heat when the bond between the three of them had unexpectedly snapped into place.

To his delight, she blushed.

"I've already trapped you into something not of your

choosing," she told him. "I won't try to curtail your freedom in any other way."

He dropped the bag. Gently brought his hands up to cup her face. "Lucinda, I wasn't trapped into anything. I'm exactly where I want to be—with *whom* I want to be. I'm happy . . . very happy," he assured her, smoothing his thumbs over the soft, tender skin of her jaw. "I know that Stefan is dear to your heart in a way that no other male is. But so am I—special to you in a way that no other person can be, not even him. Trust me, I don't regret my situation. I *belong* to you. And you belong to me and Talon. And I pray with every fiber in my being that our bond is irrevocable, unbreakable, because for the first time in my life I have a home—people I care about, who care about me. Don't waste a single moment feeling guilty," he said, and kissed her.

It was a light kiss at first. Simple and sweet.

Then it changed with one word. "Darling," she murmured against his lips.

It inflamed him, that word. Like dry tinder violently taking spark. He had been no one's darling until he had met Lucinda.

"Careful, love," Nico said unsteadily. "You know what a dangerous word that is to use around me." Oh yes, he saw as he looked into her eyes, she knew exactly how potently that word affected him.

With a faint shimmer of energy, Lucinda snapped a cone of silence around them.

"My sound barrier is only good for us now," she murmured in sultry invitation.

"Then by all means, let us put it to some good use." With a fierce, bright smile, he brought his mouth back down on hers.

She met him with hungry passion, her lips sliding over his, her tongue darting out to lick and taste him.

"Darling," Lucinda whispered, stroking the flame of his desire higher with that incendiary word. "Take off our shirts," she commanded softly.

"As my lady wishes." The tops quickly came off them both. "No, leave the gloves on," she said when he reached for them. Then forgot about them a second later as she licked and nibbled her way down his chest.

"Wait," he said, "let me lock the door." Practical matters and concerns were about to go flying out the window. And then they did, his eyes nearly crossing as she licked playfully over his nipple.

Lucinda gave a husky, purring laugh, blowing air over the wet, perked flesh. "Ruric is on guard outside. He won't let anyone enter."

"Ah, well, in that case." He spun her around and tossed her onto the bed. And felt her sound barrier slip over him, leaving him standing outside the shielding. Lucinda wasn't aware yet of what had happened, he realized, as she opened her mouth, making a remark he couldn't hear. A few seconds passed and he felt nothing: no cutting weakness that brought him down to his knees, no lessening in strength. She was looking at him with a puzzled smile, no doubt wondering why he was just standing there, staring at her with such an odd, arrested look on his face.

"I'm okay," he said, and watched horrified realization slide across her face as the sound of his voice was blocked from her.

The sound cone abruptly dissipated.

"Nico!" she cried.

"No, stay there. I'm fine," he said with growing delight, deep amazement. "I didn't feel weak at all when I was cut

off from you just now. Try it again. Raise your sound barrier and keep it up until I signal otherwise."

She did so reluctantly, perching nervously on the edge
of the bed, watching him carefully.

A minute ticked slowly by, then another and another
while Nico stood there grinning broadly, monitoring his
watch. After nine long minutes had passed, she'd had
enough. The barrier dissolved as she walked to him.

"I wasn't affected at all. You could have held it longer,"
Nico said, excitement and jubilation bubbling up in him.
He unleashed some of it in a hard, smacking kiss, a skillful
swivel of his hips, rubbing his hardness against her.

She sank against him, her body melting into his, and
cradled his erection for a moment. Reluctantly she pulled
away and retrieved her shirt, covering her delectable breasts
from his sight. "No more time for that," she said sighing.
"The others are waiting for us."

Nico snorted. "I'm highly offended. You were only
going to allot us nine minutes for a quickie?"

"Not a quickie. I don't do quickies," Lucinda said, her
eyes growing heavy-lidded, slumberous. "Ten minutes of
intense, deeply satisfying sex."

"Oh. Actually for intense, deeply satisfying sex with
you, I would have only needed five minutes," he said
tongue-in-cheek.

"Rascal," she said. "I'm sorry."

"I'm not," Nico said, all joking aside. "I can be cut off
from you and not grow weak. I've gotten stronger."

"You have. We'll have to test the limits more later; see
how long we can be safely separated."

"After giving me five minutes of intense, deeply satisfying sex first, of course."

His lady laughed, and gave him a smile filled with

such wicked, hot promise that he nigh almost spurted in release.

"If you're up for it then, lover," she purred, walking to the door.

"I'm up for it now," Nico muttered plaintively as he locked up and followed her down the steps, his bag of belongings in hand.

He heard the little witch give a low laugh.

The rest of their group, Hari included, looking quite satiated, were waiting for them at the bottom.

"All done, children?" Nico asked lightly.

"More done than you are, little man," Hari said with a sharp smile.

"Let's go home then," Lucinda said, ignoring their bladed banter.

The drive back was much more relaxed with Hari's hungry edge gone, and the subtle tension between him and Talon eased, like releasing a breath you hadn't realized you had been holding.

Back at the house, they settled into domestic life, carrying in the groceries.

Nico set his two bags on the kitchen countertop and removed a cluster of bananas from one of the bags. He recognized the fruit, but didn't know where or how it should be stored. "Um . . ." he said, holding up the yellow bundle, "where do the bananas go?"

"Jonnie and I will put everything away," Stefan said, taking the bananas from him and waving him out of the kitchen. Nico left the two of them to organize things.

"Where's Ruric?" Nico asked, going out onto the front porch. Only Lucinda and Hari were there, sitting comfortably in the shadows.

"Doing another check around the property," Lucinda said.

"We still have half the night left," Nico observed, sitting down on the top step, leaning back on his elbows. "What shall we do with the remaining hours?"

"We can do some sparring and training," she said, "when everyone's finished."

"And you can show us how soft your skills have grown, rogue," Hari jeered.

"As soft as you've gotten guarding the Princess instead of the High Lord," returned Nico with parrying ease.

A low sound came from the demon.

"You're both on the same team now," Lucinda said, leveling them a look. "Behave. The both of you."

Hari's hackles rose at her *same team* comment. He clearly wanted to repudiate it, but didn't.

Nico smiled slowly, lazily, in Hari's direction, as if knowing how abrasive that concept was to Hari.

"No baiting the demon," Lucinda admonished Nico.

"But it's so fun and easy."

Lucinda threw him a quelling look. Regretfully he subsided.

In that moment of stillness and almost peaceful calm, disaster struck. A strange energy trembled the air, and Talon cried a warning from within the house.

At first, Nico thought the danger came from inside. Then right in front of his eyes, a demon appeared, popping into existence from out of nowhere, only two feet away from Lucinda.

Derek! The very rogue demon that Hari and Ruric were here to guard against.

Shit! They should have sensed him long before he

got this dangerously close to them. But still, it was two demons against one, three if you counted the Princess, Nico thought, then watched with mounting dread as Derek splashed both Lucinda and Hari with the liquid contents of a vial. Fuck! Oil of Fibara. A substance that subdued a demon's power.

Nico didn't even see Derek move. Hari just suddenly crumpled to the ground, his side raked open by demon claws. As he fell, his hand wrapped around Lucinda's ankle, his teeth bared in a fierce snarl. Derek grabbed Lucinda by the arm. Then all three demons were gone, disappeared. Popped out of existence.

All that remained were three scarlet drops of Hari's dark blood.

ELEVEN

Humans had a saying. Hell hath no fury like a woman scorned. Well, whatever silly human came up with that hadn't known any demons. Especially one like Derek, who had been scorned by a Floradëur blood slave who had resisted him for the entire twenty-six years of his captured existence. And then, in less than one day's span of time, that blood slave had chosen me to bond with instead.

I had only a mere moment to be grateful that Talon, Nico, and the others were safe. Another brief moment of worry for Hari and I, and then it was too late. We suddenly arrived in Hell. Not the Hell I knew, but a region of it I knew only by reputation. But even with my demon senses blunted by the oil, I recognized where we were: in Bandit Land. Far away from the civilized, central state lands of Hell.

Hell's heat was even more stifling here. A low fog added to the sense of ominous oppression, rolling over the land, blanketing the peaks, and dipping down into the valleys between the humping mountains that rose abruptly up and down like sharp, spiking waves. Some of the most lethal and poisonous creatures in Hell abided here in the thick junglelike foliage. Animal-beasts that could lay slow and decaying waste to a demon's flesh with their venom, or snap him up and devour him in two quick movements of the jaw. None of them, however, were as perilous as the outcast demons who sought refuge here in this toxic southern outpost where not only the animals were a danger but the exotic, flesh-eating, giant vegetation that thrived here also.

We were in the heart of these humping mountains, in a narrow field between two of the ridged peaks. Even in my oil-blunted state, I could feel the remnant tingle of dark power here. Could almost taste the blood that had been spilled heavily and recently on the dark, tufted soil on which we stood.

Death magick. Forbidden, arcane knowledge that my father had banished a millennia ago at the onset of his reign; knowledge that was old and long unused but not completely lost, apparently. The means by which Derek had been able to snatch Hari and me and transport us without use of a portal—by using dark magick to become one himself, a portal of flesh between the living and dead realm.

I had not known Derek was this powerful, I thought, as demons crept out slowly from behind twisting trees and bushes to circle around us. Five . . . no seven of them.

I shivered as they came into sight, one by one. They were all maimed or injured in some way: a face partially dissolved, one demon missing an eye, another an ear. Another whose face was so heavily scarred that his mouth pulled up into a gruesome, perpetual half-smile. Yet another whose arm ended in a severed stump just below the elbow. The mildest disfigurement was a demon who sported two missing fingers; not cut off clean and neat, but rather gnawed down to raw, uneven stumps.

If I hadn't known where we were, seeing these demons would have unveiled that knowledge to me.

No one knew why the outcast demons in Bandit Land did not heal. Some thought it was the unnatural mist, others the distant location. Still others thought the land itself cursed. For whatever the reason, it remained a hard, unchanging truth that the demon bandits that resided here did not heal.

Only those with no other choice, with nowhere else to go, existed here: desperate criminals, outcast rogues. But with the land's abundant curses came a small blessing. It was one of the few spots in this realm that other demons avoided. Some, because of the whispers that a secret passage to NetherHell existed here, causing the strange mist and unnatural, non-healing state. Others, because it was fearfully alleged that the non-healing condition could be permanent, even after you left the cursed mountain land.

If Hell had a purgatory, this place was it. Demons existed here in precarious limbo, both cursed and guarded by that curse. Even my father's fiercest guards would hesitate to venture into this treacherous outpost. All but Hari, I thought, looking down at the stupid, injured fool. Derek had grabbed me by the arm and Hari had grabbed me by the ankle. I had tried to free myself of them both, a useless fight against Derek with my subdued strength; useless even against Hari, who had also been splashed with the oil. He had been as weak as I, but strong enough—determined

enough—to hold on to me, allowing himself to be unnecessarily captured.

Looking at him, bleeding and injured, here in this
treacherous place where you did not heal, I felt like shaking him and asking him why. Why had he stubbornly clung
to me? For someone who was supposed to be a clever and
selfish, self-serving bastard, he had acted with foolhardy
disregard for his own self.

Instead of shaking him, I quietly helped him to his feet.
Even injured, a hand clamped to his bleeding side, his full
demon strength muffled, he still managed to project deadly
menace as he eyed the motley demon bandits closing in
around us. The greatest threat, however, was the demon
who had captured us.

"Two for the price of one," Derek said with a cold,
pleased smile. "How accommodating of you. Hari, I
believe it is. Your delightful, unexpected presence might
even change my plans. It will be quite entertaining to see
how long you will be able to last here. Yes, indeed. Hold
him," Derek commanded the others.

In that demon quickness that eluded us now, he struck
Hari, sending him stumbling back, falling to the ground.
The two-missing-fingered bandit flipped Hari facedown
and yanked his arms behind him, careful not to touch the
glistening spots of oil that wet the front of him. The demon
with the macabre half-smile snapped dark shackles around
Hari's wrists.

"That was like hitting a helpless snell-kitten," I snarled
at our captor. "Does that make you feel superior, Derek?"

"Oh yes, you haughty bitch. It *does* make me feel superior. I enjoy hitting things, especially helpless things."
Moving again, too fast for me to follow, he backhanded
me across the cheek with jarring force. Had I been human,

the blow would have killed me. As a demon merely subdued by Fibara oil, it just sent me falling back hard onto the ground.

They shackled me as easily as they had Hari, while my erstwhile guard snarled and struggled uselessly, his eyes burning with deadly promise of revenge.

"Oh, my," Derek crooned, looking down at us. "This is going to be so enjoyable, a real treat for all the rotting souls here. Your capture is going to be the highlight of this cursed outland's history."

The look in his eye as he focused on me was so fervently maniacal that it chilled my blood.

"Oh, yes," he whispered. "You and I are going to make glorious history together, my dragon Queen beauty. Stunning, glorious history. Yes, indeed."

TWELVE

S ARAI FELT HERSELF slipping away. Not in the way
of the Floradëur, the physical way, though she had
often dreamed of doing so—escaping these bonds, slipping this prison, flitting up the roots of a plant to emerge
into freedom miles away. But even though it was the way of
her kind, it was a path that had been cut off to her.

She had been a captive for so long. Had endured the
burning agony of these cold irons that bound her wrists—
that had bound her soul for so many years that it was hard
to remember any other way of life. Hard to remember what
it had been like to be free—to be happy. Painful to remember those shining moments in her life of before. A life, an
existence, that would end soon. Not immediately . . . but
soon.

Hope was a cursed thing, like a weed that thrived
despite all attempts to kill it. Hope first for escape, which

had slowly faded, and finally died after the twentieth year
of her captivity came and went. Hope that her people would
search for her, fight for her, *find* her.

That wild hope had been twined with the greater hope
that her child still lived, the baby she had borne in captivity and who had been taken from her. A son, a beautiful
son, who had the look of her beloved mate—her Jaro, who
had been slaughtered during their ambush and capture. He
could have easily melded himself with one of the plant life
that surrounded them and emerged free, a safe distance
away. Sarai had begged Jaro to go, escape, seek help. But
he had refused to leave her that way, when she could not
follow, burdened by the child that was growing within
her. And so her mate had been destroyed by the attacking
demons. A male Floradëur had been useless to them, or
so they had thought during that initial flush of success. A
female would be easier to break to their will, and the child,
if it lived.

After her capture, the demons had turned like vicious
animals on each other. Two demons killed three others as
she went into early labor. After she delivered the babe, one
of the surviving demons left with her child. The scarred
one, Thorne, the bandit lord, had kept her, beaten her,
drank her blood, and defiled her body, over and over again.
Brutally, endlessly.

Thorne had ruthlessly, mercilessly taken everything he
could from her. Everything but the one thing he wanted
most. And the one thing only Sarai alone could chose to
give, she withheld.

No matter how broken her body, how battered her
spirit . . . her flesh, that one thing he could not make her do
no matter how he raged and beat her.

She would *never* willingly bond with him.

As the second decade rolled sluggishly by, something changed in her. Even the sturdiest weed dies after it has been battered harshly enough by the elements. On that second bitter anniversary decade of her captivity, hope for escape finally withered within her and died along with the selfish hope that her son still lived. Poor boy. Better that he had died than lived as she did, under the brutal claws and raping fangs of a demon. That day, as Thorne tore into her neck and drank down her blood, tore with even greater pain into her dry, unwelcoming body, she lay there without struggling, unresisting, as he slurped and grunted over her. That day . . . that moment, everything slipped away—burning hatred, cringing fear, dying hope. All that she had been was gone. All she wished for now was an end to this futile existence.

"Bond with me and you will be strong enough to break free," he whispered down into her empty face. When she didn't respond, hot temper flared in his demon eyes, ugly red.

"I have no use for you then!" he raged, smashing his fist against her, breaking her nose, painfully cracking her cheekbone. "If you refuse to bond with me then I have no use for you!" His claws ripped into her belly, and her blood flowed in a warm gush onto the cold ground. "Merge with me, you useless black bitch!" He shook her, but she was gone already, floated up into the brutal numbing pain of her body.

He tossed himself off her and left. When he reappeared three days later, she had not moved or made any effort to heal herself, as was her gift. Blood still dripped sluggishly from her face, her belly, the torn flesh between her legs.

He took her outside then. For the first time in over twenty years of hidden captivity, she tasted the fog of the outside

air. For the first time three of her shackles were removed;
only the fourth one around her right wrist remained. And
despite her will, her strong desire to seek her end, nature's
abundant energy poured into her and healed her.

He had put the shackles back on her, and taken her back
belowground. But while Thorne could force her body's
healing, he could not force her desire to live. When Sarai
touched neither food nor drink for a sennight, he shoved a
hollow reed tube down her throat and forced down broth.
She did not fight, did not move, did not speak. She did nothing, letting the hours, the days slowly pass, lying in filth, in
wetness, letting sores soften her flesh and rot her body. Each
time Thorne cleaned her up, she waited until he departed,
then threw the food and drink he had brought her on the
ground and crawled onto it, laying in the stinking wetness.
He cursed her but he no longer beat her, no longer forced
himself on her. Just continued to drink her blood, and even
that was brief and infrequent and relatively gentle now.

It was not enough. There still was no reason for Sarai
to live.

She did not waste breath begging him to let her die.
She just focused her will unrelentingly on seeking that end
passively.

In the fifth week of this silent battle, he carried something into her cell, and tossed it on the ground next to
where she lay.

"A new demon dead," Thorne told her when she didn't
even turn her head to look. "A rare demon child that my
men found wandering in our mountains. Quite damaged,
unfortunately, before I managed to convince my men to
give her up to me, but nothing you are not capable of healing, if you wish. A girl, no older than fourteen or fifteen
years of age. Not much younger than what your son would

be," he said slyly, kicking the bundle. It let out a weak, pitiful cry. "She is yours. I'll be back tomorrow. If you don't
want her, I'll take her back to my men to enjoy."

The heavy silence after he left was broken by a whim-
per, a few low moans as the ragged bundle shifted and tried
to drag itself away from her. The sound, the fear and pain
emanating from the small creature, pierced Sarai's apathy,
and she finally turned her head and saw what had been
brought to her.

A hateful demon, a hard voice whispered within Sarai.

A child, an innocent child, a gentler voice of reason
argued back.

In the end, Sarai's compassion and curiosity defeated
her. Lifting up on arms weakened from long weeks of
starvation and disuse, Sarai dragged herself over to peer
down into the frightened eyes of a young girl. A demon,
her senses told her, but a child whose skin was still white,
still so tender, not yet darkened by Hell's harsh heat. Not
darkened but not undamaged. Blood was splattered across
that white skin, and the smell of open wounds sang strong,
overriding even the bloodscent. Cuts sliced across the girl's
arms, the backs of her hands—defensive wounds scored
so violently deep that large chunks of her flesh hung like
gruesome ribbons from her arms.

That the girl's own demonkind had done this to her
sickened Sarai, along with the fear in the child's eyes. Fear
of her.

"Won't . . . hurt you." Sarai had not spoken for so long
that the words came out rusty-sounding. Weak.

The young demon, so vulnerable, showing so much pain,
didn't show any relief or belief at Sarai's hard-ventured
words, making Sarai almost smile. "Yes, wise . . . not . . .
trust words. Only actions . . . speak truth."

Even here in this stygian dark hellhole, life and energy was flourishingly abundant. The roots of trees and vegetation ran deep, some ending only inches away from the wall of her cell. Sarai thought it more a curse than a blessing that the cold iron that prevented her escape did not hinder her ability to draw energy to heal. When Thorne discovered that she was able to heal even shattered bone mere days afterward, the beatings the bandit lord gave her had grown even more savage. But here and now, Sarai could use the ability for good. And she did. She lowered the barrier she had erected and felt her body strengthen as curative energy flowed into her with a renewing surge. With a touch, Sarai shared that healing wonder. The demon girl gasped as the pain seeped out of her and into Sarai, who took it without resisting. So much pain.

A tear seeped out. By the time it reached Sarai's chin, the jagged wounds on the girl's arms had closed and disappeared. And with that willful act of healing, Sarai was dragged once more fully back into life. Thorne had been wise indeed in the lure he had cast her. Nothing else would have altered her course otherwise. And so she, a Floradëur, had came to love a demon child—Brielle was the girl's name—and the child came to love her in turn. A demon child who never grew, even as the years passed; caught forever in the body of a fifteen-year-old girl.

Brielle gradually took on the duty of caring for her, bringing her food and water, mending her clothes. The young demon roamed aboveground in the lighter day hours, and slept on a pallet outside Sarai's cell in the darker hours of the night. They became hostage one to another. The child's silence protecting the Floradëur, who Thorne threatened to kill if Brielle whispered one word of her existence to the other bandits. And Sarai willingly healing Thorne whenever he was injured, not fighting him over the taking of her blood, but even that became less and less frequent. The beatings and demands for Sarai to bond with him stopped after Thorne tried once to use the child against Sarai a week after they had become mother and daughter to one another.

"I will never bond with you, not even for the girl's sake," she had told Thorne with almost serene calm. "If you abuse her, I vow you this. I will not heal her again. I will shut myself off. And this time *nothing* you do will bring me back. Better that we suffer for a time and then find rest than suffer over and over again in an endless cycle of pain."

Thorne had heeded her vow, nay, her threat, and not touched either of them after that. During the next several years of relative peace, Sarai learned through Brielle, her tie to the world above, of the harsh existence the other demon outcasts here endured. None of them knew why the bandit lord alone healed when all other demons here did not. None knew of the captive Floradëur Thorne kept hidden deep below his private chambers in a secret cell. They whispered he was a sorcerer, a practitioner of ancient dark magicks, able to heal himself and curse his enemies with a debilitating ague. Indeed, a few of Thorne's most powerful demon foes had fallen that way, succumbing to feverish chills and sweats, taken down quickly by other bandits at the first sign of weakness, their bodies burned instead of eaten, their blood left untouched.

Brielle's physical strength was caught in the middle, like the suspended physical growth of her body, halfway between a child's strength and a grown demon's full power. None else were like her, Sarai learned. The weak did not exist long here, and that was what Brielle was—weak.

No matter how the girl tried, she could not break Sarai's manacles or bend the bars of her cell. Brielle tried, every changing season, but her strength remained as it first was.

"Enough," Sarai finally said after the sixth year had passed. "We would have nowhere else to go, even should we gain freedom. It is Thorne's protection that keeps you safe here, unharmed from the others. Who clothes and feeds us."

It was a hateful but true fact, one that made Brielle's eyes flash an angry red and slid her nails out thicker and longer; not the full length of other demons, but still lethal enough. "But *you* could still try to escape, Sarai," she said low and fierce.

"Hush," Sarai soothed and reached through the bars to draw the angry demon child into her arms as much as she could hold her. "What I have now, you and this fragile peace, is enough."

Then days later, things changed. A new demon appeared, killing Thorne and taking his place as bandit lord—the same demon who had taken away her son many years ago. Derek was his name.

The raping of Sarai's blood and body resumed, bad enough. Even worse were the taunts of what he had done to her son. If the eyes of Floradëurs turned red as demons did, hers would have been a river of blood. She hated as she had never hated before. Even more powerful an allure than the ending of her life was the ending of *his* existence.

He asked her where Thorne had hidden his book of spells. She told him she did not know. He asked that of her only the first week. When that yielded nothing, he moved on to his next desire.

"Bond with me," Derek screamed at her with a maddened gleam in his demon-red eyes, beating her more brutally, more

savagely than Thorne ever had, shattering every large bone
in her body and smiling as the splintered, broken pieces cut
her bruised flesh and more blood streamed out. "Bond with
me and I will tell you what became of your son."

She laughed then, and continued to laugh as he grabbed
her hand and twisted each finger, breaking the delicate
bones one by one. Laughed until the sound became as mad
and as wild as the look in his own eyes. Because the answer
was obvious. Her son was dead. Otherwise Derek would
not have slain Thorne and taken his place. He would not
be here in this gods-forsaken outpost trying to force a bond
with her.

Sarai didn't know who was the greater fool—she, for
staying alive all these years for nothing, or the demon for
believing she would ever willingly bond with his murder-
ous soul.

The greater the snap of bone and shudder of pain, the
louder and more feral her laughter became until the demon
was crazed by the taunting sound.

"Shut up!" he cried, slashing at her in fury with his claws,
trying to stop the sounds coming from her throat. But the
wild, taunting laughter didn't cease. Even when a piercing
claw sliced open her ribs and pierced through her lung, she
continued to choke and burble out her unholy mirth as he
cursed her to the deepest pits of Hell, not knowing that
she was already there. *Had* been there ever since her mate
was slaughtered and her babe taken screaming from her.
Dearest gods, her baby. Her poor, poor baby.

I'm coming to you now, she thought, peace settling over
her. *I'm joining you soon.*

In the bloody aftermath, the demon stood gazing down
at her, the crazed look leaving his eyes, allowing him to see
what his anger had wrought, or rather wrecked. Her.

She smiled at that thought.

"Crazy black bitch," Derek said, "look at what you made me do," and strode out in fuming fury, leaving painful peace behind. When the new bandit lord returned a moment later with a large chalice halfway filled with wine, Sarai was prepared for anything but what he did next—cut her wrist and drip her spilling blood into the chalice.

He glared down at her. "Stupid whore, making me waste your blood."

And the reason for his curious actions speared into Sarai's mind with sudden clarity. Derek thought that she might perish, and he had came back to gather as much blood from her as he could.

He didn't know, Sarai thought with a smile that made his hands tremble. He did not know that she could have healed herself so easily. That she had the choice, the ability, even now, to reach out for that flowing energy. Instead, she blocked that part of her ability and reached out for death. Begged for it to come to take her. She hovered there, so close to death, but it refused to grant her that elusive freedom from this hateful burden of life. So close, so frustratingly close, but she was not yet damaged enough, drained enough, broken enough to die.

The demon left and returned with Brielle in tow, clutching a bundle of cloth, a jar of salve, and a basin of water, trembling with fear, so small next to the angry demon who was bristling with the unnatural energy effect of Sarai's blood rushing through him. Fear changed to disbelieving horror and pain as Brielle's eyes fell on her—what was left of her.

"Sarai," Brielle whispered, tears pouring down her face in a fluid stream as Derek unlocked the door and pushed her into the cell, throwing a sack into the corner.

"Some food and blood wine to hold you until I return," he said curtly to Brielle. "See that the black bitch survives. If she passes, I will have no more mercy or use for you."

He left and the dank cell was filled only with Brielle's soft weeping as she cleaned Sarai's wounds and bandaged her. *No,* Sarai thought. *No, let me bleed, let me die.* But she had not the strength to say the words, she could merely bubble her distress, which caused Brielle's tears to flow even more.

"Don't leave me. Please, don't leave me," the young demon murmured, over and over again like a chant, a whispered prayer.

In counterpoint was Sarai's own silent pleading, spoken mute from her eyes.

Let me die. Please, let me die.

THIRTEEN

I WAS PISSED and scared and feeling really mean and nasty. Being helpless and weak, having my strength sapped and senses dulled, just brought out the natural demon bitch in me.

I was frightened, not just for myself, that was bad enough, but even more for Hari—who should not have been captured!

This was one of the reasons why I had fought my father when he had first assigned these two to me. Because even though they were supposed to protect me, when shit like this happened, I felt responsible for them. Mother of Light, when Hari saw that my capture was inevitable, he should have let me go instead of grabbing ahold of me! But he hadn't, and now Derek had not just me to play with, but Hari, too.

The games promised in Derek's crazed eyes were not going to be fun.

If I could have kicked Hari, I would have. But when another demon dared do so—kick him because he was stumbling along too slowly—I turned and smashed my heavy wrist shackles against the grinning face of the presumptuous bandit. I might not have my full strength, but the metal connected with enough force to break off two of the bastard's yellow teeth.

With an enraged bellow, the bandit retaliated with a blow that was too fast for me to see and too swift for me to dodge in my handicapped state. It smashed into my face and sent me flying a dozen feet away.

I heard Hari roar with fury, heard his warning cry, and was on my feet when the bandit came at me again. It was only when he swung and I spun easily away that I realized the demon wasn't moving any faster than I was. He had lost his demon speed. We both realized it at the same time. The bandit looked down in disgust at the oily wetness smearing the back of his hand from where he had struck me.

I swung my manacles, smashing the heavy metal again into his face. His head snapped back and another yellowed tooth went flying. With an enraged battle cry, he came at me again, but with our strength and speed equally muted now, it was easy to dodge his wild swings and land in blows of my own—punishing, hard ones, using the heavy shackles like a bludgeoning weapon. I drove them into his belly and he doubled over. Bashing the back of his conveniently presented neck, I sent him crashing to the ground. Before I could do further damage, Derek moved, too fast for me to see, and in a flash of steel, cut off the bandit's head. It rolled away from the body, and blood fountained out of the neck stump like dark, spilling oil while Derek calmly cleaned his weapon on the twitching body and resheathed his blade.

"Any other fool who allows his strength to become compromised will meet a similar fate," Derek promised with cold anger. "You." He pointed at the startled bandit closest to him. "Take off your shirt and wrap up the head. Bring it along."

The eyes in the decapitated head were still blinking, the mouth screaming out soundless words the bandit could no longer speak, not without any attached lungs. The last expression I saw on that bloody pale face was terrified dread as the other bandit obediently draped his shirt over the head and hefted it up.

Intelligence and comprehension would remain in that severed head until the remaining energy finally drained out of it. The sad thing was that in any another place, the demon had a chance to be restored into wholeness, even with so grievous a wound. But not here. Not on this non-healing, foggy land.

The headless body began to blindly push itself off the ground.

"You want the rest of him?" asked the demon with the two missing fingers.

"No, Graem. The head is all I require."

"Shameful waste," Graem muttered.

Derek smiled, a chilling stretch of lips. "Waste not, want not." He waved his hand carelessly. "The body is free to whoever is able to claim it."

Another bandit immediately challenged Graem for the body. The rake of Graem's sharp claws sliced open his challenger's face, the demon's eye spared only by the loss of Graem's two fingers. The other bandit fell back, clutching his torn face. The rest of the motley bandits stood silent, unchallenging witnesses as Graem turned to his prize and callously tripped the headless body so that it fell forward onto the ground.

With quick economy, Graem tore off the clothes, then
cut into the demon-dark skin with one sharp claw. One
clean slice down the back from neck stump to the base of
his spine. Then from there, a straight line down the back of
each leg. The body jerked and writhed in obvious pain, the
limbs flailing uselessly as Graem held it down with callous
ease. Sickening comprehension came to me when Graem
began to peel the thick epidermal layer off of the headless
body with quick finesse. Nausea swelled as I realized that
he was *skinning* the other demon, nausea so great that I
dropped to my knees and vomited.

"Quite a primitive, barbaric lot," Derek said, enjoying
my distress, his glittering eyes drinking it up. "They use
demon hide here, just as they do any other animal leather."

When Graem finished tearing loose all the back skin, he
rose and retrieved a few branches from a nearby tree. With
a few quick slashes, he sharpened the tips and returned to
the body with his makeshift stakes in hand. The headless
body was trying to scramble away on its hands and knees,
its bloody flaps of skin dragging on the ground. With a
kick, flipped the body onto its back and drove a stake into
the left hand. Then he went on to impale the right hand and
both feet next, pinning the writhing body to the ground in
a crucifix pattern. With two hard, tearing jerks, he peeled
the flap of skin down the front of its chest, and speared the
last two remaining stakes through the raw torso, left and
right side, anchoring the struggling body securely on the
ground.

Removing the stake driven through the right hand,
Graem pulled the hand down and across the body, and
stripped the skin from the limb in one smooth, tearing rip,
turning that portion of the skin inside out. He repeated the
same maneuver with the opposite hand.

With a quick, precise stroke, Graem sliced through the base of the genitalia so that penis, scrotum, and testes were left intact with the skin. A few final pulls down the front of the legs, a careful final peel down the toes, and voilá, one expertly skinned demon hide, complete with flaccid genitalia held triumphantly up for all to see.

The smell of blood, of raw meat . . . the sight of the staked, denuded body still twitching and moving helplessly . . . was too much for me. My stomach heaved again and again until I was just dry-retching.

"And that," Derek said with gloating, narrow-eyed satisfaction, "will be as nothing to what I will do to you and Hari."

His words made me glance over to see that the other bandits had sharpened the ends of long branches into makeshift spears and held these pointed at Hari; they were being very careful not to contaminate themselves with the oil smearing him.

"Enough. We move on," Derek said sharply as the bushes rustled. Yellow eyes peered out from the thick foliage as wild predators slowly began to creep forward, drawn by the sharply calling scent of blood.

No one tried to touch me as I walked over to Hari.

"If you poke me or him with your little sticks," I warned with a bright flash of teeth, "we'll play 'who can I smear Fibara oil on next?' "

We had taken no less than thirty paces when the sound of animals snarling, snapping, and fighting over the bloody body churned the air. The riotous sound of fighting eventually died down to the quieter sound of feeding—a haunting sound that stayed with us long after we had left the area.

None of the spear tips touched Hari when he stumbled and fell, or touched me when I stopped and helped him back on his feet.

After a long, winding up-and-down trek, we came suddenly upon a valley nestled among several humplike mountains. Therein, under the eerie mists that hovered like gloom, lay the ruins of an ancient settlement—a collection of smaller dwellings grouped around a crumbling temple and an old central palace. As large and impressive as the latter two were, it was the smaller dwellings that caught and held the eyes. Varied hides formed a patch-cover over the broken parts of the walls, or in some cases, were the wall. Most were furry animal hides, but quite a few were composed of bare skin with distinctive brown nipples in the chest area and shriveled male organs lower down.

"Welcome to our little community," Derek said with a warped smile. "Welcome to what we call Purgatory."

FOURTEEN

T HE GATE CLOSED behind them, locking Hari and
Lucinda in utter darkness. At least the bastards had
removed their shackles before shoving them inside here, Hari
thought. But that they *had*, made Hari even more uneasy.

"Hari?" Her voice came from nearby, sounding nervous
and unsettled.

"Here, milady." He moved closer until he brushed
against her.

She tensed, then relaxed a little, resting her shoulder
against his. "I smell animals."

"The scent is old and faint. There are no beasts here in
the darkness with us, milady. Not at the moment, at least."

"You don't need to 'milady' me in every sentence,"
she said irritably, clearly perturbed by the thick, unseeing
darkness. "Where are we? And why did they remove our
shackles and leave us here?"

His worries also. "I believe if we make our way down to the other end, we will find another closed gate."

"Leading to what? The arena?"

"That would be my guess."

"What are you doing?" she asked nervously when he moved away from her.

"Removing my shirt. You should do the same. Use it to rub off the oil."

He heard her clothes rustle. "Damn effective way to get a lady out of her clothes," she muttered.

"Just the shirt. Leave your brassiere on," he added hastily.

"They call it a bra now, not a brassiere. And no need to sound so alarmed, Hari. I have full intentions of keeping on as much of my clothes as possible."

"Were we not in such dire circumstances, milady, I would not protest the removal of as many articles of clothing as you wished."

"Back to using 'milady' again? Never mind. I'm just losing the shirt. My pants, thankfully, have no oil on them. But . . . shit! . . . my right bra strap is damp."

"Easily fixed. Just give me a moment."

The sound of ripping cloth.

"What are you doing?"

"Tearing off the stained sections of my shirt, and ripping the rest into pieces." He grunted as the effort pulled painfully on his wounds.

"Why?"

"To give you a strip of cloth to tie around the strap of your brassiere."

"Bra," she corrected again. "Here, give the shirt to me. I'll tear it up."

"Any oil on your hands?"

"No, they're clean. I wiped them on my shirt."

Hari passed her the shirt. The tearing sound of fabric continued.

"You need only the one piece, milady."

"The other strips are to bind your wounds, you idiot, so you don't lose any more blood. And call me Lucinda. None of that 'milady' crap. Not here with just the two of us."

"I call you milady to show my respect for you."

"You can do the same by calling me by my name, damn it. I'd prefer it."

"As you wish . . . Lucinda."

"Hari?" A slight pause. "You're not injured more than you're letting on, are you?"

"No. Why?"

"You're not usually this polite."

He snorted. Sour amusement tinged with sadness. "No. It's just where Derek clawed me up, and the oil making me so damn weak." Shame lanced him even worse than the physical pain as he thought of his past treatment of her. "I apologize, deeply, for not being as respectful toward you in the past as I should have been."

"Hari, you're not polite to anyone. No need to treat me any differently."

"But there *is* need. Every need. You are *drakon*."

"Don't whip yourself over believing my mother's lie when she claimed me a bastard, not of my father's blood. Even I believed it." Silence as she turned toward him. "Why does my having dragon blood make such a difference to you?"

"You do not know," he said, "how it once was to be a respected member of the dragon clan. I was born into Monère life two hundred years before you and your brother. By the time you arrived, most of our clan blood had become too diluted to shape-shift into dragon form."

"You knew others who flew as dragon?"

"Yes, many others once. The Monère used to live in separate clans, settled around their Queen. It was not all randomly mixed up in heritage as it is now. The dragon, phoenix, and griffin clans were among the most power-ful, but they slowly lost their dominance as their numbers died out. Fewer and fewer children came from pure-blood unions, only from matings outside of the clan—one of the reasons why your father chose your mother as his mate. Both were among the last pure-bloods of their respective clans. But while children resulted from these unions, the diluted offspring of these three strong clans lost the ability to shift into any animal form."

"Like Halcyon and myself."

"And Ruric and I. The mixing of blood affected the wolves, tigers, and other clans much less than it did those of the dragon, phoenix, and griffin bloodline. They still retained the ability to shift into their animal forms; we did not. Humans claim the last of the dragons were slain by knights, but that is not true. We died out simply because we could not breed pure and true anymore. But upon our death, our blood proved strong. Even those of diluted dragon blood, who made the transition to demon dead, existed far longer than any of the others, who faded away mostly after a century or two. Only those two other clans, phoenix and griffin, came close to matching our longevity.

"Dying, becoming demon dead, oddly enough, was a vast improvement over my Monère life. There were few enough of us left by then, that even those of diluted dragon blood became treasured. We lived together in Dracon Vil-lage, a few miles away from the central city. Only a few, like your father, mated to someone from another strong clan, lived outside of the village."

"I've never heard of Dracon Village," Lucinda said.

"It no longer exists. Xzavier, the previous ruler of Hell, was of the phoenix bloodline. He was a powerful and corrupt despot. Our dragon Queen gave the High Lord's procurer the food and blood tithe owed him, but she refused to hand over two of our women to serve as the High Lord's concubines—what he demanded of our village one tax year. Xzavier used this refusal as an excuse to destroy us; we were too powerful, you see. He came to our village when half our men were out hunting, and slaughtered everyone; not only the men but the women, too. He butchered every single female, including our Queen, effectively destroying our clan. Without our Queen, without our women, the warriors who survived the slaughter had nothing left to exist for, other than revenge."

"Which you took," Lucinda said.

"Your father did, eventually. He came to the village when he heard the news, and found us weeping, hardened warriors crying like children. Most of the bodies had been destroyed and burned by Xzavier's army before they left, or already eaten by scavenging beasts. Only a few remained, their bodies torn up into so many scattered pieces the enemy considered them as good as already gone. One, such, was Ruric."

Lucinda made a small sound.

"Nine separate pieces—I counted them—with his skull shattered and his face smashed up. Your father put all the pieces of him back together. Few healers could have done what your father did—heal Ruric and make him whole and functional again. Ruric was the only one we were able to save from that slaughter, and it took two seasons for him to fully recover. During that time, Xzavier decimated Griffinmass Village, and then turned to his own phoenix clan, killing all the men, thereby effectively eliminating his strongest challengers, all but your father, a handful of dragon warriors, and a few males from the other clans who lived outside their village." Hari paused, caught up for a moment in the bloody memories of that time.

Lucinda took the opportunity to gently wind the cloth she had knotted into a long strip around him.

"I can't see," Lucinda said, her voice soft, sweetly feminine. A balm to Hari's raw spirit. "You'll have to position it yourself. Try to cover as much of your wounds as possible."

He obediently adjusted the binding. "My worst wounds were dealt by Xzavier a long time ago, when he wiped out our village. A large part of me perished with our people that day. You have to understand. Ruric worships Blaec, and will always be loyal and devoted to him. But a part of me resented your father. For not being there. Or maybe I was just simply jealous. All had not ended for Blaec. He still had his family: his phoenix mate at his side, his Monère children still alive in the living realm. While your father grieved for the others, his heart was still whole and intact. His closest loved ones had not been destroyed. That was what allowed him to lead the rest of us. His heart and his spirit weren't broken by devastating loss."

"As yours was."

"Aye, as mine was," he agreed. "What there was of my family, my friends, were all forever gone. In the Great Revolt that followed, the rest of our dragon warriors fell. We won the war, but we also lost at the same time. Only your father, Ruric, and I—and then later your brother, upon his death and transition—remained of the once great dragon clan. Only a few surviving men. No women until you came to us, demon dead, and then only for a brief time before your mother took you from us with her lies, claiming that you were not of dragon blood."

"I still don't know why my mother would lie like that," Lucinda said in a small voice. "Why she hated me so much."

"Because you could have become our dragon Queen. We would have had a true dragon clan once more, while the other two powerful clans were forever gone, including her own phoenix clan. She did not hate you so much, I think. More that she did not want you to have something she could never have. But your father she hated. Your mother, Evaline, bitterly resented your father's rise to power, while she had lost all of hers. She wished to keep palace slaves as Xzavier had, but Blaec abolished the practice, keeping only a tenth as house servants, only those who desired to stay, and paying them wages. When your father did away with the tributes and cut the tax tithe down to less than a quarter of what it had been, Evaline called him an idealistic fool, someone who did not know how to rule."

Lucinda had known her parents' relationship had become strained and bitter there at the end. But she had not known why.

"Were they happy before he became the High Lord of Hell?" she asked.

"Strangely, yes. Before your father seized control of the throne, your mother was content with their arrangement, even though it was an odd coupling. She had been a former Monère Queen and descended from ruling aristocracy in the phoenix line, while your father was only a mere warrior in the dragon clan. In her eyes she married down, and not only that, had taken a mate from a rival clan. But the reason for their joining—to have children—made this acceptable. It was the sudden reversal of their power and roles here that brought out the hostility and bitter resentment in your mother. He suddenly had all the power, while she had lost all of hers. She was no longer a Monère Queen but just another demon dead woman down in Hell."

"Yes," Lucinda said, remembering. "It was quite a shock going from being a Queen, the center of my people's world, to being just an ordinary female."

"And yet you lifted yourself up from ordinary to extraordinary," Hari said. "Even after your mother did her best to destroy your new existence by claiming you bastard and taking away all the status and clan protection that should have been rightfully yours, you found a new path for yourself by becoming a guardian and walking the living realm. Becoming a legend in your own right."

"Not so much legend as maybe simply notorious."

"I disagree. Your mother was notorious, declaring you a bastard, dealing a pain severe enough to the High Lord to send him into a spiraling decline, and then cowardly ending her own demon dead existence . . . but only after doing her hateful best to leave a lasting mess behind. *That* is notorious. You, on the other hand, continued to serve your realm, your people, becoming one of the youngest demons to successfully attempt the portals. Then capturing and bringing back demon rogues—many that were centuries older than you yourself—in such numbers that you left the other guardians looking slack-witted and empty-handed. Faithfully serving almost five centuries now. *That* is legend."

"You avoided me," she said suddenly, "you and Ruric. Looked past me, through me, as if I did not exist."

"It was too painful to see what we had lost," he said simply.

"And now?"

"Now the dragon clan has a chance of existing once more with you, whole and unbroken. That is why knowing you have dragon blood flowing in you matters so much to me: seeing dragons fly the sky once more when we had thought that time forever gone. You cannot know what that means to me, Ruric . . . your father. Your young dragon form—it's such a beautiful sight."

"Young?" A soft snort. "I'm several centuries old . . . not young."

"But your dragon is. You're round, bulkier."

She huffed out a laugh. "You're saying my dragon is fat."

"Not fat. Beautiful. Adorably plump with youthful vibrancy. You will become sleeker and leaner with maturity."

But only if she survived.

"Why are you telling me all this, Hari?"

"Because Derek will do his best to try to end your existence now before you ever reach full maturity."

"That's not news to me," she said flatly. "I know he intends to end us."

"But he will not do so until after you shift into dragon form."

"He will allow us that chance, that possibility of escape?" There was a spurt of hope and excitement in her voice. "How do you know?"

"His actions. Removing the shackles from us. Allowing us to wipe the oil from our skin, knowing that the stultifying effects of the oil will wear off less than an hour after we do so."

Even with dimmed senses, they could hear the sound of movement, many voices gathering outside.

"Doesn't mean he won't just cut us down in the arena before we come back to our full strength." A beat. And then she demanded, "What do you know that you're not telling me?"

"He used death magick to snatch us, bring us here."

"Snatch *me*, not you. *You* didn't have to be captured. You should have just let me go. Saved yourself instead of dragging yourself along as an additional hostage."

"Lucinda . . . my lady. My precious dragon Queen," he said wistfully. Almost tender. "You *change* me. Make me want to be better than what I am. I abandoned you once before upon your mother's lie. I will not abandon you again."

"Tell me what you think will happen."

"Do you remember when Ruric and I brought down the giant Gordicean worm, and Ruric ate the beast's heart and I the brain?"

"I remember."

"Do you know why we did it?"

"I know those organs are considered delicacies, especially to older demons."

"The land has become almost too tamed and civilized under your father's and brother's rule," Hari murmured. "There is not much opportunity anymore to battle any of the great beasts. Eating the heart and brain of the Gordicean didn't just renew us; it imbued us with some of our vanquished foe's strength and power—a temporary effect that lasts only a day."

"Like drinking a Floradëur's blood?" Lucinda asked.

"Something similar to that, yes, but gaining less than a quarter the strength a Floradëur's blood would impart us. We're not as revved up. Nor do we crash into sleep after the effect wears off. The added strength just fades away gradually and we are as we originally were."

"Doesn't seem like much of a benefit. Not enough to risk letting me shift into dragon form and possibly escape."

"Oh, I'm sure Derek will do everything he can to make ultimate escape for you impossible. But it is not just the stealing of your strength he wishes." Hari's voice dropped low. "Does the name *Myrddhin* mean anything to you?"

"He was a mad demon sorcerer who existed a long time ago," Lucinda answered. "A Mixed Blood, I believe, one quarter human blood."

"You are correct. He was abandoned at birth, due to that mixed blood, and grew up among humans. Never knew of his Monère heritage before dying and making the surprising transition to Hell. Not many other demons would find the name he used before then significant, but you are more familiar with human history than most, having walked as a guardian for so long. Before his demon transition, he was known as Merlin. Is that name familiar to you?"

A small, quiet, "Yes."

"Myrddhin was a powerful sorcerer and seer when he was alive and thought himself human. He became even more powerful and much darker in death, devoting himself to his greatest passion, trying to find a way back to life. Not as a demon hopping a portal to the living realm, but permanently—truly having his dead body filled again with living energy. They called him the mad demon sorcerer. Not to his face, of course. Even though they did not know of his human notoriety, he had ended enough demons by then for them to know that he was quite deadly. When Myrddhin began to dabble and experiment in death magick, then they began to fear him. He is mostly known now as the originator and creator of death magick. He was also Xzavier's half-brother, almost the clone image of Xzavier's maternal uncle. Quite a surprise to the family—and him, I'm sure. But they made use of him. He was responsible for Xzavier's rise to power. When Xzavier made his bid for the throne,

Myrddhin was at his side, and all other demon challengers became afflicted with a mysterious non-healing state. They claimed they were being haunted by ghosts and perished a short time later in battle. Myrddhin never claimed anything, just returned to his hermit life after that, but a few, including your father, always believed him to be the cause of that mysterious ailment."

"So what happened to Myrddhin?" Lucinda asked.

"He appeared one last time during the Great War, emerging from isolation to come to his half-brother's aid after we staged our uprising and revolt against Xzavier. Your father severely wounded him, and it was believed he perished. We never saw or heard from Myrddhin again."

"So what does he have to do with us now?"

"Do you remember when our little flower of darkness friends and former allies, the Floradëurs, where given the new moniker Flowers of Life and became hunted? Well, that blame can be laid entirely at Myrddhin's feet. He captured a few of them for his study. We learned of this when the Floradëur ambassador petitioned Xzavier for his kinsmen's safe return. That's what started the rumor that drinking the blood of a Flower of Darkness could restore a demon back to life if you drank enough of it."

"So much slaughter," Lucinda murmured, "just because of Myrddhin's interest?"

"As Myrddhin became more and more powerful, fewer demons scoffed at him, and more began to take his pursuit and his interests very seriously. He could do amazing things. One of them you just saw when Derek popped into the living realm without the use of a portal."

"How do you suppose Derek came by such knowledge?"

"There have been whispers every now and then of a

book that Myrddhin either found or wrote himself, a book of spells."

"You think Derek got his hands on that somehow."

"Yes. I also think that this abandoned settlement was probably where Myrddhin secretly practiced his magick and conducted his research. The unnatural mist . . . I should have put it together sooner with that curious affliction that took down Xzavier's other challengers for the throne. But their demise occurred fairly quickly and we never witnessed it ourselves, just heard of it from others. I'd forgotten about it until we arrived here. But those two facts combined. . . . It makes me certain that this was once the sorcerer's hidden base."

Lucinda whispered, "Almost a millennium since Myrddhin has been gone, you said. It's a little frightening to see just how powerful his dark magick once was . . . still is."

The sounds on the outside increased. Their time was running out. Soon they would be herded into the arena.

"Yes," agreed Hari, "frightening. But that's not the most important thing I wish to tell you."

"What is?"

"During the same time that Floradëurs suddenly became a hunted delicacy, Myrddhin also began collecting information about dragons. It spawned another rumor: that life could also be regained by eating a dragon's heart and brain, its most vital organs. A very short-lived rumor since no living dragons flew the sky anymore, other than your father. But that is no longer true now. A new dragon flies the sky now. You."

"That's why you think Derek will allow me to shift into my dragon form," Lucinda said quietly.

"That's why I'm *sure* he will. Do you remember what

he called you? *My dragon Queen beauty.* Lucinda, there may be a real chance for you to get away. None of these demons has ever seen a dragon or fought a warrior with dragon blood. Derek may underestimate us. I'll do my best to keep you safe until you are given your chance. But you, in turn, must do your part. As soon as you are able to, you must shift into your dragon form and fly away."

"But—"

"You cannot save us both, just yourself. If there was a way, selfish bastard that I am, I would gladly take it, but there isn't. I will fight with every last ounce of strength in me to give you a chance—to aid your escape. But I will inevitably fall. Do not try to help me. Do not come back for me. Do as you once told me I should have done."

"What?"

"Escape. Get help and come back for me. I fully expect you to return with a battalion of warriors, you know. I'm not that self-sacrificing."

"Don't," Lucinda said roughly. "Don't put yourself down like that. Not when you're trying to be noble."

"It's not nobility. Just damn necessity. And I'm selfish enough to ask that you don't waste my intended sacrifice. If you have a chance to escape, you must seize it and not look back. You have to survive, do you understand? That is the only important thing to me. I'm a tough bastard. I fully expect you to try to salvage me when you return. But if I perish, it will have been worth it to me, *but only if you survive.*"

The inner gate groaned open, spilling in dim light. And suddenly the time for words was over.

FIFTEEN

W̲E̲ D̲I̲D̲N̲'̲T̲ V̲O̲L̲U̲N̲T̲A̲R̲I̲L̲Y̲ walk out into the pit of the arena—no, we weren't as eager as that for our trials to begin. We didn't budge until the gate we had entered through creaked open and we saw large beasts being herded into the passageway. What they were, I couldn't tell in the dim light, but the angry grunts coming our way were alarming enough to flush Hari and me out into the empty center. The arena floor was overrun with weeds and bushes and scraggly grass.

I had a brief glimpse of scattered demons above and around us. Of walls tall, old, and crumbling at various parts, which would have been good had not guards with large battle axes been posted at all these weak points. The axes were a bit of an overkill. The demons guarding those areas were weapons enough with their full strength and access to demon claw and fang—which, by the way, we did

not have. No fangs or claws for Hari and I, not as long as
the oil of Fibara still muted our abilities. Our only weapons
of sorts were our sharp demon nails; a poor tool without
full demon strength and speed to back it.

Compared to the heavy beasts trundling after us into
the arena, our modest half-inch-long nails were as nothing
compared to their sharp foot-long tusks—and those were
the smaller ones. Some were curved longer than my arm.
The animals themselves were taller than us, and weighed
at least a thousand pounds each.

Five geant boars. Hell's enlarged version of wild boars.
Only instead of a thick, hairy hide—no, that would have
been too easy—they had an almost impenetrable outer
shell much like a rhino's thick, leathery armor. Their short
curly tails looked like a cute, comical afterthought pinned
onto the thick hind quarters.

The beady, marble-dark eyes of the geant boars turned
in our direction. Some were already flaring red, not because
they saw us—no, their eyesight was rather poor—but their
sense of smell was sharp and acute.

"They smell my blood. Don't talk, don't move, and they
won't know you're here," Hari said quietly as he began to
circle slowly around to the right, away from me.

Wet snouts snuffled the air loudly and five pairs of
yellow-ivory tusks tracked Hari's movement. They began
trotting toward him. Normally they were too slow to be
of any threat to demons. Small herds of domesticated
boars were sometimes even kept by demon households
for their ready blood and abundant meat. But these geant
boars weren't acting the least bit domesticated. Their
beady, vicious eyes had turned crimson in excitement. Nor
did finding themselves inside the stadium with an injured
demon seem at all strange to them as they closed in eagerly

around Hari. Not likely this was the first time they had sur-rounded and taken down a weakened demon here. And we had nothing to fight them with!

I glared up at those who watched us from above, over seventy demons scattered loosely around the large, tiered rows of the amphitheater. Beyond them, four demon archers stood at the ready with longbows and quills, scat-tered among the axe-wielding guards. Below them, sitting on an elaborate stone throne, was Derek. He was the only demon among them not crippled, maimed, or injured in any way.

The other bandits watched Hari and the boars, but Derek's eyes were fixed upon me with shining intensity. And it wasn't because of my half-undressed state. There was nothing as simple or common as sexual desire in that avid stare. More like he wanted to inhale my essence, my very soul. His fixed, focused attention upon me, and the posted archers and guards above us made Hari's words seem suddenly far more believable. Derek was going to toy with us—have sport with us until the effect of the oil wore off. Until then, we had to survive.

The ground shook as the boars suddenly rushed Hari. I watched, helpless, a scream caught in my throat as Hari dove to the ground, rolling so dangerously close to their trampling feet. The edge of a sharp tusk from the boar nearest him caught and ripped through the skin of Hari's back. The wound was thankfully shallow, but it demon-strated that without our demon quickness, we moved as slow as the boars. Or more accurately, they moved as fast as us now.

Hari leaped back, dodging another sharp, vicious tusk, and ran to the opposite end of the arena, leading them away from me.

It was not a fair fight to begin with. The geant boars
had a far heavier mass than us, and were thereby more
powerful by simple virtue of this weight disparity. They
also outnumbered us. It should have been five to two. But
no, Hari wanted to make it even more unfair—five to one.
Screw that.

I moved as Hari had moved, slow, smooth, and unhurried, closing in on one of the great boars. What I would do
once I reached the creature, I didn't know yet. All I knew
was that I had to be closer to the action, so I could draw
some of that lethal attention away from Hari.

"Lucinda, don't. Go back," Hari said, his voice low and
intense as watched the five boars circle around him almost
lazily.

I didn't answer him; didn't want to give myself away
yet to the large, ugly beasties. I shook my head instead of
replying.

Bad mistake. That one abrupt movement was enough to
snag the attention of the boar nearest me. He snorted and
turned his dim eyes and sharp nose in my direction.

Hari muttered a harsh curse and leaped at the creature
before he could charge at me.

No, I thought. That wasn't what I wanted, what I had
intended.

Hari slammed into the geant boar and tried to shove
him onto his side. It didn't work. The big creature didn't
even budge. Hari did, however, bouncing back from the
creature to land on his butt.

"As big and as stupid as troll dung!" Hari snarled. "Here,
this way! To me!" Picking himself up, he waved his arms.
As a distraction, it worked wonderfully. The animal rushed
him, as the other boars closed in around him, leaving Hari
little room to maneuver or escape.

Hari had already proven that the creatures were too big and heavy to knock over. What else to do?

The little curly tail on the geant boar trotting away from me twitched back and forth, catching my attention. As good a part of the animal as any to latch on to it, I guess.

I ran up behind the big beast as fast as I could, which was not terribly fast. Hampered by the effects of the oil, we were reduced down to almost human strength, the lowest on the totem pole. But humans, weak as they were and even at their most primitive, still had managed to kill animals much larger than themselves by using their greater intellect.

I grabbed that little curling pig tail and used it to swing my full weight around the back of the blocky creature. The boar squealed, a loud, high-pitched sound that grated even my dull ears. It should be even more jarring to the bandits' fully functioning senses.

The big boar swung around, literally chasing its poorly abused tail. The swing of the animal's movements kept me suspended off my feet. I was actually congratulating myself on the brilliance of my smart maneuver when the boar suddenly reversed its direction. Uh-oh. A hind foot kicked out and caught me square in the stomach. A foot higher and I would have had broken ribs. As it was, I bounced and skidded across the rough dirt floor. It was, ironically, the sharp-bladed leaves of the weed plants and not the fall itself that scraped my hands and caused them to bleed.

I lay on the ground, stunned for a moment as the fresh scent of blood wafted into the air, pinpointing my location. Two boars started galloping toward me. The one leading the charge was the creature whose tail I had stretched. His eyes burned an angry, dark red as he charged, tusks lowered. I rolled as he thundered by, the swipe of those sharp tusks so close I felt their airy kiss over my skin. I rose to my knees and then had to throw myself to the ground in reverse direction to dodge the second boar's charge.

I saw Hari twist away from swiping tusks, his eyes on me. "Get up," he yelled as the two boars wheeled around and charged me again. But I was still dazed and hurt. It wasn't just the kick to the stomach, though the pain of that blow hurt like the dickens. It was more the blood on my hands, smeared on the bristly plants, so crimson bright. *So alive* came the odd thought, and I wasn't sure if it was the blood or the purple-green weed plants the thought was addressing. Another odd thought came to me—from me but not really from me—that I was more. Not just demon dead but more. What more?

As I answered the odd, seeking question in my mind, it was like a dawning revelation of myself *to* myself. Through my binding with the others, I was part living Monère and part Floradëur, not just demon.

As the revelation came to me, I tried something I hadn't thought to do before. I tried to draw from those other parts of me. The oil of Fibara muted a demon's strength; it had no effect on a Monère or Floradëur.

I felt something in me, something around me, stir as two of the half-ton creatures bore down upon me, their sharp ivory tusks gleaming.

I leaped away—and when I say *leaped*, I mean it in the truest sense. Not a little hop but a big one, covering several meters at a speed that was Monère fast. Not quite the quickness with which the demon dead could move, but much faster now than the geant boars. And with that knowledge, that sudden increased speed, I wondered: What about my strength? Is that greater now, too?

Only one way to find out.

I leaped again, not away this time but *toward* the two boars that had wheeled around to face me. I crossed the distance, and instead of latching on to a little tail, I grabbed a yellow ivory tusk. A violent pull, a powerful twist of my body, and it broke. It broke! I landed on my feet with the sharp tusk gripped like a long ivory stiletto in my hand. A weapon. I had a weapon now.

The animal screamed in rage, in pain, with an intensity of emotion that was almost human as it rushed me. I just stood there and let it come, feeling the ground tremble and shake. Waited until it was almost on me before twisting to the side and thrusting that long, sharp tusk through its eye, ramming it into its brain. It dropped, twitching and shuddering to the ground like a giant boulder, its painful squeals filling the air.

The other boar turned and tried to run away from me. Too late.

I launched myself at the retreating boar, snapped off one of its tusks with a sharp, twisting wrench, and drove it like a stake up into its eye. The great beast dropped to the ground. Snapping off the remaining tusks from the two downed boars, I charged toward the others with a wild battle cry. Two of the boars turned away from Hari to face me; the third one ran away. I slapped a tusk into Hari's hand, and went after one, while he went after another. A light spring just past my chosen target, a quick spin around, and another high-pitched squeal as I speared it through the eye.

I turned around to discover that Hari had dispatched his boar as well. He might not be as fast as I, but he was deadly accurate. A long tusk stuck out from a bleeding eye cavity as his boar squealed and grunted and writhed where it had fallen.

The last boar took only four leaps to reach and was a relatively quick and easy dispatch. I looked back in time to see Hari carve open the soft underbelly of his boar with a tusk, and rip out the heart. Didn't need full demon strength to do that; weaker human strength was more than enough for that task.

The crowd of demons watched in silence as Hari gobbled down the blood-filled organ.

Ew!

I knew now that it gave you some of your prey's strength, but no thanks—just plain old blood was more than enough for me. Plain old demon nails to cut open the soft neck and drink from it. A couple of mouthfuls and I felt even more strength return to me.

Derek's eyes bored down into me from above, and I knew that he wondered the same thing I wondered, too. If the oil's effect had worn off yet. Whether I could shift now into my dragon form.

Soon. But not yet.

They did not allow us any more time than that before the next round started. The inner gate swung open and a demon walked out of it. He was a bandit I had not yet seen, because I would not have forgotten him if I had. He was a warrior, obviously trained, wielding an old, chipped sword. But this was only noted distantly. He was whole of body, all his limb and digits intact, but not whole of face. His maiming was only one part of him—his nose. It had been cut entirely off, leaving a gruesome naked hole in his face. What most people don't realize is that the nose is mostly cartilage, not bone. The walking anatomy lesson coming toward me reminded me sharply and vividly of the fact that when you cut the nose away, you peer directly into the dark hollows of the nasal cavities. That one defect—no nose—

took away all the wholeness of his face and turned it into a garish horror.

The softening up phase was apparently over. The bigger guns were being sent out now.

The demon bandit, moving too fast for me to see, was suddenly there in front of me with that nose-missing face. "Boo!" he whispered, and I fell back away from him with a girlish scream, a sound I hated hearing coming from my throat.

That one move by him, and my reaction, answered their question. No, I had not regained full demon speed yet.

Another quick blur of movement and he reappeared standing behind Hari, the point of his sword sliding through the front of Hari's chest. The sword blade pulled back out and Hari collapsed to the ground.

I screamed, with anger, with rage, with something close to madness. "No! Fight me, you ugly noseless freak. Or are you afraid?"

His angry demon eyes focused on me, and he started to walk to me, bloody sword in hand. Just plain old walking, one foot placed in front of the other, as if he wanted me to know and see him coming for me.

On the ground, Hari twisted and latched on to the demon's right ankle. The demon turned and casually kicked him in the head with his other foot, full strength but unhurried, so I could see the blow, watch the way Hari's head snapped back, his body grow limp.

The demon continued his march toward me.

I yanked out a blood-coated ivory tusk from the weakly moving geant boar at my feet and stood holding it like a long knife in my hand.

The bandit just smiled. The gesture shifted his naked nasal plates, making him look even more garishly grotesque.

"I'm not allowed to end you. But anything else up to that point, I am allowed to do. Tell me, Princess." His words came out with an odd hollowness, without a nose to finish out the sound. "Have you ever been raped before? I hope I'm your first. Sadly, I don't think you will find it at all to your liking, but perhaps I'm wrong. You're already half undressed for me like a little bitch in heat."

I turned and ran from him, not just because he frightened me, badly, but so I could put more distance between him and Hari.

He tackled me, far faster than me, and much stronger, too. He dropped his sword and used both hands to restrain me, grab the tusk from my hand, and send it flying away.

I struggled fiercely. But I could not throw him off me or free myself, no matter how hard I tried. He lay on top of me with the hard bulge of his arousal grinding against me, that horror of a face only inches away from my own, so that I had a real up close and personal view of the cavernous hollow of his wet, glistening nasal cavities. My stomach twisted and churned in a sickening roil, and faintness threatened me. As a thing to frighten and subdue, that gaping fright-sight hole was pretty damn effective.

The demon growled and transferred my wrists into a one-handed hold. It was impossible, even then, to free my hands, and my body was pinned. That left only my head free. I swung my forehead up at him, aiming for the sharp, central nasal plate. To drive it up into his brain. Not deadly to a demon, but it should hurt plenty enough to get him off me. But he anticipated my move, avoiding my strike, and backhanding me for my efforts, a blow that sent my head twisting to the left with enough stunning force to make pinpricks of white dance in my vision.

"So you want to play rough, do you? I'll be more than

happy to accommodate you," he snarled. Grabbing my breast, he squeezed hard. It wasn't just the brutal force itself that hurt, but the sinking of his sharp demon nails into me, slicing down into my tender mound like hot dagger points.

I screamed.

"A bit too much pain for you? My apologies, Princess. Let's try to increase it," he sneered and flexed his hand, sinking the sharp points even deeper down, twisting and cutting my flesh.

I screamed again, joined this time by Hari's deep rumbling war cry and the sound of shredding clothes.

The demon was flung off of me and I looked up to see Hari, changed into his demon beast form. A much bigger, badder, stronger version of his usual lean and mean self. His hands were fully clawed, his fangs bared as he snarled, "Get out of here!" and sprang after the other demon.

The muting effects of the oil of Fibara had obviously worn off for him. But not for me. I concentrated and tried, but still couldn't manage the transition into another form.

The other demon didn't have my problem. He stretched up huge and immense, his own clothes tearing as he transformed into demon beast, and the two of them came together with thunderous impact. They fought with a speed too quick for me to follow. Feeling useless, I retrieved the sword the bandit had dropped, and felt better holding the long blade in one hand, and an ivory tusk in the other. But it only took me a second to realize how useless the weapons were to me.

On Derek's command, six more bandits dropped down onto the floor of the arena, transforming midleap into their demon beast forms. Five of these huge creatures raced to where Hari wrestled with the other demon. The last one came deliberately toward me with slow, menacing intent, twice my size and crushingly heavy, but that was as nothing to his strength and speed. The weapons I held were about as useful against him as throwing a handful of dirt at a raging forest fire.

"Now, Lucinda!" Hari said in a deep-throated yell. *Now* meaning that it would be a pretty good time to shift into another form.

Concentrating, I spiraled down into the core of myself and tried to find that spark that would open the door to transformation.

"Come on, come on," I muttered. To myself, not the demon advancing on me. He needed no encouragement.

Power flared faintly within me, stretching up, pushing against the gossamer-thin veil that blocked me from my other self. Gathering a concentration of power, I punched a tiny tendril of it through that invisible barrier, and the connection was made. A flash, a shimmering glow, as something deep inside me caught fire and started to roar up and out of me into exultant being.

I turned my eyes up into the amphitheater to where Derek sat, and saw the same triumph, the same exultation in his own glittering eyes. *Yes!* we shouted within, as I started to stretch and shift in change. I had a moment to decide which form I would take, dragon or demon beast, and chose dragon. It was a much harder transformation, slower and longer.

The approaching demon could have jumped me then, but he didn't. He came to a stop and waited patiently at a sharp command from Derek. The bandit's only deformity was a missing ear and a large chunk of meaty flesh below that, so you could see the white edge of his jawbone.

The other demon apparently didn't know I had another

shape to change into, other than my demon beast form. His eyes grew huge with shocked surprise as I surpassed even his great size and continued to grow larger and yet still larger in shape until my head rose above the crumbling arena walls.

I opened my mouth and a burning stream of fire spewed out of me toward the posted guards along the wall. Turning in a circle, I flamed the entire seating area of the amphitheater. Derek dove behind his stone throne. Others, including three of the guards and one archer, were not as quick as he, and were set afire, screaming, burning, falling backward.

My heavy tail swept the arena floor as I flamed the audience above, shifting around the bodies of the boars and knocking down all the transformed demons fighting in the pit. I tried to find Hari but could not see him.

Arrows flew at me from the three remaining archers. One struck my scaly face and glanced off, just missing my eye; another skittered off my back. One arrow swooped in at a clever angle and pierced the thinner skin under my neck. I reared back, roaring at the sharp pain, the impact of my body collapsing the wall behind me. Hari appeared suddenly up in the tiered stands of the amphitheater.

"Go now, Lucinda. Leave!" he yelled. Then winked out of sight. Bloody invisible!

A few sluggish drops of blood splashed onto the stone floor, revealing his path. A longbow was snatched from an archer's startled hands, the quiver of arrows yanked off his back. Invisible hands pushed the archer off the wall, screaming and flailing. Those same unseen hands shot arrows, one after the other, at the two remaining archers, who ducked and took cover, until he emptied the quiver.

"Hari." I growled his name in a deep rumble of sound. "Jump on my back."

For a moment I thought he was going to listen to me
as the longbow dropped to the ground. But I was wrong.
His form flickered briefly into visibility partway around
the amphitheater, then winked out of sight again, just long
enough to see that he was heading toward the two other
archers. A spate of arrows flew in his direction.

"Go! Just please go!" Hari shouted, just a voice. More
arrows flew out toward the new position his voice had
revealed.

I roared, in fury, in defeat. Hari was not going to leave,
not while the remaining archers threatened my escape, and
my continued presence only endangered him and forced
him to reveal his position to the others. I couldn't even
flame the archers for fear of burning Hari, too.

With regret, I launched myself up into the air. My wings
snapped open, and with two deep, powerful fanning sweeps,
I lifted out of the arena. A couple of arrows whizzed past
my wings, and only by the luck of an upstroke not piercing them. I didn't look down, just focused on gaining as
much altitude as I could, flying blindly through the thick
fog. An updraft suddenly caught and lifted me above the
white mist, and I soared even higher, carried along by the
powerful wind current. It was exhilarating, riding up into
the vastness of the sky. So wildly free.

Then Derek's voice drifted up to me from far down
below. "We've got him, you dragon bitch! Watch. Watch
while we tear him apart!"

SIXTEEN

T HEY CAUGHT HARI eventually by his blood trail.
That and the fact that he grew weaker with each lost
drop of blood until he was unable to maintain his invisibility and stuttered into sight once more. He lost even the
strength to maintain his demon beast form, and shrank
back into his normal size, but no matter. Hari had accomplished the most important thing. He had taken out the two
remaining archers, broken their bows and arrows into useless pieces.

Three bandits tackled Hari and brought him down into
the arena pit before he could go back and destroy the other
two longbows. They were retrieved by the bandits, who
shot at Lucinda's departing form. But soon the thick mist
swallowed her up, and blocked her from their sight.

Derek had come out of hiding once Hari was secured by
the others bandits. The bandit lord remained in his normal

demon form, but even at an arm's-length distance shorter than the four big brutes holding Hari down, he exuded a malevolence that the others lacked—a pure evil madness mixed with spewing wrath. He ripped into Hari with demon claws. "Scream," he commanded.

Blood spilled, and flesh parted down to the bone. But Hari just smiled up into Derek's furious eyes, his jaw clenched tight, not a sound escaping him.

For a brief moment, Hari thought he'd pushed Derek into a rage so great that he would end Hari's existence now, destroying the only remaining lever he held against his escaping prey in his maddened fury. But Hari had underestimated his opponent.

The bandit lord spun around and disgorged his wrath up into the fog-covered sky. "We've got him, you dragon bitch! Watch. Watch while we tear him apart!" He turned back to the four demons holding each of his limbs. "Go ahead," Derek told them. "Rip him apart in as slow and painful a manner as you can. Make him scream."

The pressure began—a slow, powerful, inexorable pull on all of his extremities.

Per size and poundage, there was almost no creature stronger than a demon beast. In the human world, the closest thing to that sheer force was the great dinosaurs. A transformed demon had more power than a bull or an elephant, so when the four demons began to pull, his body stretched until it could stretch no more, then began to give along its weakest points. His torn flesh began to rip and tear further under the steady, unrelenting force. Skin gave first, splitting the seams of his wounds wider, longer, deeper. The more resilient muscle, fascia, and tendon followed next. It was a pain that was immense and indescribable. Pain twined with silent, screaming horror as Hari felt his innards pop free, saw them bulge up like huge bloated worms along the widening split of his wounds.

"He's not screaming," Derek said unhappily. Then gave a triumphant shout as he caught sight of a large dark shape flying back toward them through the mist.

No! Don't come back, Hari wanted to shout, but he couldn't. If he opened his mouth, only horrible screams would come spilling out, not words. He fixed on the sight of her, and even under the tearing of flesh and anguish of mind, he could have wept at the beauty of what he saw. Dragon flying once more. Magnificent, beautiful, breathtaking.

The wound in his chest where the sword had run him through suddenly split under the increased pull of the four demons. Ribs separated, and his chest cavity gaped open, exposing the raw, covered organs of his heart and lungs.

"Stubborn bastard," muttered the demon stretching out his right arm. The force increased incrementally more, and Hari's shoulder popped out of its socket in sudden, wrenching give. Fresh, excruciating agony splashed through him like acid. But still no sound, not even when the other shoulder popped out, or when his hip joints followed with sickening jolts. The following spasms of the violently stretched joint muscles white-washed him further in hot blazes of pain.

The demon grasping his right leg cursed and twisted the limb he was holding, yanking on it like an angry child whose toy was not working properly. "Come on, you bloody lunatic, give us a scream."

Dots whitened Hari's vision. *No, no, no. Don't faint. Don't you fucking faint.* He had to see! Had to know what happened to his dragon Queen!

Hari fought through the searing agony of his body to fix

his eyes on the glorious sight of dragon flying down out of
the misty sky, golden scales glistening with almost metallic
brightness, fire breathing savagely from her mouth, sending all the bandits, even the four demon beast scum holding
him, running and scattering under her swooping threat.

She was so fierce and bright, so gloriously savage a
sight, that for one brief moment hope flared up in him.
Hope that she would succeed in rescuing him and flying
them both away.

Then Derek stepped into sight above him, smiling down
at him with his sword in hand. "Ignorant bandits, running
away. Don't they know that the safest place to be is right
next to you?" He sliced his blade lightly across Hari's neck
in a bloody taunt, and the dragon screamed as it hurtled
down toward them, so large, so fierce, so big a force that
Derek should have been afraid. But there was no fear in the
bandit lord's eyes, just hungry anticipation.

Fire shot out of Lucinda's mouth to burn the ground
and any bandits foolish enough to be out in the open. But
the one area she should have flamed—where Derek stood
beside Hari—she did not burn. The safest spot indeed.
That bastard was too damn cunning and excited. Derek had
something planned, and Hari was too weak and injured to
do anything to stop him.

"Now!" Derek shouted, raising his sword like a general
ordering a charge. But instead of men rushing forward,
nets filled with rocks were unearthed from the ground and
flung up into the sky by a dozen bandits. They used nothing more their own power; but demon beast strength was
as great as that of a human catapult. A hail of sharp stones
sprayed the air like buckshot.

"No." Hari moaned, watching their deadly flight. "Please.
No!"

One net, even three or four, the big dragon could have dodged. But not the vast barrage that came pelting her way in wide, spraying arcs.

Hari watched, helpless, as the projectiles struck Lucinda's face and body. But it was the sharp rocks that ripped through her wings that damaged her the most. Nothing—not even a fierce dragon—could fly with holes in their wings. She plummeted down from the sky, crashed through the far end of the arena, taking down the entire north wall, and hit the ground in a hard, jarring impact.

Derek laughed in triumph. "The nets! Cast the empty nets over her!"

With only the barest control, desperately managed, Hari weakly grabbed Derek's leg.

The bandit lord looked down at him with eyes lit maniacally bright. "A useless effort," he said and slashed his sword down, cutting through Hari's arm, cracking bone.

With gentle, insulting ease, Derek pulled his leg free of Hari's lax grip. "Nothing can save her now. Nothing." And ran eagerly toward his prize.

Hari rolled onto his side, and felt his organs, barely contained, threaten to spill out of him. He forced his other arm to move, the simply dislocated one. By stubborn will alone, he made it grip the ground, and tried to drag his body forward. But he was too weak. A scream of anguish—body, mind, soul—was all that came from the horrendously painful effort.

Hari craned his neck as far as he could to watch the bandits swarm around his dragon queen. The gold dragon shook her head, tried to heave up onto her feet, but was too injured and dazed to accomplish it.

"Please," Hari prayed to whatever power might be out there listening to him. "Please save her."

As Hari watched, his anguished eyes fixed on his queen, a shadow flickered on the ground next to her. It took quick shape, budding up from a weed plant smeared crimson with the dragon's blood, sprouting up into a slender, black Floradëur. Talon!

He looked like a slight shadow against the glittering gold scales of the huge dragon. Talon touched her and both their forms shimmered and morphed, shrinking, growing smaller, disappearing down the small plant.

It was Derek's enraged roar, "No!" that finally convinced Hari that what he was seeing was true.

She was rescued. Safe.

"Thank you," Hari whispered. "Thank you."

SEVENTEEN

THERE WAS BRIEF chaos, and then eerie silence as all the bandits dispersed to search the surrounding jungle-forest. Brielle watched them from where she crouched behind a pile of rubble—what had, a few moments ago, been part of the arena wall. Since her transition to demon dead, she had seen horrors and cruelty, pettiness and selfish meanness, which seemed to be a commonality here in all but the beautiful ebony woman hidden in the belowground cell. She, alone, had elegance and grace of body and spirit. She alone was kindness and light in this dark and dismal realm.

It was because of Sarai, and Brielle's refusal to let her die, that she ventured outside to look for a way to escape, first from the manacles and bars Brielle wasn't strong enough to break, then outside beyond Purgatory. They had to get out of here, and it was up to her to find a way. The

other two female demon servants inside the broken-down
palace were too cowed and fearful, and just as mean and
vicious as any of the males here. She could not seek help
from them. Their sole focus was their own survival, and
that did not run parallel with helping Brielle and Sarai
escape, or even acknowledging that a hidden captive
existed within their midst. They possessed eyes that did
not see what would be dangerous to their health, ears that
did not hear what should not be heard.

She had planned to stay far away from the arena where
everyone had gathered, and search the empty work sheds
and individual dwellings for a cutting tool to attack the cell
bars with. Then Brielle had heard his voice, so calm and
quiet among all the coarse mutterings and excited shouts of
the bandits. It was a voice filled with confidence and authority, rare in this place of cowards and maimed cripples, who
were as broken and bent in spirit as they were in body.

*They smell my blood. Don't talk, don't move, and they
won't know you're here.*

Brielle hadn't even registered their meaning at first.
Didn't understand what he was trying to do until his next
words.

Lucinda, don't. Go back.

Only then did Brielle finally realize that the male she
heard inside the arena was trying to protect the woman
he spoke to. It was so alien a concept, so contrary to the
laws of survival here, that hearing that voice, hearing those
words, was like seeing a golden ray of sunlight cutting
through the dense mist, a compelling and irresistible draw.
Brielle could no more turn away from it than a flower could
turn away from the light. That voice drew her to scale up
the old arena wall until she could peek her eyes up over the
edge and see within.

Brielle's first sight of him was disconcerting, like she was gazing down into a badly miscast play. She was looking for a hero, expecting someone to match that calm midnight voice. Instead she saw one of the darkest, swarthiest demons she'd ever laid eyes upon in the center of the arena floor. He was tall, lean, and quite mean-looking, with a saturnine face that was dark, cruel, and coolly cunning. His wounds leaked blood, his eyes glittered red, and his lips curled back in an ugly, soundless snarl as he faced the five geant boars circling him. He looked much more the villain than the hero his words and actions implied.

Sitting, in contrast, with graceful dignity on the throne above was the new bandit lord, handsome with a high noble brow and long aquiline nose, the kind of visage a sculptor would have chiseled onto the beautiful statue of a prince. But Brielle knew how false that outer covering was. There was no honor or nobility in the soul behind that attractive face—only cowardice, malice, and truly frightening evil.

It was only when the woman moved that Brielle's eyes were drawn to her. She was a stunning beauty, her hair and skin the exquisite color of gold. She was a small demon but voluptuously built, with large cat eyes, high cheeks, and a full, sensuous mouth. But for all her soft, lush curves, there was a hardness to her, a dark and dangerous look in her eyes much like the warrior trying to protect her. And when she sprang into action, snapping off a tusk, driving it deep into the geant boar's eye, Brielle saw that she was a warrior, too.

In fascination, Brielle watched the two of them fight the five boars, and then the warrior that came after them, Malik the Dreaded. She watched the impossible happen as the golden woman transformed into a huge, gold dragon.

Watched her protector veil himself in invisibility, and fight off the others as his lady made her escape. Watched with muted horror as they captured the dark demon and began to pull and stretch out his body and torturously start to rip him apart. She watched with dashed hope as the dragon returned and was taken down by the hailstorm of sharp rocks that ripped her wings and made her fall. Watched with disbelief as another black one like Sarai appeared out of the ground next to her, then shrank both their forms to disappear down a sprouting weed plant. It was a fantastical, almost unbelievable series of events.

Amidst all the screams and shouts and chaos, Brielle was perhaps the only one to hear the whispered thanks the bronze-skinned warrior gave for his lady's safe rescue as he lay there broken and forgotten, his body torn half open.

Brielle waited until all the demons had left the area, then crept down to the arena floor where the dark one lay, one body among so many.

Eyes noted her cautious progress. A few wounded bandits even called out to her as she skirted around them. She had to move quickly before the wild beasts crept in, lured by the bloodscent. Of them all, only *he* did not look upon Brielle's arrival with interest or cry out to her for help, even when she stood over him. He lay there with a slack, peaceful look on his dark, swarthy face, despite being so fearsomely wounded. *Please . . . please save her,* he'd whispered, and his desperate prayer had been answered. He didn't seem to care what happened to him now. A mindset that irritated Brielle, made her angry.

Moving away from him, she steeled herself and stripped the pants from two injured demons nearby, moving quickly to evade hands that grabbed frantically for her as two large carcajou scavenger beasts cautiously climbed over the rubble and entered the arena. They had the flat, pointed heads of wolves and were as big as primeval saber-toothed cats. Once they began eating, almost nothing could drive them away from their food.

Brielle froze as they looked at her with their coldly intelligent eyes, assessing her threat. She was the only demon standing, the only one not injured. They crouched with alert readiness, ears perked, hackles raised, their thick bodies poised to spring. It wasn't anything Brielle said or did, but rather the distracting movements of the injured bandits trying to drag themselves away that broke the dangerous, still moment. Instinctively the large scavengers pounced on the wounded prey trying to escape. Terrible shrieks and guttural cries rent the air and the moist scent of blood grew thicker, even stronger as the animals began ripping into flesh, feasting on the ready meal.

Moving with trembling slowness, Brielle made her way back to her felled warrior: *Hari,* the golden warrioress had called him. He noted everything—her presence, the two feasting scavengers, three more creatures slinking in—but he seemed apathetic to it all. Resigned to his fate.

Brielle dropped down beside him and began binding his torn abdomen with one of the trousers she had pilfered, tying the legs around him. Ire mixed in with fear made her rougher than she intended, but he made no sound, asked no question as four more darkly striped carcajous slipped in. One of them claimed the large geant boar lying only a dozen meters away. There were nine carcajous in total now. At this rate, they would soon run out of bodies. They had to get out of here before that happened. Quickly she tied the legs of the second pair of trousers around his opened torso.

"Try not to make a sound," she said softly as she

gathered him up. Cries, whimpers of pain, would draw dangerous attention to them.

The agony must have been immense as Brielle lifted him up, but he made no sound. Then again, he hadn't cried out when they had deliberately tortured him.

Brielle might be small, her strength not as great as a full grown demon's, but she was still demon dead and carried the warrior easily, moving with slow caution among the feeding scavengers. They were less of a threat with their attention fixed intently upon their meal; it was the new ones pouring in that hadn't claimed a body yet that were the most dangerous. By the time she reached the broken outer wall, there were only a couple unclaimed bodies left inside.

A large black carcajou slinked in and eyed them with interest. The creature took a step toward them and Brielle snarled and hissed, baring sharp little fangs. It hesitated, then loped to one of the last wriggling bodies. With a shudder, Brielle hastened away from the frenzied feeding.

She made it back to the palace and fumbled open the door. "You don't have to be quiet anymore," Brielle told him as she slipped inside and shut the door.

"You cannot save me," the demon said in a wet rasp.

"I changed my mind," Brielle said, unbearably irked by his defeatist attitude. "Maybe you should just stay silent."

Had Brielle not seen his fierce, indomitable will while he had focused on aiding his lady's escape, she would never have guessed him to be so deadly passionate and skillful a fighter as he lay there passive and uncaring in her arms. He was tall enough and she was short enough that his feet dragged the ground, his joints swinging sickening and unnaturally loose. He had to be in terrible pain, but it hardly showed on his impassive face.

The two servants had to have heard them, smelled the overwhelming stench of blood, but they didn't come to investigate, probably too frightened after hearing Hari's male voice. She strode into the bandit lord's bedchamber and awkwardly pushed open the hidden doorway on the far wall.

They descended down a black well of stairs that took them deep belowground to the hidden prison that only she, Sarai, and the bandit lord knew about—and now him. Hari's eyes noted the barred cell, the ebony occupant within, and his gaze abruptly sharpened.

"Sarai," Brielle whispered, laying Hari down outside the cell. Sarai was curled up on the floor, the same way she had left her.

Her breath caught as she peered more closely at Sarai, and saw that her wounds had healed.

"You're better!" Brielle exclaimed. "How?"

Sarai's dark eyes glittered up at her. "Something disturbed my shields, allowed energy to flow through me, and caused me to heal."

Brielle felt like a knife had been plunged into her. "You were blocking yourself from healing?"

"Why did you bring this demon here?"

Brielle shook off her feeling of betrayal. "You must heal him."

"Why?"

"So that he can save us."

Chains clinked and rattled as Sarai sat up. "That is a fool's dream, Brielle. You cannot trust any demon male. They are all evil."

"Not this one," Brielle said. "He's honorable. Not like the other bandits."

A sound came from Hari then, lightly shaking his chest.

The movement bulged out squishy intestine around his stomach binding, a disturbing and distracting sight. It took Brielle a delayed moment to recognize that the sound he was making was laughter.

"You know me not at all, little demon girl," Hari rasped. "I am far from honorable."

"This is your only chance," Brielle said earnestly. "You know what Sarai is. Without us, you will not survive. But if we save you, you must save us in turn when you are healed."

"And you would take a demon's word? You would take *my* word?"

"If you swear by the lady whom you serve that you will do so."

Brielle's words slapped all the amusement away from Hari, and his eyes focused balefully on her. Even so terribly injured as he was, she almost took a step back away from the sudden hardness in his eyes.

She let what felt like a minute pass before she tried again. "Agree to help us so we can help you." Then more softly, persuasively, "You can return to your golden lady after you bring us safely out of here."

He eyed her almost malevolently. "You are more cunning and merciless than you appear. Very well." A cynical twist of those thin lips. "I swear upon my lady's name that I will aid the two of you if you can make me whole enough to do so by some bloody miracle."

Brielle turned eagerly back to Sarai. "Please, Sarai. I know you can heal him. This is our chance, maybe our only chance. Please."

Brielle wanted to shake her as Sarai gazed at her with distant eyes. Shake both of them, so stubborn and foolish.

"Very well," Sarai finally said, after Brielle had given

up hope that she would answer. "I will try for you, Brielle. Give me your hand, demon."

"His name is Hari," Brielle said, moving Hari's hand between the bars, helping him stretch out his poor arm as much as he was able. Half a foot still remained between them.

Brielle watched, breath suspended, as Sarai's black hand slowly bridged the distance to Hari's bronze demon fingers.

The Floradëur touched him. And with the contact, power swirled.

EIGHTEEN

W ITH GREAT RELUCTANCE, Sarai touched him—
willingly touched him, a hateful demon male. Brielle was the only one of their kind Sarai did not abhor, a
child, innocent. Not so this demon, whose eyes were so cold
and dark. He had a killer's eyes; someone who could bring
death and destruction with no remorse. She did not want to
touch this demon, to heal him, to believe in him. But Brielle had pleaded, begged. And there had been something in
the demon's eyes when Brielle had mentioned his lady.

Whoever this demon served, she was important to him.
Whatever honor he held was held tenuously only by her
and the oath he swore upon her name.

It was the only thing that persuaded Sarai to try to heal
him. To lay her hand willingly upon his abhorrent demon
flesh and lift the gate she had imposed, opening herself
again to the flow of energy that came to her even here.

With will, Sarai allowed it to fill her, and ebb out of her into him. With her eyes, and a sense beyond, she watched the torn, open flesh of the demon's belly and chest begin to mend together. Watched as the bulge of intestines was smoothed down and layered over with connective tissue. Watched as sinew, tendons, and nerves came together; broken ribs and dislocated joints fit back into place. And then the pulse of energy stuttered, shut down, leaving him only half mended. And Sarai pulled away her hand with shuddering distaste.

"What happened?" asked Brielle. "Why did you stop? He's not fully healed yet."

"I gave him all the energy I could," Sarai said.

"He needs more."

Sarai's lips twisted down in an unhappy curve. "My body is . . . unwilling to give him more."

"What do you mean?"

"Sarai is repulsed by me," Hari said. "Her mind and heart reject me. It's surprising she fought her own natural inclinations enough to heal me as much as she did."

"Sarai?" Brielle said, bewildered.

"That is all I have to give. I tried . . . But it is as he said. I do not desire to heal him, or even touch him." She could not even bear to look upon him, and called herself the worse kind of fool for channeling what energy she already had into him. She hated that she was whole and healthy again, and yet still chained, still captive.

The demon moved. His hands gripped a cell bar and pulled. Despite his lean and wiry build, despite the fact that he was only partially healed, and the outermost layer of skin still left open and unhealed, the bar creaked and slowly gave way. So did his body. The muscles and fascia over his abdomen strained and popped open, blood seeping out again. Only the crude binding, still in place, kept his entrails from spilling out.

"Stop!" Brielle cried, putting her hand in restraint over his.

"You should add your strength to mine, not try to stop me. If you can shift me a foot over to the left, perhaps with our combined efforts we might be able to pry open a large enough space for your friend to crawl through."

"A second effort like that and your chest will split open, along with your belly!" exclaimed Brielle. "And just getting her out of the cell isn't enough. How will you help us escape afterward with blood and guts spilling out of you?"

"I gave my word that I would try," he said in a hard, clipped voice.

"I did not heal you fully, demon," said Sarai from within her cell.

Hari's shrug made his loose belly contents jiggle in a sickening dance. "A half-assed escape for a half-assed healing effort."

"You would still try to break me free, even though I did not heal you fully?" asked Sarai.

"I swore upon my lady that I would try."

"Well, you can't!" Brielle cried. "Not like this. Sarai, please. Heal him fully so we can escape. Please . . . I know you can do it!"

"*Can* only works if I *want*," said Sarai bitterly, "and it is as the demon says. I do not truly in my heart desire to heal him."

"We are so close. So close to freedom," Brielle whispered tautly. "Can you not make yourself desire it—for your freedom and mine?"

"How can you make yourself love what you hate?"

asked the Floradëur. "It is like asking a creature without eyes to see. *You* have a chance, Brielle. You can leave. Flee this place."

"Not without you," she said. "Not without him."

"Then we are all of us doomed," Sarai said, closing her eyes.

Brielle shook her head with despair. "So close . . . We can't give up! You could save him, Sarai. And he you. All that stops you is your prejudice. Tell her," she urged, turning to Hari. "Tell her that you know others like her—the black one who came up through the plant and rescued your lady. He was your friend, wasn't he?"

Sarai's eyes snapped open. "What is she speaking of, demon?"

"His name is Hari," Brielle said.

Sarai ignored her, her gaze fixed on Hari. "There was another Floradëur here?"

"Yes," Hari nodded. "He rescued my lady."

The slightest pause. The slightest tremor. "And you are friends with this Floradëur?"

"I would not call him friend," Hari said with a strange look in his eyes. "Perhaps a brother. We both belong to the lady."

"A demon calling a Floradëur brother." A harsh sound of laughter pealed out from Sarai. "You overplayed your hand there, *Hari*. You lie! No demon or Floradëur would call each other brother."

"I saw him," Brielle said, voice and eyes intent. "If you don't believe him, then believe me! I saw this Floradëur rescue the female demon, though I don't know how. She was huge, transformed into a dragon. He touched her and they disappeared down this little plant!"

"That's impossible on two levels," Sarai whispered. "Demons do not take on animal form, and—"

"I know, it sounds crazy, doesn't it? Disappearing down a plant."

"No, not that. We can travel that way, but we cannot transport another like that with us." Her eyes narrowed dangerously. "Unless . . ."

"I told you," Hari said in a quiet, even voice. "He belongs to Lucinda, and she to him. They are bonded."

Sarai's eyes slanted into malevolent slits. "And you think telling me this will make me look more favorably upon you? No Floradëur would bond himself willingly with a demon! Only a creature like me, enslaved, beaten into it."

"A close but inaccurate guess," Hari said. "He was indeed kept captive like you, for twenty-six years by another demon. My lady rescued him, freed him."

"Twenty-six years." The words came out of Sarai soft and strained. "He . . . bonded with your lady in return for his freedom?"

"No. She had already freed him. As you very well know," Hari said with a tight smile that was more a baring of teeth, "a Floradëur's bond cannot be forced under duress. Talon *chose* her. Willingly bound himself to her to save her when she was dying, slipping away into final death. He brought her back to us, and that is why I call him brother, for what he did."

"Talon," Sarai murmured to herself. "What a strange name." Without warning, her small black hand grabbed ahold of Hari's. With all her will, Sarai gathered all the energy that filled her and tried to shove it into the demon, but it slipped through her mental hands like spilling water. There was still too much ingrained antipathy and repugnance within her toward the demon. "Argh! I'm trying . . . but I can't!"

Driving Sarai most was the fierce need to know: Was Talon her son? With that desire most urgent, she unexpectedly flowed into Hari. It wasn't energy but herself that flowed into him, partially melding into his essence, his thoughts, his memories. *Talon,* she thought, and that name pulled her through images until she came to Hari's first encounter with a creature as black as night, standing between the High Lord of Hell and the High Lord's daughter—Lucinda, the lady this demon served! It was a jarring realization. Even more of a shock was when she caught her first glimpse of Talon, and saw in those delicate features the distinctive slanting eyes he had gotten from Jaro, the small mouth and high straight nose that looked like her own.

Immersed in memory, Sarai watched the tale the demon had spoken of unfold and become true. Watched and learned of the bond, not just with Lucinda but with another living Monère, too.

Sarai spun among the memories, the whirl of emotions, watched all that happened with a disbelief echoed by her demon host as they tried to return Talon to his people and were captured, almost killed, by them, even Talon. Watched as Lucinda drew power from her bond to transform herself into dragon. Felt Hari's awe, shock, and fierce wonder as his world turned upside down, his emotions cracking and unthawing like frozen ice coming back into moving fluidity. Felt new meaning thrill the demon's existence as he saw *drakon* fly once more.

Sarai spun along the flow of memories until the moment when Talon appeared outside the arena and rescued Lucinda, shrinking her huge dragon form down the stem of a plant along with his own. Only then did Sarai begin to withdraw. Only then, as she came back into awareness of her separate self, did she realize the coldness of the hand she gripped.

The demon's eyes were closed as if in sleep. His body was eerily still, shimmering. Becoming translucent!

"Sarai," Brielle said in a horrified whisper, "what have you done?"

"I went into him somehow," Sarai said dazedly. "I . . . I didn't know I could do that."

"You drained him of all his vitality," Brielle said, stricken. "He's fading away."

"No!" But even as Sarai denied it, a part of her knew it was true. In seeking his memories of her son, she had drained him of whatever sparked his demon essence. "No," she repeated more firmly, stronger. *No! You will not leave us. I will not stay here, captive, while you slip away free into final darkness.*

She poured herself into him in an unseen rush. All of her—willingly, wholly, gladly. Gone was the repugnance, even the hatred. She felt compassion, acceptance for the demon now, a willingness to merge fully with him. Some vital part of her found him worthy after the foray into his mind and emotions.

The melding this time was complete: all of her into all of him. A joining, a choosing.

Their bond snapped into place, and she spoke into his mind. *If you fade away into final death, I go with you.* There was giddiness, a feeling even of relief. If he ended now, she would go with him and finally be free.

A male voice, low and musing, sounded in Sarai's mind, startling her. *Freedom in death? What good is freedom then if you do not exist?*

You choose, demon. You choose. I have done all I can.

She felt shock and confusion come from him. *You can speak to me? What have you done, Sarai? Gods, what have you done?*

You know. You know what I have done. You feel it.

For a long stretch of silence, they hung teetering on the edge. Then he chose.

I wish to continue rather than end, he said. *But I, alone, cannot choose for us. You must decide, also.*

Irony struck her. *I thought as a male you would have no trouble deciding for yourself and others. Why do you insist I must also choose when I have ceded our fate into your hands?*

There was sardonic humor in his next words. *I would be happy indeed to choose for us both, if I could, but I am too weak. I have made my choice, and still we hang in precarious limbo. Decide, Sarai. Do we continue or end?*

His question reverberated down their bond like a strong wind, tossing their minds back into chaotic memory. Quick snapshots of images and emotions flashed by, a deluge of remembering. The sweet, loving face of Sarai's mother. Being held by her tall father, safe and secure. Running down a hill, the wind in her face, with her cousins, young and innocent beside her. Her first melding, that wild, thrilling sense of slipping through ground and traveling with such flowing ease. Jaro's first gentle kiss. The joy she felt as they pledged themselves as helpmates.

And then the flashes became his. A pretty Monère woman, his mother, smiling down at him. The faces of so many men, passing through, never staying long. Aristo warriors of the dragon clan, some affectionate, most annoyed and impatient with the young child he was. His mother smiling less and less frequently. The word they used for her and for him, *arlotto*, impure—not of pure dragon blood. It also described what his mother was to them: harlot.

More impressions: gnawing hunger, the blow of heavy hands as he grew taller, stronger, more challenging. More pain from the careless words and cavalier treatment of the dragon aristos toward his mother. Pretty words when they wanted her; uglier ones after they had their fill of her. The harder look in his mother's eyes.

And then, like a hot brand seared into his deepest memory, the day a tall, familiar aristo warrior found him alone in the forest collecting firewood, just before his twelfth birthday. Pretty words, unexpected compliments about how tall Hari was growing. How handsome a young man he was becoming. The flush of pleasure. The wild hope that perhaps this warrior might be his true father. That he had come to claim Hari as his son, and marry his mother. Then the brutal dashing of that dream when the warrior sprang on him, laughing darkly and excitedly as Hari struggled against him. The tearing of their clothes. The grunts of pleasure as the aristo overpowered him and forced his stiff organ into a place inside Hari he could never have imagined. Burning shame, pain, bitter tears as Hari bucked helplessly beneath the powerful thrusting body until the warrior was done, lifting from him with a mocking pat on his buttocks. "My thanks, *arlotto*. An even better ride than your mother."

No! Hari roared, his words echoing loud and strong in Sarai's mind, stopping the images with a forceful wrenching of will. *No more! Do not make me remember.*

It is you who is remembering, not I. Think of something else!

Pain flashed, vivid and horrible. A bloody sword coming down at him. His death on a battlefield.

Gods! Can't you think of anything good, demon? she cried as they began to spiral down that dark memory.

Another image bloomed, breaking past the other memory. The demon Princess Lucinda changing into dragon. The gold of her skin transforming into the gold glitter of scales. Her lunge up out of the arena into the sky. The powerful stir of wind over him from her wings.

Decide, Hari said, a whispered voicing in their minds, as if anything louder might accidentally bring them back into the darker memory.

Unfortunately, his good moments were few, and they did not last long. Pain again as they tortured Hari, tried to make him cry out. Even sharper pain as he saw the sharp hail of stones rip holes in her wings. Despair as he watched her fall from the sky while he lay helpless. As helpless as he had been when his innocence had been taken from him.

No! Sarai cried.

My only good memories are mixed with pain. The only way to stop this is to decide. Life or final death?

It was hard to know which she wanted more—oblivion in death or the continued pain and suffering of life.

Your mere wording betrays your preference, he said. *You wish more for the oblivion that death brings.*

She felt sadness in the demon and immeasurable tiredness. And yet a stubborn part of him still clung to this existence—all that kept them still on the precarious plane of continued being.

They were ripped back into his memories. Demon bandits rushing to surround Lucinda after her terrible crash. Then when all hope was gone, the unexpected sprouting of a dark Floradëur up from the bloody bent stem of a wild weed plant.

Sarai froze that image. Stopped the play of memory

there at that precise moment. And looking upon those eyes so like the mate she had loved, Sarai decided—for life. *I want to live. My son—my son . . . I want to know him!*

And with that decisive thought, the bond between them churned and tilted and flowed down the path that led them back to life and continued existence.

NINETEEN

I FELT AS if I were being squeezed impossibly thin—
thinner than water. Sliding along bright points of light.
Sometimes jumping a short distance between gaps. It was
an uncomfortable distortion. Unnatural.

I felt even worse when I returned to my natural shape.
Or at least the shape I had been in when Talon had grabbed
me, that of dragon. It felt as if a tiny mouth disgorged me.
There was a wrenching sensation and then the ground
stretched out, hard beneath me, a bumpy, scratchy surface
from all the brush and trees I flattened out beneath me.

My vision was only pinpoint brightness at first, which
slowly expanded out to tunnel vision. Enough to see Talon
sprawled next to me, a tiny streak of blackness. He seemed
to feel even worse than I did as he vomited up the contents
of his stomach. As I focused on him, the tunnel finally
stretched out into full, normal vision.

But, though I could see him, I didn't hear him. I couldn't hear anything.

Sound returned to me suddenly with a jolt as my senses settled back. It was as if the other incorporeal bits of me flowed back into the body much slower than the physical reincorporation of my flesh. Even more clearly than the sound—and smell now also—of regurgitation were the noises of pursuit: excited shouts, twigs snapping, bodies crashing through foliage. Close . . . so close. They had to see me. My body rose above the treetops, even when lying down. I was so damn large, I wondered how in holy hell Talon had managed to shrink me down a tiny plant, flow us through the ground, and reemerge what looked like only a short mile away from the arena, whose tall walls I could see from here.

We had managed to get away. But not too far away.

"Fly us," Talon said weakly, pushing himself unsteadily to his feet. "Away."

"Move back," I said, and the deep rumble of my dragon voice drew more excited shouts toward us. Damn it, they would be upon us in a few seconds.

I waited for Talon to stumble back several meters, then rolled clumsily to my feet, taking care not to accidentally crush my gallant rescuer in the awkward process. My coordination was off, discombobulated. I felt as drunk as poor Talon looked.

My wings, when I spread them, unfortunately, were as torn and bloodied as before. Whatever Talon had done, that thinning/dissipating/flowing-through-the-ground thing, it had not healed me. Flying away was impossible. For me, at least.

"You go," I said. "Fly away from here."

Talon shook his head. He might look delicate and fragile, especially from my much higher perspective, but the look on his face was as fierce and resolute as any warrior's. "Shift back down, Lucinda. Hurry!"

I hesitated, because while I might not be able to fly us away, I could fight them better in this larger form.

Trust me. Please. His words, the urgency of his emotions, flowed into my mind.

I shifted, in a process as magickal and inconceivable as how Talon had transported us. I shrank down and down until I found myself looking up at Talon in a sudden, disorienting height reversal.

Two bandits ran into the clearing that my heavy dragon body had made. Even as I spun to face them, I wondered if I had just made a mistake that would cost Talon his life. Then I felt Talon touch me. Felt myself begin to shift again, not into dragon or demon beast, but in the melting-melding way that a Floradëur morphed. It was a much slower process this time, like the sluggish pour of thick molasses instead of a quicksilver rush. Sight, sound, the sense of touch distorted and stretched out as we flowed our way torpidly down a plant. There was a feeling of emptiness—of being so long and thinly stretched out—and then a sudden jolting reemergence back into self.

I was surrounded by complete darkness, black and unfathomable. It took a slow, confusing second for my senses to return to me. Then everything snapped into acuteness. I smelled dank, musty air. Felt the touch of cold stone beneath my hands and legs. Saw the large root complex I leaned against like a thick, ungainly log. We were in an underground cavern, I think.

Talon lay sprawled next to me, his slender form a smear of pure black against the darkness. He was so still—no heartbeat, no breath to fill and rise his chest—so utterly still that concern rose up within me.

I didn't know where we were or how far away from
our pursuers we had gotten. Not too far away, in all likeli-
hood. So I mind-spoke to him instead of speaking aloud.
Talon . . . Talon, wake up. I shook him with a hand that
trembled from both weakness and worry.

He groaned, a sound that rushed welcomed relief into
me, then sparked fear that someone might overhear. I bent
and covered his lips with my own to muffle the noise.

Talon blinked into startled awareness.

I was so close to him I could see the details of his
unusual eyes—the large pupils: each individual striation
of his iris, varied gradations of black, the charcoal sclera
in place of the usual white. It was the latter that made his
eyes seem so foreign, like the eyes of an animal, a deer or
a gazelle, rather than a human or a Monère. This close, I
could see that his eyes weren't any differently constructed
than mine; all was the same but for the dark sclera, blending his eyes into a smooth sea of pure black.

He blinked again, and I realized suddenly I still had my
lips pressed to his. They were soft and smooth, no different
from any other mouth I had kissed, but for the innocence I
tasted on them. It drew me back. Broke the contact of our
mouths.

Not so innocent, he said.

You told me you had never been with a woman before.

I haven't.

I didn't understand for a moment. And then suddenly
I did. He had been Derek's possession, his slave, one
Derek had tried to break to his will. Talon hadn't just been
blood-raped all those many years, he had been physically
raped as well. The knowledge and helpless realization
boiled the blood within me for a moment then sputtered

away. I was too weak and fatigued to sustain that much intensity of emotion for long.

Wrapping his arms around his slender body, Talon focused his eyes on the ground. *You called me a virgin and I let you believe it true. I was . . . ashamed, so I let you believe a lie. Forgive me.*

Nothing to forgive, Talon. Any fault lies with Derek, not you. You are innocent.

His eyes lifted, poignantly bitter. *I am young. But I am not innocent, Lucinda.*

Neither am I. I was a stupid old bumbling fool. I should have used my hand instead of my lips to muffle the sound.

Please, do not berate yourself. It was my first kiss, a lovely one. Thank you.

How could he not think himself innocent? I wondered in a part of my mind I tried to keep shielded from him. *Where are we, Talon?*

Not far from where we were. I felt this empty space under the ground and brought us here. I was too weak to travel much farther.

You're strong, Talon, not weak. You saved me. When all was lost, you saved me.

I almost killed us. Was almost too weak to make that last effort.

Hush. Succumbing to the weariness that tugged at me like a physical hand, I lay my head back on the thick, bumping roots and closed my eyes. *Rest, now. When your strength returns, we'll leave here.*

With a delicate, almost tentative touch, his fingers brushed mine.

I wrapped my hand around his, snug and secure, and let myself slide into exhausted sleep.

TWENTY

H ari opened his eyes and a young girl's face filled his vision—a face he had seen before but could not quite place. It was unusual, to say the least. Not only that she was so close, but that she had no fear of him. Even when she saw that he was awake, she didn't back away in wariness; she edged even closer, peering down at him worriedly.

"Are you okay, mister?"

Her words made him frown, an expression that had made powerful demons step back in caution, but not this little slip of a girl.

Mister? That was a human form of address, wasn't it? And yet the girl before him was a demon—he remembered now!—the one who had saved him. Carried him out of the arena.

If we save you, heal you, you must save us in turn when you are whole and able.

He turned his head and saw Sarai asleep inside her cell—either that or she was unconscious. But for some reason, he somehow knew it was the former. He felt her slumbering presence in his mind . . . no, that wasn't quite right. He felt her through their bond.

Great Goddess in heaven. She had willingly bound herself to him! *Him*—one of the most ruthless, twisted demon souls in existence. May the gods have mercy on her, because he didn't know if he would, or could. An irrational part of Hari wondered if he had already harmed her—if the linking of his dark soul with hers had been such a shock it had torn her from consciousness. But again . . . somehow he knew that she was just sleeping. Exhausted. Not unconscious.

Hari rose to his feet and the girl scooted back, giving him room. He was miraculously, amazingly healed. Completely whole and strong, with his full strength returned to him, and perhaps even more. There was nothing stopping him from going up the steps and making his escape. Nothing holding him back but two slender females: a young girl who looked at him with concern, and a vulnerable, sleeping Floradëur. Two females and a promise: his oath upon his lady's name to aid them if they healed his broken body. Well, by some bloody Goddess-in-heaven wonder, he was healed. Though a part of him whispered, *Not a miracle . . . the bond.* Another part of him flinched away from the word. From that knowledge.

It would be hard enough making his escape just by himself. Almost impossible if he were saddled with two helpless females, one of them he might even have to carry. An honorable demon would keep his word, even at risk to his own afterlife. Hari had never been that stupid. Even Ruric, the closest thing he had to a friend, would laugh his teeth off if anyone was foolish enough to attribute *honor* to his dubious self. Hari was the furthest thing that existed from that virtue. He was the toughest, deadliest, most pragmatic son-of-a-bitch survivor that existed in this bloody afterlife.

In Hari's mind, he saw himself turning away from the two burdensome females and starting up the stairs as survival dictated. His body, though, seemed to be disconnected from his mind. He reached down and found himself bending back another bar, filling the cavernous underground chamber with the tortuous groan of metal slowly giving way beneath demon strength. He pulled until he created an opening large enough for him to step through, then crouched over the still, black form of Sarai, inwardly flinching at how gods-damn delicate and fragile she appeared lying there, while he, no doubt, looked like the devil about to fall upon the vulnerable Floradëur and devour her.

He glanced up as Brielle slipped through the opening and squatted next to him, the worry in her eyes a great relief to him. *Finally,* he thought, *some common sense in the girl.* And then she spoke and he realized that the concern was for Sarai, and not over what evil harm Hari might be intending her.

"Do you think she's okay?" whispered the girl.

Fool that he was, Hari reassured her instead of snarling, *Don't trust me.* "Ah . . . yes, she's just sleeping. Exhausted from bonding with me and healing me."

He reached over the slight, sleeping form, and four simple snaps of metal later, Sarai was freed from her manacles.

"So easy," Brielle murmured, her face closed and tight. Meaning: so easy for him to do what had been impossible for her.

As the last manacle fell away, Hari felt a powerful surge

of *something* move into Sarai. It rushed into her naturally, easily, without her conscious will, like breath filling up lungs with air. Something that should have been a part of her, but had been blocked by the metal.

He shook her shoulder lightly. "Sarai, wake up. We have to leave."

Heavy lashes snapped open as Sarai made the abrupt transition into wakefulness. For a moment, Hari wondered if she might scream, and thought of covering her mouth. It would be the smart thing to do, but he couldn't do it. Clapping a hand over her mouth would not only frighten her, it would be violating her somehow.

An edgy tension swirled around them like an electrical charge, then eased as Hari slowly and carefully pulled back from Sarai.

"You said we have to leave," Sarai said with a slight rasp, sitting up with Brielle's help.

Hari nodded. "Yes, we need to go."

She gazed at him, and it was as if those eerie black eyes saw clear down to the very bottom of his murky soul. "Then let us depart here."

Slipping through the crude opening he had made between the bars, Sarai took her first steps toward uncertain freedom. She led them up the stairs, but at the top, she paused and allowed Hari to take the lead, and with her hand clutching Brielle's tightly, followed Hari silently through the bedchamber.

Their escape outside was anticlimactic. No one came to investigate their presence. The two demons Hari sensed in the back of the palace did not raise an alarm, even though they had to be as aware of him as he was of them. The worse part was feeling so exposed walking down the front steps, open and unshielded to any eyes that might happen to look their way. Even if Hari's presence didn't stir suspicion at first casual glance, any fool would know something was up once they caught sight of a black Floradëur—Flowers of Darkness, creatures that were almost mythical.

Black Flower of Life was another name for them. Drinking the blood of a Floradëur boosted a demon's power like pouring accelerant on a fire. Drink enough of their blood and the rumor was that it could bring a demon back to life. Which was utter rubbish. Derek had remained as demon dead as the rest of them, and he'd had twenty-six years to gorge himself on Talon's blood. But still, that myth would have demons pouncing on Sarai like rabid animals. Shit. Maybe they should have taken the time to find something to shroud Sarai in; that pure black skin of hers was a deadly giveaway. But of course Hari had to have this brilliant insight *after* they had cleared the steps and were sprinting toward the nearest brush cover.

Only twenty paces before they reached concealment, a shout of alarm went up. "Ho! Intruders. A Floradëur!" The last was shouted with jittery excitement.

Sarai stumbled. Almost fell down.

Hari snagged one arm around her painfully slender form and ran with her, carrying her like a football. "Go, go, go!" he urged Brielle, right behind her, keeping his pace no faster than hers, which was much slower than what he was capable of alone—heck, while even carrying Sarai.

"Wait," he said when they reached the shelter of the trees, and set Sarai on her feet. "Keep going and stay together. I'll catch up to you."

Brielle opened her mouth to argue, but Sarai grabbed her hand and took off running. As soon as they left, Hari winked his form out of sight. It was a manifestation of his dragon blood, impure though that strain might be. In their oldest stories, legendary red dragons were able to cloak themselves from sight in such a manner for brief moments of time. Hari never made that claim—that had he been of pure blood, he would have transformed into one of the fiercest and deadliest dragons of their breed—not out loud, at least. But he had always believed it.

Silent and unseen, Hari waited for their pursuers. They came quickly: two bandits. The first demon he had not seen before. The second one was the familiar missing-nosed warrior with his chipped sword in hand.

The first one he let pass by. The second demon, smarter and more alert, stopped and looked around, alerted by the smell of Hari's blood, which Hari thought rather ironic considering his missing nose.

Hari unveiled himself, snatched the sword away from the surprised demon, and half-severed the bandit's thick neck with one quick swing. Had the blade been less dull or less chipped, it would have taken his opponent's head off completely. But it was disabling enough; the bandit toppled to the ground with a gurgle and loud crash.

Dropping the sword, Hari winked out of sight again as the second bandit turned back to cautiously investigate. The smell of blood was too diffuse now to allow the demon to pinpoint Hari's presence. To the bandit, it appeared as if the sword eerily lifted up from the ground and attacked him of its own spooky volition. Blood sprayed and the bandit screamed as his lower leg was cut off below the knee.

Hari flashed into view and yanked the pants off the first demon he had downed. He needed a clean pair of pants; his own reeked of blood, making it easy for the others to track him, which would play quite nicely for his immediate plans, but he'd need something free of bloodscent later, for the women's sensibilities if not his own. He was diverted for a moment at the sight of the bandit's naked penis. The offending organ fired Hari's fury. This was the same demon bastard who would have raped his dragon Queen as spectacle sport in the arena.

The sword sliced down, cutting off the offensive organ. "Heal that," Hari growled. He wanted to shove the demon's dick down his throat and make him swallow it, but approaching noise told Hari he had no more time to waste with further vengeance. A pity.

With the spare pants in one hand and the bloody sword gripped in the other, Hari leaped away with an angry snarl, running in the opposite direction Sarai and Brielle had taken.

Hari laid out a false trail for the others to follow that ended at a stream. Stripping off his stained pants, he waded into the water and swiftly washed the blood off his body. He tied the blood-smeared sword and trousers to a thick branch, and watched it float downstream. Jumping up into a tree, he donned the clean pants and doubled back in the direction he had come, leaping from tree to tree, veiling himself from sight as a group of bandits hurried past. He never truly understood what he did, or how he did it. It was like a partial dissipating of himself, but only in one plane, that of sight; his body was still there, clearly felt if someone bumped into him. Just not seen.

Hari waited until the sound of distant splashing indicated the bandits had reached the stream and were following the false blood trail he had laid out for them.

Good. Now he could return to the women.

Dropping his invisibility, he jumped to the ground and set off at a fast run.

TWENTY-ONE

SOMETHING SOFT BRUSHED my lips. A kiss so light it was like an ephemeral dream—wispy, almost insubstantial—drawing me gently up from deep slumber into drifting wakefulness. If it weren't for our tie, I wouldn't have known who it was, or even what it was. But even in half-sleep, our bond twanged, and through that connection, I felt how Talon felt as he kissed me. *Soft, sweet . . . my first given kiss.* The sadness I felt in him drew a sound of protest from me.

He covered my lips with his again. *Shhh, we must be quiet.*

I remembered where we were then. And remembered that last revelation before sleep: that he was young but not innocent; that he was not a virgin even though he had never lain with a woman before.

Why did you kiss me? I asked.

I am rested and recovered. We need to go, and—more whimsically—*I wanted to wake Sleeping Beauty.*

I snorted in my mind. *I am no innocent Sleeping Beauty.*

Nor am I a handsome and gallant prince.

But you are.

Am I? he asked, and since I was in his mind, I knew how he thought of himself still. As squat and ugly; a distorted being—what he had been his entire life before I rescued him and brought him back to Hell, his natural world. Down there he had painfully stretched out into the slender height and proportion that was meant to be his. And though he was handsome and tall now, a delicately refined Flower of Darkness, the ungainly self-image he had had of himself for so long was hard to throw off.

Yes. You are more handsome than any fairy-tale prince. And more gallant, although . . . Here I smiled, or maybe it was closer to a smirk . . . *you* rescued *the dragon instead of slaying it.*

His soft laughter. *Not typical fairy-tale creatures, you and I, are we?*

No, I thought, awash in the sweetness of his mind-laughter. He was beautiful when he smiled, when he laughed. I became aware of the closeness of his lips, his body slanting over mine. And felt in the faint recesses of his mind his want and desire for me—no . . . more than desire. His *yearning* for me, for everything that I was.

He saw me clearly, both hard and soft, good and bad, and still he wanted me, was drawn to me. Had been from the very beginning. The faint echo of his last thought, that I was someone far beyond his reach, humbled me and made me see clearly what I had not seen before.

I had thought to protect him from myself, not hurt him.

In my mind, it had been the reverse. I was over six hundred years demon, with over a hundred lived Monère years on top of that. I'd thought myself too old for his innocence, too cruel for his gentleness, too brittle and hard for his delicate refinement.

I had thought *him* too good for *me*, not the other way around. But we were what we saw reflected in others, and I had been rejecting him, though not for the reason he thought. Even as I grasped wisps of his thoughts and felt some of his emotions, so he caught mine, even one I tried to suppress.

You are attracted to me? His eyes widened with shock.

I felt heat rise up in my cheeks, and instinctively moved to shut down the open link between us.

No, don't, please. A faint whisper across our dampened link. A pleading that was echoed in his pretty eyes as he touched a hand to my bare shoulder. With that physical touch, our link strengthened again despite what I wished.

You think my eyes lovely? The realization filled Talon with wonder, and it was that wonder, that amazement, that kept me from bolting both physically and mentally. Being linked mind-to-mind with him was much more intimate and revealing than being nude. Truth, since it was the state I happened to be in—my clothes had ripped to pieces during my transformation to dragon. Being naked was no big deal; I was comfortable with naked. It was much harder to endure the bareness of thoughts and feelings, with hidden doubts and vulnerabilities on open display. And yet at the same time, there was such a closeness in that sharing, sweet and warm. Painful, exquisite.

I was bared to him, body and raw soul, and still he wanted me . . . as I wanted him.

Talon thought his mind and violated soul as blackened

and dwarfed as his physical form had been. But he was beautiful to me, inside and out—such heart, such valor, such purity of emotion.

With trembling slowness, I willfully opened my mind wide to him. And the warmth of our connection, what he found and discovered within me, how I saw him, my attraction to him, made his eyes blaze like a shadow moon rising up in the night.

As he had been pulled to me, so I had been pulled to him with compelling attraction, like two magnets being drawn together—something I had hidden and resisted until now. No longer. Not when it harmed more than it protected.

Kiss me, I thought, simple want unveiled. He did, and it was like sipping nectar—honey, golden, sweet and natural. Like two halves coming together.

Love me. And he began to do that, too. Slowly, gently, with a reverent touch. With the brush of his fingertips against my lips.

The pleasure I felt at that sweet caress reverberated back to him, and he half closed his eyes.

Yes, I thought.

Yes, he echoed.

Let me, he murmured as my hand lifted to touch him. *Let me touch you, learn you. Let me love you this first time.*

All before had been done to him, I realized. Never by him.

In the whole of my life, you are all that I have ever wanted. Ever dared reach for. Let me.

Yes, I answered, and dropped my hand back down to my side as I granted him that gift: to learn me at his leisure. To touch me as he wanted. To love me guided by my thoughts, my feelings, the sensations of my body openly shared with him through our link.

He started at the top, stroking my hair. It felt like silk to him, softer than he had expected, the thick, glorious mane as wild and untamed as how he saw me.

That I allowed him this—this choice, this control—awed him, humbled him. Burned his need for me even hotter, harder, and thicker so that he ached down there.

A moan rolled between our minds, his or mine, I could not tell, so willingly coupled our minds were. So open to each other, immersed in one another as never before.

Touch me! Love me!

Both our cries, both our wants, our needs, as he pulled his shirt off, shoved his pants down, and freed his stiff hardness. He was lovely, so lovely: The smooth black skin. The delicate beauty of his face. His young, supple body, leanly muscled. Wider shoulders tapering down to elegant narrow hips, drawing attention to the full frontal point of him. His male organ was a surprisingly long stretch of ebony length, less thick than my other lovers, long and slender like himself.

Oh, my, my, my . . . The luscious sight of him, turgid, full and so very long, throbbed need between my legs, an ache that sprang directly to him through our mind-link.

I had never seen anyone as long as him, and it was hard to just lie there and not reach up and grasp him—*feel* him as I so wanted to. To lie there passive when I so very much wanted to be active—to roll him over and try to stuff the whole of that length into me. See if all that long, succulent distance would fit completely inside my stretched sheath.

When he finally touched me, skin to skin, his fingers tracing lightly over my brow, my temples, my cheek, his touch so delicately light in contrast to the sharp, hungry, throbbing need in us, we both shuddered. He traced my lips—so sensitized they felt. Traced them again, testing the plump fullness of my lower rim. I licked his finger, and he stilled, letting me taste him, letting me lap again. Letting me wrap my tongue around that slender digit and draw him inside the warm, moist cavity of my mouth. My eyes captured his as I began to suck lightly on that part of him, a sweet but poor substitute for what I really hungered for.

Lucinda. He whispered my name as I twined my tongue around that slender digit and pulled it even deeper into my mouth, as deep as I could, sucking harder. He was trembling now, his black eyes blazing. Wetness oozed out, spilled from his slit. And warm honey coated my own hidden passage. My empty sheath clenched and contracted as I sucked his finger, gently nipped the tip. He pulled out and pushed slowly back in with my pursed suction, gently, tenderly fucking my mouth. *Ah, Lucinda . . . You're destroying me.*

He reluctantly pulled his finger out and used the wet tip to trace down the side of my neck—so exquisitely sensitive. To dip into the delicate hollow cup of my collarbone.

My skin tingled where he touched me. Shivered under the stimulating moisture left behind. My nipples peaked and hardened as he skimmed down the side of my chest with that light, wet touch.

Eyes glittering, he brought his other hand to my lips, let me moisten another finger with my lips, my tongue, the inner wetness of my mouth that he explored delicately with that long and slender digit. One gentle in-and-out pump and he left my oral cavity to trace that second moist finger down the opposite side of me to just below my breasts, parallel to the other hand. A moment of stillness, of indecision, that I felt clearly in his mind, then he moved the twin points down to the center of my body, one finger dipping into the hollow of my navel while the other finger swirled delicately around the rim. It felt oddly, ridiculously stimulating, more than it should have felt. He didn't need to look up into my eyes to know and feel how turned on and stirred up I was by those simple, innocuous actions—wet darkness, delving pressure.

Fuck me! I demanded.

His black eyes shone fierce and intent as he locked our gazes. *I am. In my own way.*

A little hint—move your hands down a few more inches and you'll hit the right spot.

Humor lit his eyes and made them sparkle like black diamonds.

Black precious diamonds—I love how you see me. How you want me. How you're letting me touch you like this.

Hush, I admonished gently, *and get to it—that touching you're rhapsodizing about.*

He laughed, and the joyous sound in my mind made me smile softly, tenderly, despite my aching frustration.

The look in your eyes ... The sweetness of your mind ... So beautiful, so generous, your thoughts, your heart, your body.

With his eyes tenderly on mine, he ran his fingertips down until they reached the tangle of wispy hair.

Your hair is even curlier down here, he thought as he played his fingers in the crisp thatch.

A light gasp as he tugged gently, zinging unexpected sensation through me that arched me up in need. *Talon!*

Soon, he promised, and settled himself with lithe grace between my legs.

Not what I wanted to hear.

May I kiss you?

His sweet mix of bold and shy turned my heart yielding. *Of course. Anything you want.*

His eyes softened at my words. At how he knew I truly meant them.

Ah, Lucinda . . . As if my words, my offer, broke his careful control, he kissed me, his tongue gliding in my mouth with gentle exploring strokes to learn me, claim me, mate with me. And I discovered that the surface of his tongue was rougher, coarser, like fine raspy sandpaper. I had a moment to wonder: *How would that feel against my breast?* And I had the answer to my question.

It was divine. An incredibly stimulating sensation that became even better as he reached my sensitive areola. His agile, rough tongue laved over my peaked nipple, and sharp shards of pleasure burst like a kaleidoscope within my mind. My pleasure seeped in and mixed with his as he lavished more attention on my nipple with that wicked and wonderful tongue.

Moving to my other breast, he dispensed the same detailed attention on my other hungry peak.

Another thought barely formed: *How would that wonderful rough tongue feel lower down?* And he was suddenly down there, spreading my legs wide with his hands and shoulders. A lick along the outer lips had me throwing back my head, arching my pelvis.

You taste so good, he whispered hungrily. Lapping his way up to my apex, he searched out what he saw in my mind, what I could not help but picture.

When that gently rough, abrading tongue grazed lightly over my hard, swollen pearl, my eyes crossed at the sublime burst of sensation, which backwashed into him with strong eddies of pleasure.

It was a most unexpected find to Talon. A discovery about a woman's body he would never have known or guessed without our mind-link. Delighted pleasure, eagerness for more filled him as he spread my folds, gently pulled back the hood, and swiped that light, abrasive tongue over the secret pleasure organ he had exposed.

Sweet Goddess!

Sparks flew. A tumult of sharp, sweet sensation that spiked through me and blew me apart in a hard climax. He pulled back and watched me with wonder, feeling all that I felt: the bright shards of fracturing pleasure, the clenching contraction of my womb, the spasm of my empty sheath as waves of powerful release pulsed through me. He cupped me with his hand to feel the gentle, hidden convulsions of my flesh. Slid a long finger inside my wet sheath to experience physically what he sensed through our mental joining.

Lord and Lady, how sweet that slight fullness felt. But I wanted . . . needed more.

This is how it will feel when you're buried deep inside me, I crooned to him. *Your finger is nice but an inadequate substitute for what I really want: something bigger and much longer than what you have inside me now.*

My words squeezed another drop of wetness from his tip.

He lowered his weight down onto me, his finger still buried inside me until the last of my spasms ebbed away. The press of his body was nice—satisfying. Being held by him even nicer. From our linked minds, I knew he enjoyed the pillowed feel of my breasts, the soft cushion of my body, just as he knew that I savored the long, ready hardness of him pressed against my thigh.

For now, in that languid moment of post-orgasmic bliss, it was enough to hold him. To lightly run the sharp tips of my nails up and down his back in a gentle, dangerous caress. To have him hold me and let the closeness of our bodies and his hard, sweet ripeness begin to stir me once more as satisfaction faded and hunger grew anew like a rising tide. It grew even more when he pulled his finger out of me.

I mourned the loss. Wanted . . . needed something else to fill the empty space he left behind. Wanted and needed him—my sweet and gallant, beautiful Flower of Darkness.

I am none of those things, he protested softly.

You are all of those things in my eyes. You know I speak true . . . that I cannot lie to you.

I am the worst of cowards.

How can you say that? Think that? You came and saved me.

Because I selfishly wanted you.

Oh, Talon. You are much braver than I am, reaching out for what you wanted while I hid myself away from what I secretly desired.

Because you thought to protect me—from yourself! An inelegant snort. *How can you think of yourself as bad for me?*

How can you think yourself ugly when you are so exquisite, so finely built?

I'm different from everyone else—utterly black.

I let my eyes drift over the smooth, pure lines of his midnight-dark face, his features exquisite enough to belong to a girl: large eyes, thick lashes, bold nose, delicate mouth.

With that face, the tall, slender build and lean muscles smoothed across his graceful body, he would put top models to shame.

Models? he asked, not knowing what that was.

I flashed him images of fashion magazines and scrumptious male models gracing the covers.

I tried to suppress my next thought as my gaze traveled slowly and appreciatively down his body but it squeaked through to him.

Underwear? You think I could attain great wealth modeling underwear? He thought the idea quite funny.

Different, in your case, is very, very nice, I assured him, my eyes lingering longingly on his long, tumescent stretch of hardness.

A smile slowly teased the corners of his mouth. *I think I might like being different in this way for you.*

I guarantee that you'll like it even better if you put that big, long thing inside of me where it belongs.

A thought, a vivid image of him sliding into my wetness moved him back over me. He held me with his gaze—held me with the still, suspenseful waiting of his body . . . then slowly began to push his way into me.

A shiver, a shudder shook my body. Hitched him a little deeper into me.

We must be quiet. His voice sounded strained as he gave the mental reminder. Quietly he forged his way into me with killing slowness, filling me more and more.

Talon . . . Oh, yes . . . yes . . . more!

I bit my lip as he continued to forge his way into me. Ye gods! He was so deep I felt him nudge up against the cervical end of me. The sensation had me crossing my eyes.

Through him, I felt how he felt: the tight, wet, and warm squeeze of me all around him, the firm noselike resistance there at the end, pushing back against his sensitive tip. How unbelievably good all of it felt and yet incomplete; he had an inch or two more to go, and a strong instinctive need to sheathe himself all the way in, all the way home. And through me, he knew that never before had I ever felt what I did now. That sharp, sweet rain of pleasure and bite of pain as he knocked with gentlemanly politeness against the door of my womb, as if to politely ask if I would be good enough to let him in?

A half-laugh strangled in my throat and his mouth sealed across mine, ate the sound down. *Hush,* he murmured in my mind, *no sound.*

No sound when I wanted to scream, to cry, to grunt and groan and thrash beneath him. But I did none of that. I held it all back, restrained in so many different ways—in sound, in movement, in all but my mind. In my mind I let him know, let him see, how I felt and what I wanted to do.

I know you wish me to take you wildly, he said, *but I can't. I don't want to hurt you.*

He pulled out slightly and pushed firmly back in, bumping against my cervical door. It was the most unusual, exquisite, pleasing-painful thing I'd ever felt or experienced.

Don't worry . . . Oh, Goddess! . . . just keep doing what you're doing.

I'd never had a lover this long before. And sweet blessed moon, he wasn't all the way in yet!

I had been content to just pleasure Talon, to make this a sweet experience for him, knowing that he was too gentle a soul to give me the edge of pain and sense of danger I enjoyed with sex. Those expectations flew out the window as he pulled out then plowed back in another insistent half-inch, his teeth bared, his eyes locked on mine.

This little bit of sweet pain I don't mind giving you, he said and danced that long length in and out of me again. Slip, slide, deep nudge—oh!—in just a little bit deeper.

His eyes grew even more heavy-lidded as he took on a gentle rhythm, his body moving over me with strength and grace, sliding in and out, pushing, knocking harder, deeper within me. That sharp, sweet, edgy pleasure had me arching up, sweeping the peaked points of my nipples against the lean muscles of his chest—extra stimulation that was suddenly too much and not enough.

I'm sorry, I'm sorry, I have to move, I cried out, and drove my hips up with a strong thrust. The jarring jolt of pleasure and sweet pain was blissful, divine—almost overwhelming.

He cursed and snarled within our minds, and began a faster, harder rhythm, pulling out—long, so long—pushing back in with deep and powerful drives, rubbing slick and snug and hard through my swollen channel, his end meeting my end with more and more insistent force until with a soundless pop he didn't push through but *past* my cervix into a little cup of space beyond it, impaling me deeper than I'd ever had anyone inside of me. Sinking his entire long length home, buried full in me.

At the sweetly painful, full joining, we both cried out, silent, within our minds, and held there unmoving, his hips ground against mine, my pelvis lifted up to his in arched symmetry. My hands lifted without thought, on pure instinct, and gripped the tight muscles of his buttocks to me even harder. The added shove of him so deep . . . my sharp nails piercing his meaty flesh . . . my teeth biting into his chest to keep the scream of pleasure locked inside my throat . . . it all combined to flash us into a convulsive climax.

He spurted inside of me, one hot, fluid burst that I felt physically through our joined bodies and mentally through our joined minds as my own contraction hit, making me clamp down so tightly down on him that I cut off his ejaculation, halted it for one hot, clenching moment of blissful agony. Then my closed-fist contraction relaxed and he came in three more hot, wet bursts, his release coming

harder for having been delayed and interrupted, shoot-
ing his wad into me like hard bullets as I squeezed and
spasmed tightly around him until he was wrung out, completely dry.

We had made love with hardly a single sound; with
emotions and sensations linked and layered deliciously on
top of each other so that ecstasy spiraled and reverberated
within us still like undulating after-ripples.

Wow, I thought as my body gave one last tired twitch
around him. *That was different.*

He smiled and relaxed down over me, covering me like
a hard, firm blanket. With a heroic heave of effort, he rolled
until I lay on top.

In this case, I definitely like being different, he purred
contented and happy.

We drifted off to sleep still connected.

Talon's mind brushed lightly against mine in welcome
when I woke up a short time later. He rolled until I was
once again on the bottom, then eased out of me, a long pull
that had me shuddering and him smiling.

You liked that, he thought.

So did you.

*Oh, yes. Most definitely. Although putting it inside you
is even nicer.*

The smell of his blood filled my nostrils. *I hurt you!
I'm sorry.*

No need. And I felt the ease in his mind. *I liked your
nails, your teeth, there at the end. The bite of them felt
surprisingly good. I loved most knowing that I'm not too
gentle for you. That just my size is enough to give you what
you like and need.*

I shuddered in remembered pleasure, a reaction that had
him smiling even more.

We have to go, he said regretfully. Rolling to his feet, he helped me up.

Standing, my eyes were level with the raw bite mark on his chest, skin bruised but not broken. *Your wounds aren't healed,* I said puzzled. *Neither are mine.*

We had healed that first time when the bond had snapped into place between the three of us with Nico buried deep inside of me, and Talon joining us in orgasm. We'd been healed, I thought later, because of Talon and our bond with him. Floradëurs healed far faster than demons and Monère through their tie with nature and their ability to tap into its plentiful energy.

There is something about this place, Talon said, frowning as he pulled on his pants. He slipped his T-shirt over me. *The area feels enclosed somehow. Like a capsule.*

His observation had me looking around uneasily. It was a tiny cavern hidden below the ground. Nothing unusual about it but for the long, unusually thick tree root complex that tunneled out through the wall to lay on the ground like a giant foot—that and the sense of containment I sensed now through Talon.

I think it comes from this thick tangle of roots, Talon said thoughtfully. The gnarled structure was thicker around than a man's body.

That must come from one heck of a big tree.

Let's find out. Without any more warning than that, he touched me and merged us with that heavy root system, flowing us up it. There was no easy sense of travel this time, only a jarring sensation of something wrong, something off in the life force of the wood and sap we flowed up through.

There was sharp relief when we emerged aboveground and physically separated from it. Then all that relief died as I looked up into the branches of the large tree above us . . . into the *heads* that hung from it. Demon heads.

I shrieked, but only in my mind. Outwardly I made not a noise, moved not a single muscle of my frozen body.

It was a gourd tree. Green gourds hung high in some of the branches, but you didn't see them at first. Your eye was drawn first and foremost to the demon heads hanging beside them, far outnumbering the natural fruits of the tree, although "hung" wasn't really quite the right word. The heads had apparently started that way but then as time had passed, branch tips had connected into the severed necks, thickening and distending into rootlike structures, so that the heads became perched atop these supports.

Most of the heads were dried and brown, shriveled and shrunken effigies. The rootings beneath these necks were like the heads they supported—thin, old, and dried out . . . as dead and gone as the husked heads they were attached to. The rootings beneath fresher heads, though, bulged thick beneath their still-moving, still aware heads, draining them of—what? Their blood, their energy?

The eyes from these alert heads were focused on us; jaws opening and closing, tongues moving inside like large obscene worms. The freshest head belonged to the bandit Derek had beheaded, the one the other demon had skinned.

Jesus! Now I know why Derek had wanted his head: To feed this damn tree. *That* was the wrongness I had sensed traveling up this thing. Power had thrummed from it, and I knew why now. The energy I'd felt running through the sap, built into the wood itself, must have come from the blood and vitality drained from these demon heads. But to serve what purpose? I wondered.

Gods! There were so many heads. Forty or fifty of

them, maybe. Then the fog around our feet swirled and thinned enough to see the ground, and fresh horror stabbed me anew. The ground we stood on was strewn with dried heads fallen from the tree. Holy Mother! Not fifty but *hundreds* of them!

The fog swirled again, and out of the thick white mist stepped Derek, two demon heads swinging with bloody freshness from his hands.

"Ah, perfect." Grim surprise and pleasure lighted Derek's face as he dropped the heads and drew his sword. "You found my Tree of Death. No need to hunt you down. You came to me."

Derek had taken one eager, ominous step toward us when the ground suddenly began to shudder and tremble violently beneath us. A large circle of soil shot up like a geyser, raining chunks of dirt over us as something leaped out of the hole that had been formed in the ground—a male creature. He felt like a demon to my senses, but with an altered flavor to his essence like nothing I had ever encountered before. Broken bits and pieces of something that looked like bark but wasn't quite that—it was smoother, thinner—hung around him like a ragged mantle. Beneath that bizarre covering you could see old and rotted remnants of cloth, what had once maybe been his clothing. The face . . . no, actually his *head* was the most eye-catching of all. Not so much the blood smeared across his mouth and chin like gruesome paint, but the thick, bulbous structure perched atop his head like antlers; they looked eerily like the strange branch-roots that drained the demon heads in the tree above us. The end of it looked as if it had just been freshly broken off, inches above his head. The bottom half seemed anchored into his skull.

He should have looked utterly ridiculous standing there.

But there was some sort of odd power that emanated from him that made him more frightening than funny. You could even *see* it—a sheer rim of whiteness that outlined his body and almost made him seem to glow.

"Whose blood woke me?" the strange thing demanded in a hoarse and rusty croak. He glanced at Derek, noted the offering of heads tumbled at his feet, then turned to study Talon and me with more careful scrutiny. His gaze took in the deep cuts and scratches on my arms—the damage the sharp stones had done to my wings. His scrutiny, however, lingered the longest and with the most interest upon Talon. Nostrils flared as the strange apparition scented the wounds my sharp nails had cut into Talon's buttocks.

Derek's reaction was quite strange. He paled, his dark demon skin going ash gray. "Tree Lord," he said in a strangled whisper.

Tree Lord? I had a second to wonder. Then Derek sprang at the strange demon with a harsh cry, his sword raised.

Derek never reached him.

With the simple languid lift of a finger, the strange demon froze Derek and held him suspended in the air, halted mid-leap. There was an ease and elegance and *effortlessness* to the gesture that bespoke great power. It was easy to stop and hold a Monère in such a way; much, much harder to do to a demon whose own mental strength should have battled and negated your own. Perhaps my father, maybe my brother, had the sheer brute psychic power to do such a thing. I, personally, could never have held Derek suspended so.

Then an even stranger thing happened. The limbs of the Tree of Death above us reached down and twined around Derek's wrists and ankles, holding him bound and suspended above the Tree Lord.

At this point I'd seen enough to know I could not fight this thing.

Run, I screamed to Talon.

He tried to. And so did I. But what the Tree Lord had done to Derek, he did now to us. His will swept out and overpowered us like a giant rolling wave, freezing us into immobility.

I was captured, but not necessarily Talon. He was a Floradëur. He didn't have to move a muscle to slip his way down a plant.

Go! Slip away while you can!

Whether Talon would have listened or not, I never knew. I felt something thrust through me, so horribly cold and painful and *wrong,* it stole all my strength and shocked a breathless gasp out of me. At first I thought it was Derek's sword, run straight through me, but no blood spilled out. It was only as I saw it happen to Talon also that I came to know what it was.

Something white and slim and shaped like a spear thrust through Talon's slender back and came out the front of him. It wasn't until it dispersed and dissolved its form, and became just white mist once again that I realized it had been formed from the pervasive fog that blanketed this land. It was only because I had felt it go through me that I knew now what that white mist really was: spirits. Demon spirits that had been captured and chained to this land somehow through the Tree of Death.

Death magick.

Death magick had enslaved those poor souls. Death magick that I watched being wielded by a master's hand as more of that white mist formed and thickened around Talon and me in imprisoning bubbles of his willing. It lifted us up several inches, separating us—separating *Talon*—from the ground through which he might have escaped.

The weakness was temporary. I was already getting back my strength, enough to rake demon claws down the wall of my misty bubble. It was like scraping down solid stone—no give, no weakness. No way to claw my way through this thing. I retracted my claws, curled my hand into a fist, and punched the damn thing. Curse it, but it hurt! Not from the physical force of the blow but rather from the harsh contact of my bare skin against that misty white. I was standing in the sphere with my bare feet flat against the white surface, but that passive contact didn't give me the flash-burn feeling the violent action of punching my prison had. Emotion speared through me much like that mist-spear passing through my chest. Hatred, fear, despair, violence. Guilt, grief, and anger—so much anger. I felt the emotions of those imprisoned ghosts—because that, I realized, was what they were—and that brief flash of contact with them sapped me of energy, strength, vitality.

I lay there fallen, cocooned by that white prison bubble, and looked across to Talon. He stared back at me with concern, standing docilely in his own white-mist cocoon.

Lady help us . . . because it didn't look like I could. I had a dreadful feeling not even my father or brother could, even with scores of their best men. That belief became even more certain as I watched Derek struggle uselessly against the entwining branches that held him suspended. It boggled the mind to know that the tree was stronger than a demon.

Ceasing the futile struggle, Derek opened his hand and dropped the sword he still clutched, and thrust the weapon forward with pure strength of mind. The sharp point of the blade thrust straight and true at the Tree Lord's heart. It stopped with an audible loud *clink* as it hit the white shimmer that limned his body, revealing what it was. A shield! Much like what imprisoned Talon and me, only it protected and armored the Tree Lord.

The sword turned easily, like it was nothing for the Tree Lord to take control of it. It swung around in the air to face Derek, and became a battle of pure mental will. Derek's face was strained and furrowed, while the Tree Lord's was unlined, uncreased, with a slight smile even.

As effortlessly as if a real hand guided its course and intent, the sword sliced down Derek's neck in a cut deep enough to start the dark flow of blood.

The sword swung back into position in front of Derek.

Giving up the uneven mental battle, Derek renewed his struggles against the binding branches of the tree. But that, too, was an uneven match. As he wriggled like a fish caught on an unbreakable line, the sword shot forth, much as it had under Derek's guidance. But this time the weapon met its target true, and pierced through Derek's heart. The shuddering cry he gave rang loud in the misty air.

The sword slid wetly out of his chest and dropped with a clatter to the ground to lie among the shrunken, shriveled heads.

The Tree of Death swayed two of its free limbs toward Derek and inserted its branch tips delicately like fingers into the open wounds of his neck and chest. A frightened gargle came out of Derek as those branch tips pushed their way inside his body, and then he screamed and screamed and continued to scream as those inserted tips started to thicken and swell, bulging obscenely with the blood it began to pull out of him.

I watched as Derek's swarthy skin turned paler and paler. And probably paled myself as some of the tree's roots pulled themselves out of the ground and reached for the Tree Lord. The ends of them, broken off and leaking blood-tinged sap, aligned themselves perfectly, and connected to the antlerlike crown atop the Tree Lord's head. As I watched, the roots there swelled and thickened also. At first I thought the tree was drinking from him, too, until I saw that the Tree Lord was growing flusher, not pale. No, not drinking. Feeding! The tree was disgorging Derek's blood into the Tree Lord!

I realized finally what those broken, barklike remnants covering him from head to toe were. That thick man-sized tree root complex down in the cavern below had grown around him, covering him, surrounding him. Talon and I had been *leaning* against the Tree Lord, positioned right next to him when we had made love. The tree fed him, sustained him. And we, our blood, maybe Talon's and mine combined—dragon and Floradëur—had woken him up when some of our blood had smeared across his mouth.

As if that were not horror enough, what came next was even worse. That thin, white barrier that limned the Tree Lord's body disappeared suddenly, and he began to pull Derek's energy, his vitality, out of his body—a white mist substance that flowed from Derek's neck and chest wounds.

The Tree Lord not only fed on the blood being siphoned out of Derek's body into his, he stole out his essence, his very spirit.

One last, horrendous blood-curdling shriek from Derek and then his body went slack and still, truly dead. Only an empty shell now.

I had a somewhat similar ability to this. I could drink

down a spirit's essence into me, take in its vitality. But I could not capture that essence and enslave it to my will. Finally—someone who was capable of doing something far worse than what I did.

It was a discovery I was very unhappy to make, I realized, as I watched Derek's body, emptied of blood and spirit and soul, shrivel down to less than one-quarter its original size.

When he was as drained as completely as he could be, the supple branches unwound themselves from his legs and arms and dropped him to the ground, a discarded husk. The tree roots detached themselves from the Tree Lord's head, reddened clots visible at the ends of the broken connection.

He looked much better now, no longer thin, dried, and brittle. His flesh had filled out, his weight increased by almost a stone. He moved much more fluidly now, like the deadly, dangerous predator he was. The ultimate predator who fed off what had once been the top of the food chain down here—off of demons themselves.

He looked rested and relaxed, almost cheerful, as if he'd just had the best sex of his undead life, no matter that his partner had not survived the experience.

I shook my head to dislodge that macabre analogy and watched the Tree Lord rummage through Derek's remains. He wasn't content with simply stealing Derek's blood and spirit, he had to steal his clothes, shoes, sword, and food pouch also.

"Who are you? What is your name?" I asked. Even though I had pretty much guessed already.

"Merlin," he replied. "Or perhaps you might know me better by my demon name. Myrddhin."

The mad demon sorcerer who had been obsessed with

the blood of Floradëur and dragon. The father of death magick. The infamous seer who Talon and I had inadvertently awakened from his centuries-long death slumber with our blood.

We were fucked. Truly and hopelessly fucked.

TWENTY-TWO

T HE DEATH MAGICIAN pulled Talon and me along in our misty bubbles. It was a relief to leave that creepy Tree of Death behind. A pity we couldn't leave its even creepier master also. But no, it seemed he was keeping us for a later snack.

Good thing Derek had come upon us or his fate might have been Talon's and mine. It still probably would be, sooner or later. But later was a much better option than sooner. Time was our friend, no matter that we had awareness of the horror awaiting us. I was learning things—for instance, about the shield that protected him. He had to shed it before he could yank our spirits from our bodies and turn it into the mist that crawled this land. Cursed this land was indeed by the enslaved spirits of demons. No wonder we felt so uneasy entering these misted mountains.

Myrddhin pulled us along to a flowing stream and

parked us along the bank while he waded into the water
and immersed himself in it. It would have been nice if he
had drowned, but alas, demons could not drown. We didn't
need to breathe, and the stream was only waist high, the
current not strong.

He ripped off the remaining shreds of cloth and root-bark
from himself, and scrubbed clean, emerging naked. Someone so malignant and evil should have been as ugly and
repulsive as his actions were, but nature had camouflaged
the monster he was inside with a pleasing outer countenance. He was not wickedly handsome like Hari or beautiful like my Stefan, but he was attractive, pleasing to the eye.
And that was just *wrong*. He should have had a beaked nose
with a wart at the end, a hooked chin, and rotting teeth.

He shook himself like a dog, slicked off as much wetness as he could with his hands, and donned the shoes and
clothes he had pilfered from Derek's corpse. Wearing his
stolen clothing, he looked ordinary, just your average, ordinary demon. Not like the most infamous black sorcerer
and dealer of death magick that ever existed, and, unfortunately, still did.

Taking out a strip of yaro jerky from the food pouch, he
bit off a piece. "Ah, food," he murmured, chewing slowly
with relish. His gaze shifted over to Talon and me. "What
year is this?" he asked.

I told him the truth—why not?—and watched his eyes
widen in surprise.

"Almost a millennium," Myrddhin said, gazing blindly
down at the dried stick of meat in his hand.

Time was our friend, true. But unfortunately it was also
Myrddhin's. He was a formidable enough opponent weak;
he would be even more so after he had recovered his full

strength and power. If there was any chance of taking him down, it had to be done now.

I shifted position to kneel down on one knee, as if tired of standing. The movement straightened my back, thrust the mounds of my breasts into even greater, more eye-catching prominence, and the hem of Talon's T-shirt gaped an enticing hole between my knees. I knew what I looked like with my alluring gold skin, long curly hair, and full lush curves. If his appetite for food had stirred, so soon would his appetite for other things. I did my best to help it along, not by being seductive but the opposite. By appearing helpless, feminine, frightened, and weak. It wasn't always a matter of how to get to your prey. Sometimes it was simply a matter of how to draw them to you.

"W-what are you going to do to us?" I asked, my body and voice shivering with fear. It wasn't hard to fake. Truthfully, it wasn't even really faked.

His eyes fastened on the quivering slopes of my breasts, the round nipples clearly outlined by the softly stretched material. For once I was grateful for the large boobs and pretty face my mother had bequeathed me. Mad sorcerer or not, he was male. A male who hadn't had sex for almost a thousand years. Talk about a dry spell.

He'd met his other needs—clothed himself, sated his thirst for blood, taken the edge off of his physical hunger. The want and need for sex had to be rearing its ugly head now with my helpless, quivering female display.

That's right, you crazy son-of-a-demon bitch. Come to me.

Only when he did, I quivered and quaked even more, and nothing of that was at all faked. I had come up with a horrible plan, you see. A way to destroy him. Unfortunately, it involved him getting really, really close. Intimately close.

"Please me and I might keep you around longer than I planned," he said, coming to stand beside my bubble. His eyes lingered on my breasts for a long, slimy moment before trailing down the rest of my body.

"No," Talon said angrily, "leave her alone." He'd been standing there calmly in his bubble, not fighting or trying to escape like I had. Part of it might have been seeing how useless my efforts had proven; another part might have simply been that he was used to captivity, it was nothing new to him. But now that calm acceptance flew out the bubble, so to speak.

His talons flashed out long and thick. Before, he had had small pointy black nails like the claws of a kitten, stunted and half-formed like the rest of him had been. He'd been named Talon in mockery for the talons he did not possess. Then after I had brought him back to Hell, and he had stretched into his tall, willowy self, his fixed, stunted nails had retracted. I hadn't seen what they had become until now, when he used them to slash at his spherical white cage. He didn't look like my gentle Talon with those impressively long talons viciously scraping at his bubble-cell, his eyes flashing dangerously with rage.

"Please," I begged, looking at Myrddhin. I didn't even know myself what I was begging for—for him to come to me, or leave me alone. My body didn't want him anywhere near me, but my mind knew the necessity and protested it vehemently.

Myrddhin dissipated the sphere that surrounded me. Before I could move, he froze me with a mental flex of will. Bloody saints, he was strong! Not just natural demon strong, but with the added power of hundreds upon hundreds of other demons' stolen blood and vitality. It was frigging terrifying how helpless I was against that great mental strength.

He touched me and I couldn't even shudder in revulsion,

locked still by his will as I was. Talon howled protest, throwing himself against his bubble. It was distracting enough to make Myrddhin look up and frown. From the corner of my frozen eyeball, I saw a sliver of white peel off the inside of the sphere and stab through Talon, exiting out his back to blend back into the misty white bubble. The attack dropped Talon to his knees.

Hush, Talon, I said as quietly as I could through our mind-link. *Be still. Don't make him hurt you again.* Then I closed my mind off, not wanting to give a hint of what I was planning.

Everything—all worries, concerns, conniving plans— flew out the window as Myrddhin lifted my arms and tugged the T-shirt over my head. It was humbling and deeply disturbing the way he moved my limbs around like that of a plastic doll—lowering my arms, positioning me on the ground to lie down on my back, straightening out my legs, spreading them open.

Somewhere deep inside, I screamed, *Noooo! I don't want this!*

Panic suddenly exploded within me, a wild, feral thing. No matter how my mind argued that this was the plan, the frozen and spread state of my body ripped away all my control and I fought. I fought with everything I had, trying to break his control over me. And couldn't.

Terror surged and battered within me like a giant riptide. And there was nothing I could do—not even blink as Myrddhin disrobed and knelt between my spread legs.

It took far more effort than was pretty to push back the tide of panic and terror flooding me, drowning me. To grab desperately for control, for coherent thought. To find a faint thread of reason and frantically hold on to it, and not let it slip from me. The one thing I needed for him to do—drop his shield—he had not done yet. It glowed faintly white around him still.

Talon, recovered enough to regain his feet and breath, opened his mouth and unleashed a powerful echoing cry, a forceful sonic blast that he could use like a weapon. But it didn't shatter the misty bubble. It reverberated against the barrier and bounced back on him, knocking him unconscious as Myrddhin put his hands on my breasts. It was the oddest sensation, those shielded hands—not the pain or strength-stealing jolt I was expecting. His hands just felt solid, like hard stone touching me, lifting, squeezing my breasts. The way he ran his hand down my stomach, brushed his hard fingers through my thatch of curls illustrated that he knew how to touch a woman, how to please her. And that somehow made this violation worse—that he could not only control my body, he could ignite unwilling pleasure in me, too.

Alarming dismay mingled with the wet moisture that started to dew my folds as his shielded finger probed the opening of my inner sheath, and grazed over the sensitive bud of my clitoris, giving me another sharp jolt of unwanted pleasure.

Just fuck me, already, I screamed the only way I could—in my mind. Maybe he heard me, or maybe it was simply because my body was lubricated enough now for intercourse. For whatever reason, he followed my wish and positioned himself over me.

I had a horrible moment to wonder if he was going to fuck me while still shielded—surely not! Could he even *feel* anything that way?—and then the whiteness limning his body disappeared. At the same moment, he pushed his way inside of me.

A lot of things hit me at once. How *good* it felt—

Goddess curse him. A sting of panic that maybe all of this was for nothing, that what I had planned wouldn't work. Another stronger wave of panic that it *would* work and I would destroy not only myself but Talon and Nico, too.

Fear, anguish, and panic passed through me in that endless, timeless moment when he penetrated me. He had full control of my body. But not all things I could do required physical control or movement. I sent up a brief prayer to the Goddess to help me. Then I threw up a cone of silence around me—around *us*. I hadn't known that it would work. If I would still be able to do that while under Myrddhin's control. But, yes—silence snapped into place around us.

I'd seen it once briefly visible, my cone of silence. It was a type of shielding I could erect around myself that kept others from hearing or sensing me, tapering to a point above my head and stretching several feet around us, impenetrable to sound, encasing us fully like his white bubble had. In addition, in a nice bonus I hadn't expected, my sound barrier cut Myrddhin off from some of his power. I hadn't known until then that he drew some of his power from that ghost fog. The barrier cut off enough of his power so that I could move my legs, wrap them around his back, hold him to me tight and secure. He didn't know, wasn't aware yet, of what I'd done. Simply cried out as my maneuver pushed him deeper into my body.

Sharp, undeniable pleasure mixed with hatred and loathing for the one who gave it to me, a really fucked-up sensation.

"Gods, you feel so good. So warm, so hot," Myrddhin muttered.

His eyes, which had closed during the penetration, opened when he tried to pull out and plunge back in . . . and found that he couldn't move, not with my legs wrapped like a vise around him, holding his abhorrent self to me, in me.

"Let's see how you like this." My teeth-baring smile must have been more alarming than I thought, or maybe it was simply that I had spoken to him and given him a clue that things weren't completely under his control anymore.

Heat was another gift of mine. It resided in me like a simmering, dormant volcano. I'd used it to heal before, had channeled it into my fingertip to cauterize Jonnie's bleeding artery. Now I used it to hurt—to destroy. I yanked it out of me, from the depths of my inner core, and it roared up in a molten flash-fire flood.

Burn, I thought, *burn you bastard* as I felt the heat fill me up, encompass me, and spread out to him. I held him to me, arms and legs wrapped around him like the most ardent lover, and let the heat overtake my body, burning not just him but me as well. Everything that was contained within my protective cone.

Myrddhin screamed and shrieked and then wailed, horrible sounds as he burned and sizzled where I touched him, clung to him.

Dredging up every last power I had, I set us both aflame.

TWENTY-THREE

I T WAS A surprise to open my eyes and find myself still alive, so to speak.

I heard the murmur of voices, not just one or two, but many. Several of those voices I recognized; they were familiar to me. But it was the gentle hands that held me, the hot splash of tears on my face, the raw, broken voice that murmured to me, "Please, Lucinda, please come back," that pulled me out of the floating darkness I had been drifting in.

I emerged from darkness and opened my eyes to even more darkness. But a dear, familiar kind: Talon's sweet face. I was wearing his T-shirt, my head and chest cradled in his lap, the rest of me sprawled out naked along the ground. He was crying.

Two tears plopped onto my face. Startling wetness that had me swatting at my cheek, where they were starting to slide down in slow, irritating crawls.

"Tickles," I mumbled. The word emerged in a weak, faint sound that surprised me. The effort it took to move my hand was both startling and alarming. I was incredibly weak. It brought out a flare of panic in me that increased with a loud drumming noise that sounded foreign and yet familiar at the same time. Even looking around and recognizing the faces around me—my brother, Halcyon; my father, Blaec; their men and mine, Ruric—and realizing that Talon and I were safe didn't totally dispel the panic. The misty fog that surrounded us made me very uneasy for some reason. And the impressions of *safe* and *not safe* bombarded me with conflicting messages.

"Why are you all staring at me," I rasped. "Like I've come back from the dead or something."

Sitting up, I found, was quite an effort.

"I think it's the *or something*," murmured a voice that jolted an odd flutter through my chest that coincided with that loud drumming sound again, a double assault. I twisted my head around to confirm that, yes indeed, it was Hari who had spoken. And standing next to him was—I blinked my eyes twice—a female Floradëur. A young girl—a young *demon* girl—stood next to her.

The unlikelihood of seeing what I was seeing was enough to make me wonder if I was having an odd dream. But the pain squeezing my head and the nausea twisting my poor empty stomach dispelled that theory. I had never felt this lousy in my dreams. This had to be real.

"Hari," I croaked, feeling worry and relief at the sight of him but not knowing why. I leaned heavily back against Talon's chest, the only reason why I was upright. Talon's silent tears continued to drip down his face, wetting the back of me.

"Don't cry, Talon," I muttered.

Talon wrapped his slender arms around me, and buried his face in my hair, giving himself over to silent, soundless sobs. I didn't know what else to do other than pat his arms awkwardly and make what I hoped were soothing sounds at him.

"Hey, hey, it's okay. I'm all right," I murmured, all the while feeling quite dazed and confused. For the life—or rather afterlife—of me, I couldn't remember what had happened.

"You were gone," Talon said, his voice thick.

"What do you mean? What happened?" I asked because I really, really wanted to know, and memory was proving to be a real slippery bastard.

"You destroyed him," Talon said in an almost-whisper.

"Who?"

"Myrddhin."

That one name brought it all back, and had me stiffening, freezing against Talon. I unwrapped his arms and carefully turned around so I could see him. "Where?" I demanded.

"There," he pointed. The demons who were in the path of that pointed finger cleared back, allowing me to see a small pile of ashes a couple of body lengths away.

"Myrddhin?" Hari repeated, sounding as shaken as my father looked. "The mad demon sorcerer I told you about?"

They were the only ones who seemed to recognize his name—my father, Hari, and Ruric. The old guard, all that remained of them. The rest, including my brother and I, hadn't been around a thousand years ago.

That loud drumbeat came again.

"What is that sound? Make it stop!" I cried, clutching my temples. "Holy Hell, my head hurts."

"We can't make it stop," my father said. "It's your heart."

"What?"

"What you're hearing is your heart," Blaec explained again patiently. "Your heart is beating."

I just stared at him, understanding the words, but not truly comprehending them. Then I laughed. "Wow. I must have taken some blow to the head. I thought you just said my heart was beating."

My father's face remained sober and serious. "I did."

It came again. Two tripping beats that I not only heard this time, I also felt them in my chest like the tiny kicks of an agitated sparrow.

My hands flew up to press between my breasts. In that still, quivering silence, I waited for it to happen again. It took an unusually long time for it to do so.

Baboom.

Holy shit! My heart was beating!

I must have paled or something because Ruric rumbled with alarm, "Don't faint on us, Princess."

His words snapped me out of that momentary whirl of light-headedness. "I don't faint," I said, scowling.

"Talon said you were gone." Halcyon crouched down in front of me, his dark chocolate brown eyes, so like my own, fixed with piercing intensity on me.

"What's happening to me?" I asked, bewildered, confused, more than a little frightened.

"According to Talon," my brother said, "you deliberately set yourself and this other demon, Myrddhin, on fire. Hot enough to burn the both of you down to ashes."

"Must have been one hell of a fire," I quipped, but it was done mostly on autopilot. I remembered it clearly now—the indescribably painful flames consuming my flesh. "But obviously only Myrddhin burned. I'm still here."

Blaec knelt beside Halcyon. "You were gone," my father said, grasping my hand.

"There was nothing left, Lucinda. Just ashes," Talon said in a low voice behind me. "Our bond . . . it was gone. Nothing but a gaping hole. And then you came back—"

"Well, that's good to hear."

"—as a bird."

"A bird?" I twisted around to look at him.

"This red and gold bird," Talon said.

"A phoenix," Blaec said softly, "rising from the ashes. The other half of your bloodline. We arrived in time to see that part of it."

"A phoenix?" I squeaked.

"You were reborn," my father said, "into life."

"That's . . . crazy."

Right on time, my heart sounded again. *Baboom.*

"Obviously not," returned my brother.

It was too much: the odd flutter in my chest, the sound of blood rushing through my vessels, pumped out fast by the squeezing contractions of my heart.

White light flashed my vision and I spun away into fractured darkness.

≈

I CAME TO again lying on the ground, in Talon's lap, surrounded by the concerned faces of my father, brother, Ruric, and Hari, his two strange female companions, and an outer ring of demon guards.

"Why am I still having the same dream?" I muttered, frowning.

My brother laughed, a nervous, relieved sound.

"Okay, now I know it's definitely a dream," I said.

"Why? Just because I laughed?" Halcyon asked, helping

me up enough to recline against Talon's chest. It was much
easier to do this time around.

"You haven't laughed in decades." My brows creased.
"No, centuries, I think!"

"Well, it's not every day my little sister comes back
from the dead," Halcyon said with dry humor.

Right on cue, my heart kicked up again. *Baboom.*

"Oh!" My hands flew to my chest as if to try to hide that
unsettling sound. "It wasn't a dream."

"Don't faint on us again," Halcyon said sternly.

My hands dropped as I scowled at him. "Demons don't
faint."

"Lucinda, maybe you're not just a demon anymore,"
Halcyon said gently, no sign of levity at all in his face.

I stared down at myself. "I still look like a demon, and
smell like one."

"Demons have no scent," Ruric said, frowning.

"Exactly! Neither do I."

"But your heart beats," Talon said in his soft voice.

Wait for it . . . wait for it . . .

Baboom.

"It guess it does," I reluctantly admitted, "but real slow.
No more than four or five beats a minute. Much less than
a human or even a Monère." Human hearts ran at sixty
beats or higher; Monères at half that rate. "I'm not sure if
five beats per minute would even be considered technically
alive. In human standards, at least."

"But you're not human," said the High Lord, "or just
demon anymore." Taking my hand, he pressed it tenderly
against the side of his face. "Whatever you are, I'm glad
you're still with us."

"Father . . ." It still was an odd pleasure to call him that.
To know that the title was true. "You don't really believe

what you said . . . about me being reborn. That's simply a fairy tale."

"An old legend," Blaec corrected, "not a fairy tale. Just because a gift or ability has become lost to us does not mean it did not once exist."

"But . . . my phoenix blood . . . I'm only a half-blood."

"You are only half-dragon blood, and yet you can take dragon form" was his response—logically illogical reasoning that I could not argue with.

I glanced around and counted all the oddities present here. Two Floradëurs—count them, two!—and one very rare demon young. And yet all eyes were fixed on *me*.

Even among freaks, I was the greatest freak show here. Nice to know.

My heart thumped again.

I pushed onto my feet, feeling too vulnerable sitting on the ground with all those demon eyes fixed on me. There was uneasiness and confusion in many of those eyes. My heartbeat proclaimed me prey and yet my appearance declared me demon, hunter.

Standing, I was able to see Talon's face. He was still crying, his face so sad. "Talon, what's wrong?"

"You're here, you're still with us," he said, a quaver in the sweet melody of his voice. "But I don't *feel* you anymore. I don't hear you."

He was mourning, I realized. I had shut myself completely off from him when I let that tumultuous heat rise up in me and overtake me, desperately hoping and praying that in destroying my enemy, in destroying *myself*, I was not killing the two others bound to me.

I lifted that block now in my mind. Reached down the familiar pathway and touched Talon's mind. *I'm here. I'm still here.*

Talon's knees buckled as joy flooded his mind. *Lucinda!*
he cried as I caught him against me. "I thought our bond
was broken," he said in a broken voice.

"No, just closed off, shut down tight. Not broken. If it
was in my power to do so, it would have happened. I certainly tried hard enough."

I never want our bond broken, even at the risk of death,
he said.

Wiping the tears from his face, his greatest fear relieved,
Talon turned and looked curiously at the other Floradëur.
"Who are you?" he asked, voicing the question I had been
wondering for some time now.

The dark female had been observing us with a strange,
keen intensity, very reserved and contained until Talon
asked her that question.

Now her face twisted as strong emotion gripped her. "I
am Sarai. Your mother."

Strange expressions flitted across Talon's face and then
hers as he walked to her. It took me a moment to realize
they were speaking to each other, mind-to-mind, but on a
different channel, one I could not hear. The two of them
drifted slightly apart from the others, lost in their silent
conversation.

Hari took the opportunity to make his own report and
recount what had happened to him. How the young demon
girl, Brielle was her name, had rescued him, and how
Sarai—Talon's mother!—had healed him by bonding with
him. "She was too weak and I was too injured to save me
any other way."

"You bonded," I said with something like wonder. "The
three of you?"

"No, just Sarai and I."

"And Brielle?"

"Brielle is under my protection," Hari said in answer to my question. His declaration drew a startled look from the young demon girl. From *everybody,* actually.

"Many miracles have happened today," Blaec murmured. And I didn't know if he was commenting on the demon-Floradëur bonding, only the second one to occur in his long existence, or the astonishing responsibility Hari had just taken on. Then there was, of course, me. The new me that felt so shaky and vulnerable with all those male eyes on me and so few clothes on my body; it was not a safe pairing. I felt like prey, in more ways that one, not just my beating heart, but me as a woman surrounded by too many males. I absolutely hated that new fear and did my best to suppress it, but it remained a shivery, ghostly feeling along my spine.

"There is still a lot that needs to be done to clean up this mess," I announced briskly. "For one thing, we have to destroy the tree."

"What tree?" asked Blaec.

"The Tree of Death. It was what nourished Myrddhin this whole time while he was in that hibernating sleep-state until we accidentally woke him up."

I explained as we walked, and every one gazed uneasily at the pervasive misty fog, spooked now that they knew the white mist surrounding us was really demon spirits chained to this land somehow, maybe through the tree.

I knew some of the demon guards didn't believe me, until we arrived. The sight of the tree itself and the ghastly heads it fed upon shocked them all. More than a few ended up retching into the bushes.

"Sweet Goddess, that's evil," Hari said.

"Yes," I agreed. "We have to destroy it."

"Will that free all the ghosts?"

"I don't know, we'll have to see. I hope and pray that it does."

The tree was eerily still as we surrounded it. An odd thing to say about a tree; you expect them to be still, after all, but I'd seen this thing in action. I just didn't know how much of what it had done before it was still capable of doing, now that Myrddhin was gone.

"Careful," I warned. "It's not like other trees."

"That we can see," a warrior muttered. He was of darker countenance than the other guards standing near Halcyon—a captain by his insignia ranking.

"What do you wish us to do?" Halcyon asked.

"I don't know. I guess hack it down, pull it up by the roots, and burn it all. But treat it as you would any other armed opponent."

"A tree?" the captain asked.

"It was capable of moving before, almost like a sentient creature."

Even after all the unusual things he had seen today, I had the distinct feeling the good captain didn't quite believe me. But at a nod from Halcyon, he turned and gave orders to his men. "Red and yellow team, stand guard. Blue team, you heard the Princess. Take the tree down but proceed with caution."

There was palpable tension as the eight warriors in the blue team approached. One of them leaped up and chopped down a thick branch with his sword. It dropped with a heavy *thunk* to the ground. Bloodred sap spilled out but nothing else stirred. A second warrior hacked off another heavy limb, this one housing two heads. The second branch dropped down, and the two heads bumped and rolled across the ground like ghastly coconuts. Disgusting, but nothing alarming.

Everybody relaxed; all but me. And in that unguarded moment, the tree moved, lightning fast, impaling six of the guards. Sharp branches stabbed through their bodies, skewering them, lifting them up into the air. The remaining two warriors were lashed around their necks by supple limbs, while more branches twined like rope around their arms and feet. In one concerted pulling move, arms and legs were torn from torsos, and the two demons' heads were yanked off their bodies. Agile tree tips stabbed into the open necks of the dismembered heads like dark, sucking fingers that quickly swelled with repulsive thickness as they began draining the still-moving heads. The faces of the beheaded demons twisted with horrible spasms, their jaws opening in silent screams while the other six impaled guards hacked at the attacking branches with swords and claws, desperately trying to free themselves and escape the gruesome fate of their comrades.

"Mierde!" the captain whispered beside me.

Ruric and Hari launched themselves at the whirling, writhing tree like two missiles, one heavy and thick, the other slender and thin, approaching from opposite sides with drawn swords, Hari snatching a weapon from another guard. I had never seen them work in tandem before. It was an odd pairing but one smoothly honed by many centuries of fighting together. The tree stabbed viciously at them and had those limbs hacked off for its trouble as the two of them battled their way closer to the trunk, slashing at the whirling branches that speared down at them, attacking from above.

It was what was belowground that tripped them up, literally. Roots exploded up from the ground like long brown fingers and wrapped around their ankles. Ruric, with his heavier bulk and weight, was able to stay on his

feet, slicing at the entrapping roots with the claw of his free
hand. Hari, though, was lighter and less fortunate. The tugging roots pulled him to the ground and tree limbs swung
down and wrapped around his neck and arms like ropes,
lifting him up. The yellow team rushed in at the captain's
shouted command, and I started to move. But I would have
been too late, for all of my preternatural demon speed. It
was another who saved him.

A black form morphed up out of the ground below
Hari, and with a whirl of clawed talons, the Floradëur cut
through the thick branches wrapped around Hari's arms
and neck. He tumbled to the ground with the Floradëur,
and rolled both of them away, dodging the branches spear-
ing furiously down at them until they rolled beyond the
tree's range. At first I thought it was Talon who had cut
Hari free, but he was still standing next to me. Then I realized it had been Sarai—Hari's bondmate.

There was a loud *crack* and I turned back to see Ruric
cleave his sword halfway through the thick tree trunk. Only
thin fingerlike roots were wrapped around his ankle, tugging
ineffectually at him; all the other branches capable of reaching him had been hacked away. With muscles bulging, his
big form straining, he yanked his sword back out and, with
a roar, struck again, cutting almost through the entire thickness of the trunk this time. A great heave, and the Tree of
Death toppled over with a loud crash, its limbs still moving,
but weakly now, slow and sluggish. Blood was everywhere,
and the thick red sap that bled from the tree was not much
different from what leaked out of the injured demons.

With edgy fear and anger, the guards chopped up the
downed tree into smaller pieces.

While they did that, Hari yelled at Sarai for putting herself in danger.

"And what about you, fool?" Sarai yelled in return. "Endangering yourself like that was endangering me, also."

Hari opened his mouth, but words choked in his throat as the truth of her words struck him. Her eyes glaring black daggers at the idiot demon she had just saved, Sarai turned her back on him and strode away.

I walked over to Hari. "She's right, you know." Both of us watched Ruric grab the stump and yank it up out of the ground. The squirming roots were so long, the final bits of them had to be pulled out by hand. "Things are different now that you are bonded," I told him. "What affects you affects her, and vice versa."

"Are you saying that I cannot put myself in danger anymore?"

"Sometimes that's not possible. I'm just saying that you do have to think twice before you risk yourself again. Be aware of the consequences. That it affects not just you alone anymore. Different, huh?" I said with a dry smile.

"Yeah, it sucks." He grimaced. "But it's better than being snuffed out, not existing anymore."

"Much better," I said pensively, my eyes wandering to Talon's slender form. "You may even find with time that it doesn't even suck, that it's something wonderful."

The look on Hari's face said that was highly unlikely, but I had high hopes for him. "There's more depth to you than you would have anyone believe . . . even yourself," I said, smiling at my own words. They were hard to believe. "Thank you for saving me."

"Talon saved you, not I," he said, looking away.

"You both did," I returned softly.

We watched the guards carefully sweep up all the last bits and pieces of the Tree of Death into one great pile.

They used broom-branches they had fashioned from neighboring trees. I didn't blame them in the least for not wanting to touch the weakly squirming tree parts with their bare
hands. The multitude of heads, old and new, was swept into
another pile, along with Derek's shriveled and desiccated
corpse. And the two bodies of the demon guards, whose
heads had been torn off and drained by the Tree of Death,
were gathered into a third, separate pile.

"I guess they need to start a fire," I said, and moved
forward to help them do that. Provide fire.

"No!" Hari said sharply. He reached out to stop me, and
I leaped back away from him like a frightened deer.

A crushing moment of startled silence.

"Forgive me—" Hari started saying.

"I'm sorry—"

"—let someone else start the fire."

"—I guess I'm still a bit skittish," I said shakily.

"There's no need to use your gift, Lucinda," my brother
said behind me.

I swung around, my eyes wider and more wild than I
would have liked. I was more than just a bit skittish. My
heart was pounding in my chest.

"It would be more prudent to let Father take care of
starting a fire," Halcyon said in a calm and even voice, "in
light of your recent ordeal."

"You mean after I burned myself up along with Myrddhin." The words tripped quickly, nervously out of my
mouth. "A novel way to destroy your enemy, but I wouldn't
recommend it. Hurts like the dickens."

"If Myrddhin was as evil as that cursed tree . . ."

"More," I said.

"Then you did us all a huge favor. Father and I can
handle the rest of the cleanup." Halcyon's eyes, damn his

hide, were too knowing and compassionate as they rested on me.

I couldn't hold his gaze.

Blaec had no problem supplying the fire they needed. He stepped forward, and the guards retreated from the three piles. Power rode the air like an unseen current, and the faint image of a much larger shape overlay the image of my father's lean form for a moment. Then he opened his mouth and a powerful jet of fire streamed out and flamed the separate piles.

"Dragon fire," Halcyon murmured. "Highly effective."

"Those poor guards," I said, watching the headless bodies writhe as they burned.

"Once the Tree of Death got ahold of their heads, they were doomed. It would be too dangerous now to try to heal them. Hopefully their souls won't be chained here like the rest."

As fire lit the three piles, and burning smoke drifted up to mingle with the fog, the mists around us thickened and took on a more defined substance until you could clearly see the ghostly forms streaming above and around us, gathering and twirling around the rising black smoke like a powerful whirlwind, tunneling up. It was quite a sight.

"*Mierde*," the captain exclaimed again, while others mumbled curses and imprecations in other languages.

With one last, powerful, hot stream of dragon flame from my father, the wood, flesh, and even bone incinerated until nothing remained of them except floating ashes and sparks of ember that twined and lifted up with the ghostly whirlwind, burning the ghostly forms away until none, not one white wisp, remained, leaving just smoke. No fog, no mist. No more ghosts.

"Ashes to ashes. Dust to dust. Be at peace," I murmured

and looked up at the first clear sky these cursed mountains had likely seen in over a thousand years. The third red moon, Rubera, was arcing up as Kantera, the yellow second moon, slipped down the horizon—red and yellow. Or red and gold, like the phoenix bird I had been.

A rebirth, like mine? Or simply the ending of a curse?

Poor souls. They were at peace now. But I wasn't—far from it, as the noisy thump of my heart reminded me. Its pounding beat proclaimed that I did not belong here anymore. Not just in Bandit Land but in Hell itself. I looked like a demon, smelled (or rather didn't smell) like one. Did not sound like one, however; no more echoing demon silence. So what was I? I pushed that away to deal with later.

"Now we have to find and destroy the book," I said quietly.

"Book?" Halcyon asked, turning to look at me.

"An old book of death spells that Myrddhin or someone else wrote. Derek must have found it, because he used death magick to pop into the living realm and grab me. It's one last piece of evil we have to destroy before leaving this gods-forsaken place."

We ended up dropping back down the hole Myrddhin had emerged from. We searched the walls, floor, and even the ceiling of the subterranean cavern where the mad sorcerer had lay entombed for almost ten centuries, and where Talon and I had come together. But there was nothing down here, just a gaping maw in the wall where the roots of the tree had ripped themselves out. It felt suffocating down here. An odd thought since I didn't need to breathe. Or had that changed, too?

When we resurfaced, Ruric, along with the help of the entire red and yellow team of warriors, pounded the ground above until the roof of the cavern caved in and was buried in dirt.

It didn't take us long to make our way back to Purgatory. By the time we reached it, our wounds were beginning to heal—a comforting thing to see. Three other teams
of royal guards had secured the settlement and rounded up
most of the bandits, who were, also to their bewilderment,
starting to heal old wounds and injuries they had probably
borne for years, maybe even decades. I doubted any of
them were lucky, or unlucky enough, to reach a hundred
years here.

The guards in our three teams hissed at the sight of
the skinned demon hides strung on the shoddy dwellings.
I almost didn't even notice them anymore; there were so
many other more horrible things I had seen and experienced today.

A word with the captain of the other teams told us that
no unusual book of spells had been found. But then they
hadn't known to look for it. We split up into several groups
and went hunting. Ruric and Hari, and his two ladies,
paired up with Talon and me. Brielle led us to Derek's bedchamber, and after we tossed it thoroughly, took us down
to the hidden subterranean cell where Sarai had been held
captive for all these many years. Brief shivers shook my
body as I ran my hands and probed my senses along the
walls and ceiling of the dank prison. I had been at Myrddhin's mercy for less than an hour, and that short amount
of time had been scarring enough to me already. I couldn't
image twenty-odd years spent as his prisoner.

We searched every corner of the old palace but came
up empty-handed. The other groups had just as poor luck.
A thorough hunt through the temple, private dwellings,
work sheds, and surrounding ground turned up one book,
and two old scrolls from the temple, but none of them contained anything about spells or death magick.

Questioning all the captured bandits was equally as unyielding. No one had any knowledge of such a book. Nor had they ever seen Derek or any of the previous bandit lords in possession of any book or scroll.

"It's not here," Halcyon said.

"One of the bandits may have found it and taken it," my father said. "Not all the bandits are accounted for. But sorting out who perished and who managed to escape will take some time."

"Maybe it doesn't exist," I said pensively, "or is hidden so well that no one can find it."

"If that is the case, we'll do our best to make it even more so," my father said grimly. With the help of his men, he demolished everything there—the old palace, the temple, all the surrounding structures. Even the crumbling arena was torn to the ground. Then, everything that could be set on fire was torched and set ablaze, including those vile demon skins.

"That's it," I said, watching everything burn. "That's all we can do for now." Only time would tell if that elusive book and its evil contents—death magick—would ever resurface. "Thanks," I said, turning to my father and brother. "For coming to rescue me."

"We were on our way, but your bondmate got to you much quicker than we were able to," my father said, and passed along his gratitude, in turn, to Talon. "I am in your debt," he said nodding to the dark Floradëur.

"I'm sorry," I burst out, interrupting, "but I can't stay here any longer." A wild yearning to be gone, away from here, shivered my skin. Rippled through my soul.

"I'm returning to the other realm," I told Hari and the two females he seemed to have accrued. "My thanks, Hari, for saving me so heroically and selflessly. But Derek . . .

he's gone now. And you seem to have new responsibilities, a new path to follow. I free you from your honorable service to me."

The High Lord nodded agreement. "You have accounted yourself with great valor and distinction, Hari, a true dragon lord of our clan. But my daughter is right. Your feet are set upon a new path. As such, I release you from your service to me as well, and open the doors of my home to you and your two ladies." Blaec's gaze drifted to rest meditatively upon Sarai's painfully cautious reserve. "With your son's ties to my daughter, milady," he said, addressing her, "we are family. And your bond to Hari puts you under the protection of our dragon clan. You are welcome to stay at my home while you decide what you wish to do. But I would be quite delighted should you decide to stay on as permanent residents. My home has been long empty. I would enjoy the company."

With simple grace, my father solved my greatest dilemma—what to do with Hari and his two females. Brielle was too young and too weak to risk crossing the portal to the living realm. Nor could I stay here in Hell and offer the protection that Sarai and Brielle so obviously needed, not with my loudly beating heart, which had startled *everyone* here, bandits and royal guards alike.

I didn't belong here in Hell anymore. Things had changed. Not just for Hari but for me as well. My awakened organ loudly drumrolled again. *Away! Away!* it seemed to cry with each unsettling beat.

"Talon." I turned back to my dark Floradëur with a small pang in my heart. "I know you have to stay, to speak with your mother . . . get to know her. Come back to me when you can," I said softly.

One last duty to discharge, I thought, looking at Ruric.

He dropped down heavily onto his knees, shaking the ground. "Forgive me, Princess, for failing you."

His words didn't surprise me. I knew he'd feel that way. "You didn't fail me, Ruric. Nothing could have stopped Derek from taking me. You shoulder guilt that doesn't belong to you. But you, too, are discharged from your service to me. Honorably."

"I would still serve you, Princess," he said with his head bowed.

"There's no more danger, no more rogue demon. Derek is destroyed." I glanced at my father, seeking his help. It was he, after all, who had first peeled Hari and Ruric off himself and assigned them to me as my bodyguards. *Take him back,* my eyes begged.

The High Lord shrugged. "It is Ruric's choice."

"Please, Princess, I wish to remain with you," Ruric said humbly.

"But . . . I don't need a bodyguard anymore."

"Then how about an honor guard," Blaec suggested. "It would make me easier knowing he was with you."

"And I," chimed in my brother.

Both ruler and former ruler of this realm ganging up on me. Not fair. Especially when Ruric lifted his pleading gaze to mine.

I sighed, wondering just how much of his desire to serve me was influenced by a certain blind human. "Then come," I said, gesturing for him to rise. "Let us go home."

"I left the others at High Court," Ruric said. "Safer, I thought."

"Then first we stop at High Court." I glanced over to the other half of what I had thought of as the bronze pair. It felt odd breaking up the two of them. "Hari," I said, catching his gaze one last time, "if you ever have need, send word to me and I will come." Then I was striding away. Running across the ground.

As I called up transformation from deep within me, I wondered how much of me had changed? Had I kept my abilities or lost them? Then I had my answer as the power stirred, rose to my will. It was like calling up my demon beast but even wilder, more primitive, pulling deeper from within my blood—Dragon. It rushed out of me, stretching my cells, changing me to something both beautiful and monstrous. Gloriously strong.

As I transformed into the dragon of my blood and bloodline, my limbs lengthened, my spine bent, and my T-shirt ripped away as golden scales rippled over me and covered my skin.

"Hop on," I said in a deep resonate growl to Ruric. He sprang onto my back, and the ground trembled and shook as I ran. I spread my wings, snapping them open like taut leather sails, and we lifted off the ground in a rush of wind.

Ruric clung to me and shouted, "Your father."

Looking down below I saw my father running after us, several alarmed guards trailing him. As I watched, the High Lord's slight demon shape began to shimmer in a remarkable transformation that stretched him out and out and up into a huge and long, black serpentine dragon. It was a glorious sight, one I'd never thought to see. He launched himself gracefully into the air amidst shouted protests from his guards, a large dragon smile on his face that showed more free and delighted emotion than I'd ever seen on his face.

He was a stunning creature, differently formed than I. Where I was big and bulky, my father was sinuously lean, a mature dragon. While I flapped my wings to catch and ride

the wind, he flowed with wings outspread, gracefully air-
borne, the most dominant predator of land, sky, and maybe
even sea.

His fierce dragon cry trumpeted the air, and I threw
back my head and added my bugling call to his.

His poor guards. An eight-member team set out at a
dead run after us. They must be having a hissy fit over my
father taking off like that, alone, unguarded. Although
I couldn't imagine what could possibly be of threat to a
four-ton, fire-breathing dragon.

Blaec playfully arced and twisted through the air, unbur-
dened by a rider, executing a couple of tight and graceful
somersault loops—definitely something I wanted to try at
the next opportunity.

Flying in the company of another dragon was exhilarating, and time literally flew by. In less time than I imagined,
the dark spires of Darkling Hall, my father's residence,
came into view. Shouts came from the sentry as he caught
sight of us: easy enough to do with my booming heartbeat presaging our arrival; it was an arresting sound, much
louder in my huge dragon form.

Four royal guards—all that had remained behind—
raced out into the courtyard. Thankfully, they didn't try to
shoot us down. I doubt any of them had ever seen the High
Lord in dragon form, but it was a well-known fact that we
were the last existing members of the dragon clan. Hopefully they knew that the gold dragon was me; Ruric, riding
on my back, large and recognizable, should have been a
big clue. But if they had any worries or doubts, they were
firmly put to rest by the unusually tall and gaunt demon
who rushed out into the courtyard.

Winston, the butler of Darkling Hall for as long as
I could remember, gazed up at us with moisture glistening

in his dark eyes as he watched the High Lord swoop down to land with perfect, light precision—no rustiness at all—and shimmer back into his less prepossessing demon form.

"It has been a long time since you've flown as dragon, my lord," Winston said with more emotion than I'd ever heard before in his voice. For a moment, I thought he was going to break form and say something personal, but he reigned himself in. Ever the perfect butler, he handed my father one of the cloaks he had brought out.

Blaec swung the cloak around himself, grinning broadly. "There are two dragons that soar the sky now; maybe even a third one soon. It is good not to be the only one anymore."

I landed not as lightly or as gracefully as my father. The ground shuddered under the hard impact, and clumps of dirt and lawn sprayed up into the air behind me, but at least I kept my feet and didn't plow my nose into the grass. Ruric bounced off my back to spring lightly onto his feet instead of trying to hang on, saving me a scraped hide.

"Sorry," I rumbled. With a moment's concentration, dense dragon flesh slowly condensed down and reshaped into my petite demon form. Ruric draped the cloak he had taken from Winston around me. I was grateful for the covering.

As the exhilaration left me, fatigue crept in, and I sought refuge inside the Hall, leaving Ruric and the High Lord to pass the news on to the others. In the bedchamber my father kept for me there, I washed myself thoroughly, scrubbing my skin almost raw as I soaped and rinsed every single reachable inch of my bare skin, washing four times over everywhere he had touched me. But even clothed, I still felt sullied. Dirty and unclean.

I was so tired, so weary. I wondered if it was because my
heart had to labor now. Or if it was because I had burned
myself down to ashes? That would be enough to make anyone tired, I imagined.

Winston was waiting for me outside my room, his tall,
gaunt form ruler-straight, looming over me. "Princess." He
bowed. "Is there anything you require that I can provide?"

The few unfortunate occasions we had brushed together
in the past, I had enjoyed tweaking his poker-stuffed ass,
giving him grief and sass while he frowned disapprovingly
at me. We'd always rubbed each other the wrong way, more
intentional on my part than his, but for whatever reason—
maybe the joy on his face when he had seen my father flying as dragon, the tears in his eyes—my usual animosity
toward the oh-so-proper butler was gone now.

"Hey, Winston," I said, greeting him, if not with joy,
then minus my usual jeering disrespect. "No, I found
everything I needed." And I had. My favorite hair cleanser
and soap had been in the bathing chamber. Placed there by
Winston, I realized suddenly. Whatever his opinion of our
individual family members, he served us well, took care of
my father. Whatever his feelings for me, he seemed to care
genuinely for the High Lord.

My mild response seemed to take the butler aback.
Why? Just because I hadn't snapped his head off? Looking
back, I could maybe admit that I might have been a serious
pain in the ass myself in the past.

I smiled up at Winston's tall form, which made his brow
crease into a frown. "As you can see, my father is doing
much better."

"Miraculously so," Winston replied. "And yourself?"

Me? I was feeling suddenly old and tired and lonely. I
missed Talon—even Hari—felt their absence. Talon, like

a gentle ache. Hari, like a teddy bear I had grown accustomed to that had been suddenly taken away from me. How maudlin of me.

I shrugged. "I'm fine," I replied without my usual snap and fire—an uncomfortable thought, that . . . heat and flame.

Wincing, I started down the hall, then stopped, swung back to face Winston. "I just wanted to say . . . thank you, for all the years you've taken care of my father."

"He is a great man," Winston said.

I smiled and watched his brows furrow even more. "Yeah, well, I can't believe I'm saying this, but he's lucky to have you."

"He's lucky to have you, Princess Lucinda, returned to him. As much as he loves Halcyon, he loves you, too, equally as much. You bring him great joy, and renewed life."

"Literally." I grimaced as my heart kicked out a loud beat. "I guess my father told you everything."

"The general events, yes."

"No need to hover. I'm fine, really."

Winston cleared his throat. "Pardon me, Princess, but you do not seem fine."

"Why, just because I'm not insulting you?"

"Well, yes, I guess," he admitted, looking worried and puzzled. "You would have normally called me a cretin or a toad, or some other obnoxious thing by now."

"How's this? I'm fine, you freaky dipshit. Now back off. Don't crowd me."

A rare smile creased his austere face. "Thank you, that's much better, Princess."

I curled my lips up at him. Waited until I hit the stairs before letting my own smile slip across my face. Maybe I wasn't the only one who took comfort in familiar routine.

My father had also bathed and changed, and sat with Ruric, waiting for me in the front parlor.

"You ready to go, Ruric?" I asked, feeling the itch to be gone.

"Yes, Princess, but—"

"Maybe you should take a day to rest and recover here before you attempt the portal," Blaec suggested.

It took me a moment to register the concern in both of their faces, and realize why. Gah! They were worried about me, wondering if maybe my new altered state had changed my ability to traverse the portals. Demons who didn't have enough power ended up dissipating in transit, never to be seen again.

Gods, wouldn't that be an ironic? To be alive again, yet kept from the living realm.

"No, I'm ready to go now." Ready and eager, *wanting* to go with every thump and kick of my heart. The set expression on my face told them clearly that I was not willing to wait or delay.

Sighing, my father gestured to the door.

As we walked down the front steps, the team of guards who had set out after my father came running up, their clothes drenched with perspiration. Blessed Lady, they must have broken records getting here. They met the High Lord with not one word of remonstration. At his acknowledging nod, they simply fell into place behind my father as we crossed the field to the south portal.

Just in case, I kissed my father on the cheek, the first time I had done so since my mother had broken us apart with her lie.

"Love you, Dad," I whispered. Then, with Ruric beside me, I stepped into the shimmering portal.

As one of the oldest, strongest demons, I had traveled

the portals with impunity and ease. After the three-way bond had snapped into place between Talon, Nico, and I, that had changed. Traveling this very same portal had caused a stinging discomfort. Now it changed yet again. It prickled in mild discomfort, an improvement. That was certainly nice.

My heart beat once, accelerating the prickling to a sharper, clawing sensation along my skin. Then we were in the living realm. Arrived at High Court.

TWENTY-FOUR

O UR SECOND ARRIVAL at High Queen's Court was much more discreet than our first visit had been—what was it?—several days before. Gods! So many things had happened during that time. Relationships had changed, a mother and son had reunited, afterlives had been destroyed, a new life reborn.

Captain Gilbert had posted two duty guards to watch the portal. One of the guards dove for the alarm gong at our sudden appearance. The other went for his weapon, not a sword but a very modern shotgun, which had my eyebrows lifting in surprise since few Monères were proficient in the use of modern weapons, preferring the traditional sword and dagger. Silently I commended the captain's wise judgment. A sword was pretty useless against a demon. A wide spray from a shotgun had a better chance of hitting its target. Well, at least a far better chance than an arm's length of steel.

I laid a restraining hand on Ruric's arm as he tensed, readying himself at my side—a move so quick, so fast, the guards
didn't even see it. I could have just as easily pounced and dis-
armed them both in that same split fraction of a second.

"If you shoot us, I am going to be very pissed," I told
them, standing very still.

The guard thankfully lowered his shotgun, and bowed.
"Princess Lucinda."

The second guard bowed as well, the gong mallet
clutched in his hand.

More points to the captain for posting men who at least
recognized me.

"And you are?" I asked.

"Zaquiel, milady," said the guard standing next to the
alarm gong.

"Irwyn at your service, Princess," said the gun-toting
guard.

I turned and slanted a look at Irwyn from slumberous,
half-lidded eyes that sped up his heartbeat, something I
had done without thinking, instinctively slipping into my
natural armor of smoldering sensuality.

"Do you know how to use that shotgun, Irwyn?"

I asked because I was curious. It was an oddity, a Monère
warrior holding a shotgun with such comfortable familiar-
ity. Only, the simple question came out in a suggestive, sensual purr, still locked at I was in my defensive state.

"Yes, ma'am . . . milady . . . I mean, Princess," said
Irwyn, his face growing redder and redder as he tripped
over his tongue. Beside him, Zaquiel snorted in disgust.

"And you, Zaquiel?" I asked, turning the full force of
my glittering eyes onto the other guard. "Do *you* know
how to use a shotgun?"

He swallowed, flustered. "No, Princess. I, uh, don't."

I grabbed hold of my control and toned it down. It took concentrated effort. "I've come for my men," I managed to say in
a much blander voice, "and to report to the Queen Mother."

"Yes, Princess," Irwyn said, recovering his composure.
"Just one moment, please." He whistled, three short blasts,
and another guard came bounding up the path.

"Armsman Talbert will accompany you to the Queen
Mother," Irwyn said.

"And my men?" I asked.

"They are supping at the dining hall, Princess. We'll
have them meet you at Council Hall."

No witless Queen raised up a hue and cry as Ruric and
I and our chaperoning armsman stepped out onto the main
path.

Being met by two armed guards instead of one silly,
screaming Queen was a vast improvement, but still I
mourned the heightened security. Permanent guards had
once been routinely posted at the portal but that had been
long ago, before my time. It had never been manned during
the five hundred years I had served as guardian. No need
to, before Derek. The stray demons that slipped illicitly
into the living realm didn't come to High Court. They went
to other places to wreak their bloody havoc.

Lunar New Year festivities were apparently over, thank
the Goddess, and High Queen's Court was once again its
usual tranquil self. We strolled our way down to Council Hall, where the Queen Mother resided and presided,
without any alarm being raised, although more than a few
guards we passed cast wary glances at Ruric. But then, he
drew the same guarded attention even in Hell.

As we walked, I became aware of something I had not
noticed before. My heart had sped up. I had not registered it
until now because it beat in the same rhythm as those around

me—at around thirty beats per minute, the same heart rate as the other Monère, blending me seamlessly in with them.

I entered Council Hall focused entirely on my inner self until we came to a stop before two duty guards stationed in front of a door. Armsman Talbert knocked and opened the door, bidding us enter. Ruric looked relieved when I asked him to wait outside.

I stepped alone into the Queen Mother's private study.

"Lucinda!" Shock, relief, and pleasure crossed the Queen Mother's face as she rounded the desk and embraced me. I tensed involuntarily at the brief hug.

"I was so worried when I heard you had been taken by that rogue demon," she said. "Your being here . . . it's good news, I take it?"

"Yes, Derek is no longer a threat."

"Ah. That is good news indeed. Sit. Tell me what happened."

She drew me to the sofa instead of the armchairs set before the desk, making our meeting more casual. I waited until she had seated herself next to me, before asking, "Do you notice anything different about me?"

She frowned, studying me, this Monère woman I had known throughout my long afterlife of existence. I'd known her when she was young and beautiful. Over the unnaturally long centuries of time, her skin had grown softly creased and wrinkled; she was the only Monère to ever reach such an aged and human-looking state. But then, she had lived over twice a Monère's normal lifespan. Only her eyes were the same— crystal blue, vibrant and intense. Eyes that were capable of being coolly calculating, impartial, ruthless even. But none of that aloofness was in those blue eyes now as she scruti- nized me carefully. It wasn't until she delved deeper beyond the skin's surface that her eyes lit with shocked surprise.

"Your heart is beating! Dear sweet Light. I hadn't noticed because, well, everyone I come across here has a beating heart."

"But not demons. Except me. I'm different now from others of my kind. Just as you are, Giselda." Here, in this privacy-bespelled chamber, we could speak openly of long-kept secrets. Here, I could call her by her real name and not by her title.

"But how is that possible, Lucinda? Your heart is *beating*. Did your father . . . ?" Her voice trailed off, not knowing how to ask if my father had done to me what he had done to her—give her one drop of his demon blood. One mere drop. Not enough to turn her into *Damanôen*, demon living, so that she acquired our physical demon traits and bloodthirst. But enough to kick her power far beyond that of any other Monère, any other Queen. One drop of forbidden demon blood mixed with her Queen's blood, and Monère history and survival had changed for the better. Giselda had been there, a Queen powerful enough to guide her people during a confused and chaotic time when the pure bloodlines of powerful clans had fallen away into extinction as death from battles and skirmishes took their toll on all.

Clans fell apart as the last of their pure-blood Queens died or were killed, leaving them lawless, homeless, and desperate to steal or capture another Queen to survive. It was a time of great upheaval, a time when Monère social structure slowly unraveled and fell messily apart. In that rough and unstable time, High Queen's Court was hammered into existence by the iron will of the most powerful Queen, who was backed by the High Lord of Hell's even more intimidating demon clout.

New territories were formed, and Queens of mixed clan blood ruled over an assemblage of people who had been taken from different dissolving clans and thrown to live in peace together under these new Queens—a peace and order that was strictly and ruthlessly upheld by the Council and, on the rare occasions it was needed, by Blaec's enforcing hand. In time, the young Monère Queen named Giselda became simply known as the Queen Mother.

Wrinkled, old, and motherly, Giselda was, in truth, more of a sister to me. After all, my father's blood, a tiny bit of it, ran in her, same as me.

"No," I told her now. "My change came about much differently than yours. After Derek snatched me, another bigger and badder demon came along and destroyed him, and took me prisoner."

"Lucinda," Giselda said, looking at me with frowning intensity. "I know for a fact that there are not many demons more powerful than you. Derek, they said, used some sort of dark magick to sneak up on you."

"He used death magick."

"That sounds ugly."

"It is. The bigger, badder demon who came along was the originator of this death magick." I started from the beginning and told her the tale. Told her how either my blood or Talon's had awakened the millennium-old sorcerer. "His psychic power was far greater than mine. Maybe even greater than my father's. I couldn't escape him, so I burned us up—heat, you know, is one of my gifts. I managed to destroy him but also ended my own afterlife. Talon said we both burned down to ashes, and that I rose up out of these ashes as a phoenix."

"New life. The symbol of rebirth," Giselda said in soft wonderment. "And the other half of your blood."

"Yes, well, my heart has started beating again. Slowly, at first, but it's sped up since I came back here. I've changed . . .

am still changing." I must have looked more unsettled than I realized because Giselda gently squeezed my hand in reassurance.

"Are you frightened?"

"Yes," I whispered.

She smiled. "So was I after I took your father's drop of blood into me. My change was more subtle than yours, but I know how frightening, how bewildering change can be. How you feel as if the very foundation of who you are is crumbling beneath you."

"I feel so . . . vulnerable now."

"You feel *alive* again."

I shook my head. "I look like a demon but my heart beats like a Monère. I don't know what I am anymore."

"You are who you always have been," Giselda said with earnest wisdom earned from a long life, "and you are also the new person you are becoming. Life is change—that is its very meaning."

"I was content being a demon."

"Were you, really?" Giselda asked kindly, her eyes so piercingly blue. "You were alone, an outcast of sorts among your own demonkind. It wasn't until you encountered your two Monère rogues and bonded with Nico and Talon that I truly saw you as you say you were—content. Lucinda, even when you were demon dead, life called out to you, and you embraced it. Don't stop now, girl."

I laughed, a short ragged sound of involuntary mirth.

Giselda grinned at me, her blue eyes twinkling. "I may look like an old lady, but my heart is still that of a young Monère."

"Has living this long been difficult? Do you ever regret it?"

The sharp clarity of her eyes softened as they turned to look inward. "A people cannot survive long in lawless disorder. No, I do not regret it, but sometimes I am tired, and eager for someone else to take over the reigns of responsibility from me. I thought for a time perhaps it might be Mona Lisa," she said, speaking of the new human-Monère Mixed Blood Queen. Another Queen had blood-raped my brother, gulping down mouthfuls of his blood, and Mona Lisa had sucked that demon-tainted essence of this other Queen into herself.

"She is not like you, merely enhanced with demon strength and dragon longevity," I warned. "Mona Lisa is *Damanôen*, becoming a true living demon complete with fangs and bloodthirst. I saw it myself."

"Yes, Halcyon mentioned that she is having some difficulties. Only time will tell what becomes of her," Giselda said with a sigh, then looked up with a small smile. "So you see, you are not as alone as you thought. And you will likely have an easier time adjusting to your new changes that Mona Lisa to hers."

"I thought my brother a fool for entwining his fate so much with hers, drowning boat that she is," I said. "Only more recently do I understand."

"That he is desperate to save the one he loves," Giselda said with a sad smile, "just as I was desperate to save our people. You are strong, Lucinda, and you have many others now willing to help, who are no doubt anxious to ascertain your safe return with their own eyes. With so many ties to life, and to love, it is not so surprising that you were pulled back, reborn into life."

Those ties she spoke of twanged within me now. "Thank you, Giselda," I said, rising. "It helps . . . everything you said."

"Anytime," she said, clasping my hand, a beautiful smile on her softly wrinkled face.

TWENTY-FIVE

M Y MEN WERE waiting for me by the front entrance.
They didn't notice me at first, having heard my slow
heartbeat and automatically discounting me as Monère. It
was Jonnie who spotted me and rushed to me with a cry.

I had a moment to brace myself, to get my skittering
nerves under control, so that when he flung himself against
me, hugging me tight, I was able to endure it and not fling
him instinctively away. At eighteen he was no longer a boy
but he was still boyish, not quite a full-grown man . . . a
full-grown threat. Still, the suddenness of a tall male rushing at me, boyish or not, had me stiffening so hard that my
muscles almost spasmed. With gentle care, I pulled free
from him.

"Lucinda, are you okay? We were so worried!"

"I'm fine," I reassured him, though that was not entirely
the truth; my own tense body contradicted my words but

he was too excited and happy to notice, and my men too stunned.

"Lucinda," Stefan said, confusion in his face as he looked behind me to Ruric's looming presence and his still, demon silence, contrasting sharply with my now much noisier one. Neither of the two Monère duty guards posted near the entrance seemed to notice anything amiss. Only Stefan, and the man beside him—Nico, my bondmate. The weakest among our triad.

"Nico." I ran my eyes over him anxiously. "You are well?"

"Yes, and you?"

I nodded and gave a happy smile as I took in his hale and hearty appearance. Nico had grown stronger, but a part of me had still worried that he might have collapsed or even died when I had destroyed myself along with my enemy.

I should have gone to them, my two precious men. But already my body was shaky from Jonnie's exuberant embrace, so I just stood there, looking at them, one as beautiful, dark, and compelling as a fallen angel, the other light, fair, on the rougher side of handsome.

I couldn't bring myself to hug them, but other things I could do. I held out my hands to Stefan and Nico, and they came to me, slipped their hands into mine.

Questions, the most burning one, *Why is your heart beating?* went unvoiced. They were reluctant to ask that in the presence of the posted guardsmen. But other questions they could, and did, ask. First and foremost being, "Where are Talon and Hari?"

"Talon stayed behind to become acquainted with his mother."

"His mother!" Jonnie exclaimed.

"And Hari acquired some other new obligations that I'll tell you about later." Later wasn't until we arrived home.

The house in Arizona was still bland and brown and nondescript, but now—with all the bedrooms claimed and filled—it was a home, truly a home, not just an empty box I briefly stayed at. It was quite modest, even a little shabby, compared to my elegantly appointed residence in Hell, but I'd much rather be here with them, living simply, than alone, existing in lavish luxury. Besides, things could be fixed up, the interior furnished better, more comfortably. I'd just never bothered before. Never had any reason to do so when it was just me.

"We still have to buy two more beds," I said abstractedly, doing a mental count in my head. With Hari gone and Talon absent, everyone got a bed to themselves, except for Jonnie and Stefan. Stefan would likely cede the bed to Jonnie, who was still recovering from a bullet wound . . . although, come to think of it, he had *run* to me, no hitch to his stride at all. A rather unexpectedly fast recovery for a Mixed Blood . . .

"We'll get them tomorrow," Stefan said. Simple words but so incredibly sweet, implying companionship, a shared future together.

Tomorrow . . . I was damn grateful to have a tomorrow.

"Why is your heart beating?" Nico finally asked once we were inside the house. "Can you tell us now what happened?"

We ended up in the living room, and they listened in silence as I recounted the morbid events, leaving out only one intimate detail—how close I'd had to get to Myrddhin before I could destroy him.

"You ended your existence." The white knuckles of

Stefan's clenched fists belied the seeming calm of his voice. "Deliberately."

"I had no other choice. Believe me, if there had been any other way, I would have taken it. But there wasn't."

"Jeez, Lucinda," Jonnie breathed. "Death magick, Merlin as a demon, a Tree of Death, demon ghosts, and you rising out of the ashes as a phoenix." He shook his head. "If I didn't hear your heart beating, I wouldn't believe you."

I looked at him sharply. "You can hear my heart beating?" As a Mixed Blood, Jonnie's senses should have been blunted.

As it turns out, I had not been the only one to change. Jonnie had also. Only days after being struck down by a bullet and undergoing major surgery, the boy had healed. Not normal healing, but completely. No scar marred his skin. It was smooth and perfect, no evidence that he had almost bled to death from a gunshot wound. And not only was his hearing keener but his eyesight and reflexes were sharper, his strength and speed much greater.

Of Goddess, I thought, as my heart surged in sudden, fast-thumping rhythm. Had my demon blood somehow mingled with his? Had I broken one of our greatest taboos? Accidentally made him *Damanôen*, a living demon? Had I delivered a death sentence to this boy while trying to save him?

I had inserted a searing hot fingertip into Jonnie to cauterize his bleeding artery. But there had been no open wounds on me.

My mind searched desperately back in time but could not remember any occasion that could have allowed the mixing of my blood with his while I had been conscious.

What about when you were unconscious? whispered my mind.

"It was my blood," Stefan said, his voice drawing me out of my dangerous thoughts.

"What?" I said, looking without comprehension at him.

"I believe it was my blood that caused these changes in Jonnie. The bullet passed through me first before hitting him, remember?"

I remembered quite well. Stefan had used his own body to try to shield Jonnie. But even Monère flesh gave way beneath a bullet; it had left a fist-sized hole in Stefan's back, and a fragment of that bullet, coated with Stefan's blood, had struck Jonnie.

Monère blood. Not my demon blood. With all my might, I prayed that it was so.

The simple fact that Jonnie's wound had healed indicated it was a Monère ability, not a demon one—demons did not heal in the living realm—supporting Stefan's theory. I clutched that comforting piece of fact to me as I collapsed into bed and slept for twelve straight hours.

~~~

I AWOKE FEELING surprisingly hungry. Not for blood, but for food.

Ruric looked on, appalled, as I scooped up a bowl of chicken noodle soup that someone, probably Stefan, had prepared. The poor demon looked like he was watching a train wreck taking place before his eyes as I proceeded to eat the delicious-smelling soup. Because demons did not eat solid food in the living realm; we only drank blood. Attempting anything more solid made demons vilely sick. But I ate without any problem. In fact, I slurped down a second bowl.

As the days passed, I also found that sunlight no longer

harmed me. Exposure to it no longer drained my power or softened my flesh. I explored my new tolerance for sunlight under the wary, anxious eyes of my men, who I had insisted stay inside the house while I curled up on a blanket outside, soaking in the bright warm rays like a small, sleepy dragon. One hour the first day became three hours the next, then five hours the day after that. And all I got was a slight tan that deepened the golden pigment of my skin.

Only Jonnie wasn't driven crazy as I tested the new limits within myself, because he was as busy exploring his changes as I was mine.

His strength came to a peak two days after my return, falling just short of full Monère strength, then started to wane until he was once more as he had been, only just a touch faster and stronger now. No sign of bloodthirst or new demon wildness.

My greatest fear faded but my lesser ones still remained. I slept alone.

I got the call one day that my own personal funds had finally arrived. I had asked Halcyon to sell the herd of blood cattle I owned down in Hell. He had transferred the proceeds of this sale to Donald MacPherson, who in turn had deposited the money into a new private account that had been set up for me. I was no longer a guardian. I had given my official notice to Halcyon, and no longer felt free using guardian money to support myself and my new expenses, which had quadrupled. Before, I had just drunk blood, which had been of no cost to me—my donors maybe, but not me. Now I ate food, and had three, possibly four other mouths to feed.

Halcyon had undoubtedly been more generous than he should have been converting demon currency into human dollars. But I was fortunate he was there to act as my bank. I doubted any of the human banks could have accommodated me.

We finally purchased the two extra beds we needed, and Jonnie began classes at the new high school.

The first day of school, Jonnie drove off in Stefan's car, unaware that Stefan and I surreptitiously followed him ten minutes later in my car. Ruric and Nico wanted to come along but we made them stay behind. We wanted to be discreet, not draw attention.

Jonnie seemed to ease into his new classes without any difficulty. It was the end of January, so the timing wasn't too bad, considering. Through snippets of conversation we learned that Jonnie wasn't the only new kid; several other students had also just moved into the area.

In school, Jonnie was much more subdued than he was with us at home. Only now did I realize how comfortable he felt with us—with me.

Stefan and I watched and listened from the car, parked in the shade across the street, keeping easy track of Jonnie's slightly slower heartbeat as he moved from classroom to classroom. When at the next period bell, he headed toward the back of the building, we left the car to slip quietly into the woods behind the school and continue our watch beneath the shade of a tall pine tree.

"I can't believe how nervous I feel," I muttered as we kept vigil. "I know he's supposed to be safe in there, but there are so many kids in there—thousands of them! A shame that boost in strength he gained from your blood didn't last longer."

"I'm glad it didn't," Stefan said in a quiet, thoughtful voice. "I think Jonnie is, too. Easier for him to blend in. I want him to have a real life; to feel a part of human society.

Goddess knows he spent enough years with me, feeling
like a fugitive."

Stefan had been a rogue before I had met him, a Monère
warrior who had grown too strong for his Queen and fled
her, becoming an outcast. I had saved him from that drifting, precarious life when I had claimed him and his ward.
They were safe now, under my protection, as was Nico.
But the few white strands of hair scattered among the thick
black silk of Stefan's hair reminded me of another need
they had. The need to Bask in the renewing rays of the
moon, which I could no longer draw down; only a Monère
Queen could.

Bereft of a Queen for almost twenty years, Stefan had
aged prematurely. White hair should not have started
appearing until after two hundred years of life, but he had
these white strands because even though Stefan's chrono-
logical age was one hundred forty-five, his true biological
age was that of a two-hundred-five-year-old Monère. He
had aged sixty years instead of twenty in the two decades
of his exile without Basking.

Nico had also been a rogue, but his banishment had
only lasted months, not years; he had not been cheated out
of prime years of his life as Stefan had.

The full moon was only a week away, reminding me that
arrangements had to be made for Stefan and Nico before
the next Basking period came.

Stefan held his head very still as I ran my fingers
through his thick hair, touching one of those offending
white strands. He guessed what had captured my attention
by the more agitated rhythm of my betraying heartbeat.

"I should dye my hair like humans do," he said.

"No need. It reminds me of your other needs, and that
I need to make arrangements for you and Nico to Bask

somewhere. If not at a neighboring territory then back at High Court with the Queen Mother."

"My white hair upsets you." He turned to face me, catching my hand unexpectedly in his.

I flinched and jerked free with blind terror, falling back away from him as if he had clamped his hand cruelly around my wrist in restraint instead of holding it in a soft and gentle grip, easily broken.

We stared at each other in a tense and frozen silence.

"I'm sorry—" I began.

"You no longer want me," Stefan whispered bleakly, looking stunned and viciously wounded by my violent rejection of him. "I . . . I know you don't really need me. You have so many others now."

"No, I still want you," I said, begging him with my eyes to believe me.

"Then why did you pull away just now? As if you could not bear for me to touch you?"

I groped for words to answer him, but they stuck in my throat.

Stefan's eyes narrowed. "Something happened. Something that you didn't tell us about."

I didn't want to tell him. Didn't want to remember Myrddhin's foul presence sliding into me. Shame twined with fear that Stefan would look at me differently. That he would no longer want me. But if I said nothing, didn't explain, I risked losing him that way, too.

"The part I left out, that I didn't tell you or any of the others," I said, looking blindly at the school, "was how I got Myrddhin to drop his personal shielding. He was fucking me, of course."

His next words came gently. "You were scared and frightened."

Fear and shame thickened my throat. "Yes, you're right. I was scared and frightened and helpless—truly helpless. His power dwarfed mine. I'd never encountered anything like him before. My father and brother are stronger than I am, but they never used their greater strength against me. And they weren't *evil* like he was."

"He raped you."

I shook my head. "No, Stefan, he didn't. I lured him to me, and when he fondled me, when he entered me . . . it felt good. He made me feel"—I had to choke the next word out—"pleasure."

"That does not make it any less a violation," Stefan said. "Inside your mind, did you desire the act?"

"I told you already, I needed him close and unshielded, and sex was the only lure I could think of to get him to drop it."

"No, not your intent—your emotions. How did you feel when he penetrated you? Not the physical sensation but in your mind?"

"I felt panic, fear, revulsion. My mind was screaming: *No, I don't want this.* But I didn't push him away. I wrapped myself around him and pulled him even deeper into me." A wet tear overflowed, trickled down my face.

"So you could end his sorry existence."

I braced myself and glanced at his face. He looked anguished, not angry at me.

"Oh, love. You should have told us."

"I didn't want you to know," I said, slow, ragged. "It's so dirty. So ugly."

"He wounded you in a way we couldn't see but should have been aware of. You should have told us so we didn't accidentally hurt you more. Like grabbing you suddenly, the way I just did."

"Y-You don't think I'm dirty . . . disgusting?"

"No, love, never. I'm *awed* at how brave and smart you are. Grateful that you came back to us. Look at me." He stretched out his hands so I could see the fine tremors shaking his long, elegant fingers. "I'm *relieved*. Literally shaking with relief knowing that it wasn't me you were rejecting but him . . . your body's memory of him. It was killing me when I thought you didn't want me anymore."

"No, Stefan. I'll always want you. I was worried you might not want me anymore if you knew."

"Lucinda. I love you."

His words ran a thrill through me. Loosened a tight ball of anxiety that had been knotted up tight within me. The deep, unseen wound Myrddhin had inflicted on me didn't heal right then and there, but it did begin to mend, continued to do so with the soothing balm of his words.

"I've never loved a woman before," he said softly, "not really. Not any of my Queens. But I love you. There was this empty, aching hole inside of me before you came along. Now you complete me, make me whole and happy. So happy that I have this constant dread that it'll be taken away. That maybe you'll tire of me."

"No—never. I love you, too," I whispered, and crept into his arms.

He didn't try to hold me or make me feel trapped in any way. He let me go to him. Let me slowly relax against the solid wall of his chest. Let me rest my head down on his shoulder. "You complete me, too. Don't ever leave me."

"No, love. I won't." He kissed the top of my head, a soothing and comforting gesture.

I rested against him and felt the reassuring beat of his heart. Felt my own rhythm match his. Felt old stagnant fear wash away and new desire flow in and take its place. This was Stefan—my love. The beacon that drew me to my new life, one that had began even before my rebirth.

He called to my heart, as he always had, since the first time my eyes fell upon him. And his blood, so tantalizingly close to me, called up my dormant hunger. A thirst for blood stirred awake within me and drowsily stretched, lengthening out my fangs. I hadn't drank blood for several days now, just eaten food, something that had been worrying my men.

I nuzzled Stefan's throat. Played the sharp tips of my fangs lightly across his pale, white skin.

He groaned, tensing against me. "Lucinda . . ." he murmured as the flow of his blood quickened to an even more tantalizing beat.

I stood and pulled him to his feet.

"No," he protested. "You're hungry. Feed from me. I want you to."

"I want me to, also." I smiled and pushed him back against the trunk of the tree. "But I want more than just your blood. Loosen your pants for me," I whispered, and licked my tongue over his beating pulse.

"Lucinda." He said my name again, but more cautiously. "We don't have to—"

"I want to," I said with a smile that kicked up the rhythm of his heart even more.

"We can wait."

"I don't want to wait."

"Maybe you should just take my blood," he suggested in a strained voice.

"Hush." I brushed his lips lightly with mine, and removed my clothes, quick and efficient. "Please," I whispered in his ear, pressing my bare flesh against him, "I need you."

Laving my tongue over his beating pulse again, I drew the deep rich scent of him into my lungs.

"I don't want to hurt you," he said.

"You won't."

"Or frighten you."

"You won't! Please, Stefan."

With a tortured groan, he finally nodded, and—glory hallelujah!—loosened his pants. His organ sprang free. When I didn't shriek or jerk back from him in horror, he kicked off his pants and removed his shirt.

He was gorgeous. Breathtakingly beautiful. All of him. Nothing repulsive, nothing to be frightened of. And he desired me—the bold, rampant length of him, bobbing upright, was irrefutable evidence of that.

He wanted me. He loved me. He didn't want to frighten me. And that sweet, tender concern softened not only my heart but my body, so that my arousal perfumed the air as wet dew slicked my secret passageway.

I sank my sharp nails down into the bark, caging him against the tree. Out of sight, my claws extended further, embedding into the hard depth of the wood. Pulling myself up, I wrapped my legs around him, and sank down on him, taking him into me with a soft, purring groan.

He ceded control to me, his hands at his sides, his body still and trembling, growing luminescent with light, his heart speeding, his breathing fast and ragged now as I began to move myself slowly up and down his length.

It wasn't until I bit him, punctured my fangs deep into his tender neck and started drinking down his rich, powerful Monère blood, that he cried out, jerked against me.

I hummed with pleasure, the vibration of my mouth spilling inside him and mixing with the wash of sensation

I let flow out of me and into him like an ambrosia splash of ecstasy.

My body stilled as I drank him down, spurring him into motion—a surging dance of his hips moving against me; noises pulled from his throat. Hot washes of sweet blood. Rapture spreading in us both until it crested and he arced and grew still and spilled inside me.

His release triggered my own, a sweet and blissful shattering that pumped through me like the pulse of his blood.

Retracting my claws, I pulled my nails out of the tree, and without my anchoring hold, we slid down until we rested against the base of the trunk, my legs wrapped around Stefan, him still inside me.

The last of Myrddhin's ghost, one I hadn't even known had been hiding inside me, drifted out in a wisp of white and dissolved.

And the wound inside of me healed.

TWENTY-SIX

R URIC RAN THE entire eleven miles into town.
   Bounding through the forest was the easy part, the
fun part—sheer exhilarating speed. Concealment was not
an issue; he was going too fast for people to see. It was only
when he reached town that it became more difficult, especially since it was daylight. He didn't have Hari's ability to
disappear or Lucinda's camouflaging gift of glamour. His
gift was more of a deflection, a blurring and repelling ability, so that when human eyes landed on him, they skidded
away without consciously noting what they had seen. He
used that ability now to cloak himself as he moved, track-
ing Mary's scent.

   It had been over a week since he had seen her. He had
unexpectedly missed her—her sweet voice and feisty spirit.
The wonderful, casual way she spoke to him, touched him,
even hit him, without fear.

He trailed her fresh scent to a small café. She was sitting at a table near the window front, sipping tea, eating a croissant. The sight of her, safe and unharmed, dispelled his disquiet. She looked so peaceful and beautiful, a young and vibrant life.

He could have watched her without making his presence known, but he wanted to be closer to her. Wanted to see her smile at him, or scowl at him, if she wished to. And a thought, a possibility had occurred to him. Something that he needed to confirm or invalidate.

Uncloaking himself, Ruric opened the door and several pairs of human eyes glanced his way, widening. Several customers hastily left, clearly heeding the aura of danger that clung to him. But Mary remained oblivious, even when he stopped by her table and spoke to her, making her aware of his presence.

"You repaired your glasses," he said in his deep bass rumble.

Mary's empty gaze swung up and a smile lit her face. "Ruric, is that you?"

He nodded, relieved she no longer seemed upset at him, then remembered she couldn't see the gesture and said, "Yes."

"Join me. Sit down."

Obediently he pulled out a chair and gingerly sat across from her, setting his gloved hands on the table. The chair creaked and groaned in protest but thankfully held his weight.

"It's been a week since we bumped into each other," she said with a small smile.

"I had matters to attend to."

She waited but nothing more was forthcoming. "Wow, you just talk so much I can't get you to shut up about yourself."

He flushed. "I do not often have much to say."

"That's okay," she said, her lips quirking. "I can talk enough for the both of us."

Some of his tension faded beneath her easy manner, and he sensed it then—what he had suspected, hoped for.

Mary was a Mixed Blood.

It was so small a trace it was almost unnoticeable, unless you looked past the surface distraction of her blindness to what lay beneath in her blood. No more than a quarter of her blood was Monère, maybe even less—the reason why none of them had detected it before. But it was there, a faint and unmistakable signature. It explained how she was able to compensate for her blindness so deftly. Her loss of sight had probably triggered her other non-human senses into play. It also explained why she was able to detect everyone but the demon dead among them. Even full-blooded Monère had a hard time sensing demons.

Ruric stood up abruptly, scraping his chair back. "I must go."

"Oh." A look of disappointment crossed her face. "More matters you must attend to, I guess."

"Yes."

"Okay. Well, maybe I'll bump into you again. Though not literally, I hope," she said with a small teasing smile.

"Likely not. I do not come often into town," Ruric said gravely. Not in the daytime, at least. He paused, hesitated, then walked away, heavy with the knowledge that this would probably be the last time he ever spoke to her.

∽

"MARY, THE BLIND girl, is a Mixed Blood," Ruric told the others later that afternoon. Lucinda and Stefan were back. Jonnie had returned a short time after them.

"How do you know?" Nico asked, stretching and yawning. He had just risen from bed, earlier than his usual time, stirred awake by the others' return.

"I went into town and saw her," Ruric answered.

Nico frowned. "I didn't even know you were gone."

"You went into town?" Lucinda said with surprise.

Ruric's eyes dropped to the ground. "Forgive me, Princess. I should have asked your permission."

"Don't be silly, Ruric. You don't need to ask my permission. What you do in your own free time is your business as long as you abide by the rules I set. But we could have dropped you off had we known you wanted to go into town. We were going that way anyway." The idea of him running outside in sunlight clearly bothered her.

"The possibility of the girl being a Mixed Blood only occurred to me after you had left," he explained quietly.

"Where did you guys go today?" Jonnie asked curiously.

"To the supermarket," Lucinda answered. Not a complete lie. They had indeed stopped by to purchase a few quick items on the way back home.

"So what's so important about her being a Mixed Blood?" Jonnie asked.

"If she's a Mixed Blood," Ruric said gravely, "she might be able to be cured of her blindness."

"How?" Nico asked, intrigued.

"By mixing a few drops of Monère blood with her blood. Like Jonnie."

There was a moment of stunned silence as they took in what he was suggesting.

"I don't see how that will help her," Jonnie said. "The boost in my senses that I gained from Stefan's blood only lasted a few days before it wore off."

"Your wounds healed," Ruric pointed out. "Mary eyes might be able to heal their underlying damage, the way Jonnie's skin healed without scar or blemish. If so, she would continue to see, even after the enhancement of her senses wore off."

Stefan considered the idea thoughtfully, "This would have to be done without her awareness."

"If we go to her at night," Ruric suggested, "it would be easy for me to keep her in a deep sleep state and heal her wound afterward. There would be no evidence of what we did. If she regained her sight, she would never know the reason why." Thereby keeping their secret.

Stefan glanced questioningly at Lucinda.

"As long as our secret remains safe," Lucinda said, "I see no reason not to try this."

And so it was agreed and carried out that very evening in the late twilight hours of the night. They followed Mary's scent to a small ground-floor apartment where she lived alone. Using compulsion, Ruric kept her deeply immersed in sleep as he sliced a shallow cut on her arm with his nail.

Nicking the tip of his finger with his dagger, Stefan squeezed a few drops of his blood into her wound.

Ruric waited several seconds to allow the mixing of their blood, then sealed his mouth over the wound and injected the healing agent. A moment later, her skin knit together, smooth and whole.

They slipped out as silently as they had entered.

"Will you see her again?" Stefan asked once they were back inside the car.

"Not if she regains her sight."

"Why? It's obvious you care for her."

"If she regains her sight," Ruric said slowly, "she can

have a normal life, find a human to love. She is . . . too fragile for me."

Hard to argue with that.

They drove home in silence.

❧

T HE NEXT MORNING, Mary opened her eyes, and for the first time in her life saw things with sharp, vivid clarity.

My God, she could see!

She traced the blue and yellow design of her blanket with a trembling finger. Touched the smooth brown wood of her bedside table.

Color. Pattern. Precious detail.

The doctors and specialists Mary eventually saw couldn't explain the sudden restoration of her sight. They shook their heads and called it a miracle.

TWENTY-SEVEN

T HE REAL MIRACLE occurred several days later.
      I had contacted Mona Cara, a neighboring Queen.
My tiny province bordered the western part of her terri-
tory. Had been an original part of it, actually, before High
Court had broken off that little piece and given it to me.

The previous Queen who had ruled there had been
coolly distant and wary of me; we had coexisted by pretty
much ignoring each other. She stayed out of my territory,
and I passed lightly through hers. This new Queen, Mona
Cara, was a nice surprise, readily and graciously agreeing
to allow Nico and Stefan to Bask with her and her people.
So here we were the night of the full moon.

A tingle passed through me as I walked into their circle
of power set deep in the woods and stepped into the clearing where a Queen gathered her people every month to
draw down the rich, life-renewing rays of the moon. Oddly,

unexpectedly, I could *feel* the lunar energy soaked into the ground from countless centuries of Basking. Spilled power drawn down by Monère Queens in an unending, unbroken chain.

Mona Cara was much younger than her predecessor had been, and far perkier, if one could say such a thing about a Queen. She smiled at me and my men, which was just Stefan and Nico; we had left the others at home. Didn't want to scare the nice Queen off the first time Basking by bringing Ruric with us. Ruric had stayed home to baby-sit Jonnie. Pretty much my role tonight also. No way was I going to send Stefan and Nico alone into a strange new Queen's territory. I might not be as big and scary as Ruric, but I could be as formidable a foe as he, maybe even more because I came clothed in attractive sheepskin. I didn't *look* like the big bad demon I was. But if anyone threatened my men, I was more than ready to kick ass. Of course, I didn't tell Nico and Stefan that. My reasoning to them was that I had wanted to meet and greet this new neighbor Queen, that it wouldn't be polite to just send them in alone this first time. They thought I was being diplomatic. Hah! Yeah, right.

On second thought, once I got past the knee-jerk rejection, I guess I *was* being diplomatic. We were all spiffed up and had even come bearing a present: a simple, elegant black dagger made for me by one of Hell's finest demon craftsman.

Mona Cara was delighted by the present. "It's lovely," she said, the amazed expression on her face telling me that she fully realized the significance of the gift. No Monère had ever been gifted with such fine demoncraft before. "I am honored."

"I am indebted to you for this service to my men," I returned with a small dip of my head. Gee, maybe I had a future in demon-Monère politics after all. I was being as kiss-ass polite and proper as any official. But hey, she was doing me a huge favor. And it wasn't as if I was giving her demon blood. Now *that* was a definite no-no. Anything else was fair game—or gift—as far as I was concerned.

It wasn't until we gathered within the Basking circle that I grew jittery. It wasn't so much the large crowd of Monère that gazed nervously upon us, but the fact that I suddenly felt it—the moon. Round and ripe, hanging above us like a giant Christmas tree ornament pinned up in the sky, glowing and shimmering, eagerly waiting to spill down upon us. I had lost that connection, that awareness, of the moon when I had died and become demon dead over six centuries ago. But I felt it now. And when Mona Cara called the light down, I felt it even more: a tugging, pulling sensation deep within me. Different yet similar to what I had once felt as a Monère Queen.

As the lunar light hit her, a tiny bit of it spilled over into me. And that taste, that familiar taste of power and light, opened up something inside of me that connected above with the full, ripe moon. It *sensed* me, *recognized* me, and beamed down a separate ray of lunar light that washed into my demon-dark skin with shimmering incandescence, lighting me up until I glowed like a gold lightbulb, filling me up so much until it felt as if it would burst out of me, and then it did, spilling, flowing into Stefan and Nico standing beside me, while next to me Mona Cara bathed her people in another blanket of lunar light. You could see that my Basking light was a different color than hers: dark streaks were mixed within the glowing light.

Then it was done. What came down from heaven, from the moon, was no more, and the bodies that had been lit with incandescent shine—scores upon scores of Monères . . . and one very surprised demon—drank the luminous energy of the light into themselves, and skin became normal skin once more and no longer glowed.

"Well," Mona Cara said with a breathless, giddy laugh. "I guess you won't be needing to come here anymore. Can I still keep the present?"

"Absolutely," I said, feeling as giddy and light-filled as her.

"Sweet Goddess," Mona Cara said with a crooked smile. "Wait until the other Queens hear about this."

EPILOGUE

RURIC AND I went back to Hell to recharge—more him than me. I think I could have gone a couple of weeks longer. My battery seemed to be of a different construct now since I had been reborn. Not wholly demon anymore, but not quite Monère either. I seemed to be a mix of both— demon dead tossed with living Monère into one unusual smorgasbord of a salad. My heart beat like a Monère, but I didn't need to breathe. I still looked like a demon, lacked scent like one, but I had a beating heart. It slowed down quite a bit in Hell, but didn't still into silence.

Talon was happy to see us. Hari, too, even though he was a bit overwhelmed and frustrated by his new charges.

Talon and Sarai had gotten a chance to know each other better—mother and son bonding. A different sort of tie than what we had but just as strong a connection in its own way.

Speaking of strong, I guess that word could apply quite nicely to Talon's mother. Hence Hari's frustration. He and Sarai butted heads loudly and frequently, arguing with each other worse than any mated couple I'd ever seen. With Talon and Brielle, Sarai was gentle and patient. With Hari, or any other male, she was abrasive and rude. Only the High Lord she treated with cool respect. All other males, excepting her son, felt the blisteringly sharp lash of her tongue and temper.

There were tears in the eyes of both mother and son when Talon returned back home with us to the living realm. And maybe even tears in Hari's eyes, though these were more of the *please-don't-leave-me-with-her* kind. Because Sarai was talking of returning to her people, not for a happy reunion but rather to seek revenge. Sarai was certain that one of the Floradëurs, maybe even one of her close kin, had betrayed her and her mate into that demon ambush those many years before. Remembering the hostile reception Talon had received from them the last time, and how we had barely escaped with our skins, Hari was vehemently opposed to the idea.

I was surprised when Ruric returned with Talon and me. I had expected him to stay down in the familiar, comfortable realm of Hell, a demon's natural home. Mary, the human girl who had so captured his interest, could see now, even after the temporary effect of Stefan's Monère blood subsided. His mission had been accomplished. And he remained adamant in his desire to stay out of her human life.

I gave Ruric the option of returning to his former position as my father's senior guard, but he declined and returned topside with us.

Ruric never spoke to Mary again. I would have known.

I would have smelled her scent on him. But even though he never got close enough to talk to her, I didn't doubt that he was still keeping an eye over his human. He went off alone on occasion, returning without word of where he had been.

I thought he was being stupid and stubborn and more than a little afraid—that she would reject him, his brutish, ugly appearance, now that she could see. But who was I to argue how the big, taciturn demon lived out his existence. Life was already complicated enough for me. Complicated and wonderful.

Maybe the miracle wasn't being reborn or being able to Bask once again. Maybe the true miracle was a demon finding love, and holding on to it.

AND NOW A SPECIAL EXCERPT FROM
MELJEAN BROOK'S SEDUCTIVE AND
DANGEROUS WORLD OF THE GUARDIANS

DEMON FORGED

Available now from Berkley Sensation!

ONCE UPON A time, all roads led to Rome. As a human girl, Irena had been marched into Rome on the Via Salaria, as frightened by the imposing city walls as she had been of the shackles binding her mother's wrists. Frightened—and forbidden the comfort of remembering the home that had lain at the beginning of their journey. They hadn't been allowed to look back; all that lay ahead of a conquered people was service to the Empire.

Twelve years later the Visigoths had sacked the city, and Irena had escaped by the same road. She'd looked back then, but only because she'd hoped to see Rome burning behind her.

It hadn't. To Irena's bitter disappointment, the barbarians had shown restraint. Although fires had lit the nighttime sky, the city hadn't been consumed by flames.

Time consumed it, instead. Over sixteen hundred years, all that Irena had known of Rome slowly crumbled. In another sixteen centuries, the celebrated remnants of the Empire might collapse into nothing. Humans labored to preserve and restore the ruins, but Irena wouldn't be sorry when they were gone. She preferred what had risen in their place.

Now, as she jogged across the Via Salaria, she relished the feel of smooth concrete beneath her leather soles rather than paving stones under bare feet. Automobiles with their blinding headlights and blaring horns swerved to avoid her. One driver shouted obscenities, and Irena grinned at him through the windshield. One of the few things she'd liked about Rome had survived—and Italians were still inventive.

Irena suspected she'd soon be coming up with a few curses of her own.

The vampire she was scheduled to meet at the nearby Piazza Fiume shouldn't have been here. Not in Rome. Less than a year ago, the nephilim had slaughtered every vampire within the city. The demons might still be here, hidden within the bodies of their human hosts and shielding their psychic scents.

The nephilim still might be here . . . but they weren't just demons, Irena reminded herself, and her amusement leached from her thoughts, leaving them sour and dark. The nephilim had come from Hell, but they hadn't been created when Lucifer and his angel comrades had rebelled against Heaven and been transformed into demons. No, the nephilim were the offspring of two demon-spawned grigori who'd once called themselves Guardians.

There were *still* other grigori who called themselves Guardians. Until a few weeks ago, Irena would have fought to the death for one of them: Michael—the first Guardian, and their leader.

She would not die for him now.

Michael hadn't explained why he'd lied about his parentage for millennia, or why he'd written in the Scrolls that he'd been human before slaying the Chaos dragon. Not that an explanation was necessary. As the son of Belial and a human woman, Michael was half demon—and lies were as natural to demons as their scales and horns.

Since she'd learned the truth, Irena couldn't make herself trust or believe in him. Not while Belial's blood ran through his veins.

But although she'd lost faith in the Doyen, she was still a Guardian. Still believed that every demon and nosferatu needed killing, that humans—and some vampires—needed protecting. And she would have met with Deacon even if the vampire hadn't been a friend.

A friend, but not close enough to know what this part of Rome had meant to her. She'd never told Deacon that she remembered the walls when they hadn't been ruins, and the gate that had opened Rome to the Via Salaria. This meeting and location had nothing to do with her past. And she could have avoided this road and the memories associated with it by flying directly to the piazza, but she'd wanted to be reminded of the changes in the city. She wanted the stink of exhaust burning her nostrils, rather than the stink of bodies and animals and waste.

And she'd wanted to see the metal. So much metal.

Yes, she liked what had risen—and *who* had risen. Whether they lived here or were tourists fascinated by the past, humans experienced the same emotions they always had, but they governed those emotions differently. There were still too few with too much power, but despite the corruption at its foundation, the civilization that humanity had built was impressive.

Impressive, but not perfect. There were always exceptions, large and small.

On the sidewalk ahead of her, beside the entrance to a wine bar, a small exception slouched at a wrought iron table. His jacket and shirt were unbuttoned despite the crisp autumn evening, and a medallion winked from a bed of dark hair. Empty wine bottles stood next to an overflowing ashtray.

His bleary eyes sharpened as they fixed on Irena. *"Mi sento come un buon pompino. Quanta puttana?"*

How much? She studied his face as she drew nearer, and dug into his emotions—arrogance, overblown machismo, a need to humiliate, a sharp loneliness—but she was unable to summon either pity or disgust.

And she felt no surprise at his suggestion. No matter the century, there were always men like this. Men who would see the brief top she wore, the cling of the soft suede from her hips to her upper thighs beneath the belt and straps of her leather stockings, the face that had aroused a Roman senator before she'd reached her ninth summer, and assume rights they didn't have.

At least this one offered to pay—and she'd known too many whores to be insulted when mistaken for one. She dismissed him, and her gaze moved on. Ahead, a fenced monument marked the Piazza Fiume.

The human's derisive command returned her attention to him.

"Venite a succhiare il mio cazzo." He cupped his crotch, jiggling his hand as if Irena were a horse and his balls a bag of oats. His mouth slid into a leer. *"E si inghiottire troppo."*

At that, Irena smiled. She would swallow—but only if she bit off a chunk first.

She didn't need to tell him so; her expression served as a reply. He dropped his gaze to his table.

Cowed, but not quieted. Even if she hadn't heard the word he muttered as she reached him, its shape was unmistakable on his lips. *"Stronza."*

Bitch.

Irena's breath hissed from between her teeth in a thin stream. This one, he did not know when to quit. She halted in front of him and bent over to grip the arms of his chair. Her smile was still vicious, but he didn't glance at her face. Unease slithered through his psychic scent as he took in the winding blue serpents tattooed from her wrists to her shoulders.

"You are a handsome man," she told him, and didn't attempt to suppress the accent that chopped at her Italian, "but you use your tongue in the wrong way." Irena crooked her index finger beneath his necklace. Gold. Such a worthless metal. Far too soft, even when blended with stronger materials. Irena favored steel, iron, or platinum. She tugged lightly on the chain. "Stand, and I will show you what your mouth is good for."

Like a dog, he obeyed. Her fingers drifted down over his chest as he rose from his seat, and she shape-shifted subtly, increasing her height so that his tobacco-scented breath gusted heavily over her lips. His breathing stopped when she reached the waistband of his tight jeans, and she paused to test his emotions. Fear trembled in him, lust also.

And this one had no resistance to lust. Even as his flesh hardened beneath her hand, his arousal left him as malleable as gold. Left him easily manipulated. Demons loved humans such as these.

Irena did not.

She dragged her fingertip up his brass zipper, and her Gift melded the teeth together.

The human wouldn't sense the psychic touch. If Deacon had already reached their meeting spot, however, he would know she was near.

And if she'd revealed herself to any other creatures who might be in Rome, she looked forward to meeting them. Killing them.

Excitement fermented within her, and she imagined rending a demon's crimson skin when she placed her mouth to the male's. The flesh behind his zipper swelled as her tongue slid over his, pulling, sucking.

He reached for her chest and she stepped back. He panted, his eyes glazed.

She wiped his taste from her lips with the back of her hand, leaving a sneer. "Not good for much, after all."

His face reddened. Rage choked him; she'd turned away and walked half a block before he managed to roar *"Stronza!"* after her.

She continued on. The insult did not anger her so much now that a plea lay beneath it. A small-minded man, frustrated by such a small thing.

He would know true frustration as soon as he sought release for his bladder or his arousal.

Her good mood was restored and her steps were lively as they carried her to the piazza. The evening was cold and clear; on the tundra, this was the kind of night when only the sharp, freezing air separated the earth from the heavens. A night for hunting. All that this moment lacked was the use of her blades. But if a nephilim or demon had felt her Gift, perhaps bloodshed wasn't far off. She couldn't detect any nearby, but they could block their minds and hide from her psychic probes.

She *had* expected to find Deacon—a vampire's mind wasn't as powerful as a Guardian's, and his shields weaker—but she didn't sense him, either. Only humans.

She rounded the stone blocks at the corner of the monument, her gaze sweeping the piazza. It froze near the monument entrance. A tall male stood in front of the iron gate. His dark eyes met hers.

Olek.

Her step didn't falter. She didn't betray her surprise with movement or breath, but her heart became a sledgehammer against her ribs. Did it pound with anger, shame, or need?

It did not matter. With Olek, they were all the same.

He was Alejandro to every other Guardian, but always Olek to her. Try as she might—and she *had* tried—she couldn't think of him as anything else.

Olek, the silk-tongued swordsman whose idea of honor was to die for nothing.

Like Irena, he dressed not in modern clothing, but clothing comfortable to him. A black long-sleeved shirt hugged his torso, loose enough to allow movement but leaving little for an enemy to grab. His fitted trousers were tucked into knee-high boots. She knew their soles were as soft as hers—and as sure-footed. Both she and Alejandro would sacrifice a hardened boot and the damage a heel could inflict in order to feel every aspect of the ground beneath their feet.

Old-fashioned garb, but it hardly drew a second glance from the humans milling near the monument with cameras in hand. There had been centuries when Guardians had been careful to blend; these days, almost anything was acceptable, if unconventional. For all Irena knew, her leather leggings and the ragged cut of her auburn hair might have even been fashionable.

Alejandro's haircut was severe. Gone were the overlong, thick curls that he'd worn when she'd met him. Now his dark hair was short, with edges as sharp as his face. It was not a style that invited a touch.

And she hated her desire to comb her fingers through it. She refused to clench her fists against the urge.

Alejandro was as controlled as she. He held his lean body still and his mouth in a firm, immobile line.

Her gaze rested on the sharp point of his beard. She had seen his facial hair diminish over time, according to human custom, until it was short and tight. The beard no longer extended past his chin; the mustache curved just past the corners of his wide mouth. A devil goatee, her young friend Charlie had once called it.

The description was more accurate than Charlie knew.

Irena pushed away the memory of a silken brush against her inner thigh, of heated lips. Pushed away the anger, shame, need.

"Alejandro," she said deliberately.

Dark and unwavering, his gaze lifted from her mouth. "You tread near a line that cannot be uncrossed, Irena."

With the human whose zipper she'd ruined. Any Guardian who broke the Rules by killing a human or denying his free will had to Fall or Ascend. But kissing a man without his consent didn't interfere with his free will—only kissing one who resisted did.

"Did he refuse my touch? Attempt to escape?" With his Guardian senses, Alejandro would have heard everything that transpired between her and the male.

Alejandro didn't reply with words or a change of expression.

"Obviously he did not," she continued with a shrug as light as the French on her tongue. There was no reason to feel defensive. Yet she did, and resented it—she wanted to strike at him for it. She turned and examined the piazza again. "Has Deacon already come and gone?"

"No."

Irena frowned. Deacon hadn't known how to contact her; she hadn't met with him since she'd begun using the satellite phone that allowed other Guardians to reach her no matter where she traveled. But the American law enforcement agency, Special Investigations, had made itself known to vampire communities worldwide, offering them the Guardians' protection against the nephilim, demons, and nosferatu. Deacon had called SI and asked for Irena specifically. The text message had come through her phone—sent by Lilith, the hellspawn directing the agency . . . and who often directed Alejandro, as well.

And if Alejandro had come, he must have thought *she* wouldn't have.

"I would never shirk my duty," Irena said.

"You shirked it when you didn't respond."

He left the rest unspoken: that, because this was Rome, whatever Deacon had to tell them might be critical in the Guardians' fight against the nephilim. SI couldn't assume she'd received Deacon's request. They had to be certain.

She met his gaze again. "I don't answer to hellspawn. Send the message yourself, or have another Guardian or vampire do so. Then I'll respond."

Alejandro's dark eyes glinted with emotion before he concealed it. Did she anger him? She wanted to, but wasn't sure if she had. Reading his face was impossible. His only reply was a short nod.

"Have you sensed Deacon?" she asked.

"No."

"Any other vampires?"

"None."

The flash of a tourist's camera whitened the right side of Alejandro's face. Even in shadow Irena could clearly see his features, but the burst of light made her realize how her gaze had been tracing the angular lines of his cheekbones, his jaw.

She looked away, scanning the square. Their reflection in a passing vehicle window revealed that Alejandro still watched her.

Always, he watched her. She didn't know what he searched for.

Even pinched by the French, Alejandro's voice tugged over her nerves like fine kid gloves, tight and supple. "You will recognize this vampire?"

"Yes."

"You know him well?"

"Well enough," she answered simply, though Alejandro would want more than that. After a moment of silence, she gave it to him. "Forty years ago, I tracked a rogue vampire near Prague. He'd already murdered several humans. I caught him and returned him to his community."

"You didn't slay the rogue yourself?"

No, she'd wanted to see what sort of community it was. "I let them decide the proper punishment. Deacon leads them, and he carried it out." Once Deacon learned of the murders, he hadn't hesitated to execute the rogue. It was one of the reasons Irena liked the vampire so much. "I return now and again to see that all is well with him."

And the last time she'd visited, all *had* been well. Why, then, had Deacon come to Rome? Had he brought the entire community?

She couldn't believe he'd be so foolish.

The nephilim, led by the demon-spawn Anaria—one of the grigori, and Michael's sister—intended to overthrow Lucifer's throne in Hell and enslave human free will in the name of Good. And, because of a prophecy that predicted the nephilim's destruction by vampire blood, the nephilim had been killing vampires, one city at a time. Just because the nephilim had already slaughtered the vampires in Rome didn't mean the city was safe for others to move in.

Not remotely safe. And Irena was beginning to worry now.

Relief replaced her concern when a man with a farrier's shoulders came out of a hotel several blocks down the road. "There he is," she told Alejandro. "Black hair, dark gray suit."

A wrinkled suit, as if he'd spent his daysleep in it. His white shirt was untucked and half unbuttoned. Peach lipstick stained the collar. Deacon pushed his fingers through his shoulder-length hair, tying it into a queue as he walked.

"Are those your swords that he wears?" Alejandro asked quietly.

"Yes." Vampires had no mental cache to store their weapons, so Irena had designed Deacon's short swords to be concealed beneath his clothing, yet still easily accessible. Deacon carried the swords in sheaths that crossed between his shoulder blades; he only had to reach behind his waist for the handles. When he lifted his arms, as he was doing now, the grips disturbed the line of his jacket over his hips.

His hair and clothing rumpled—who had he been with? The vampire was upwind. Irena tested the air, and caught the odor of alcohol, sex, and blood mixed with Deacon's individual scent.

Human blood.

He'd fed from a *human* woman? Irena did not like this. She had not expected this. What had forced him to use a human?

Vampires were slaves of a different sort: to bloodlust. The accidental offshoot of the nosferatu, their existence was the result of an attempt—a failed attempt—to honor a proud and strong girl. Though nosferatu and vampires both burned in the sun, the similarities ended there. Vampires, though stronger than humans, were much weaker than nosferatu. And although nosferatu suffered from bloodlust, they didn't need to feed to survive; vampires had to regularly consume living blood. Drinking it from humans threatened exposure, however, and so vampire communities required their members to find a vampire partner—or partners—to feed them.

Where were Deacon's partners? He wouldn't have left them behind. Eva and Petra didn't just share blood with him; the two vampires were his friends and lovers, as well.

Yet they must not be with him if he'd used alcohol. Vampires weren't affected by the drink. But after a human drank enough, she'd probably forget that a vampire had fed from her. Even if she did remember, a few drops of vampire blood would heal the bite and erase evidence of it.

From behind her, Alejandro said, "I trust that, despite the drink, she was willing."

Irena clenched her teeth. Though Alejandro employed polite words and phrases, he was lying; he didn't trust it.

She slid her right hand behind her back, and used the Guardian's sign language to reply. *Of course she was willing. Deacon knows the Rules.*

Although vampires weren't bound to follow the Rules as Guardians and demons were, Irena had made it clear to Deacon that if he didn't she would slay him. Feeding wasn't the same as hurting or killing humans, however. Guardians would tolerate his drinking from human women if he had no other option.

On silent feet, Alejandro came to stand beside her. *Willing to invite him into her bed* and *to take her blood?*

Irena gave him a disbelieving look. When a woman invited a man into her body, what did it matter if, in addition to her mouth and her sex, he also tasted her blood?

"You split too many hairs, Olek."

"You clump them all together."

And that, Irena thought, was the difference between them: details. She refused to focus on them.

There was a saying in English that the devil lay in the details—the little flaws brought down the whole. And that was exactly how the demons worked: focusing on the details, boring at tiny weaknesses until the entire structure was so brittle it collapsed. They talked in dizzying circles until nothing was left of meaning, and only their purpose remained. They smoothed everything with slick words, until nothing was left to grasp.

Irena preferred rough edges, even though they scraped and tore. But Alejandro, he was all sleek speed and elegance, from his words to his body. The leopard to her bear, the fox to her wolverine. Solitary predators who avoided one another, respecting too well the teeth and claws of the other—and when they couldn't keep apart, they ripped pieces from one another in passing.

Wounded predators, she admitted . . . and wounds were weaknesses. Irena had been trying to excise hers for centuries. But this one wouldn't heal, so she tried to ignore the pain.

And Alejandro was correct: she did lump many things together. But wounded predators were also dangerously short-tempered, so she gave him no response but a sneer before heading across the piazza to meet Deacon.

Olek did not follow her.

She had not expected him to.

T HE FIRST TIME Alejandro had seen Irena, she'd been standing with a group of her friends on the opposite side of a courtyard in Caelum—the Guardian realm. It had been almost one hundred years after his transformation; although his training neared completion and he would soon return to Earth as a full-fledged Guardian, Alejandro had still been a novice.

And he'd known *of* Irena, who—at the time more than a thousand years of age—was one of the oldest Guardians. He'd known of her Gift to shape metal. He'd known she had created the exquisite swords he practiced with, and that Michael had assigned her to oversee Alejandro's final weapons specialization and his transition to Earth.

He'd known all of that, but he'd not yet met her.

And so he hadn't known who had mesmerized him with a single toss of her head, her long braids bright auburn beneath Caelum's sun. Hadn't known who had hardened his body with one shout of her loud, brash laughter. It had fallen silent when his gaze had caught hers. Without hesitation, she'd stridden toward him across the white marble square—just as she was walking toward Deacon now.

He'd been arrogant enough to think that she'd be impressed when he introduced himself. His talent with the swords had been praised by Guardians centuries older than he, and there were already predictions that, given another century, his skill would surpass Michael's. And when she'd said her name, he'd been bold enough to challenge her, to suggest there was nothing she could teach him.

She'd accepted his challenge. When she'd offered up a single dagger against his swords, he'd been foolish enough to imagine that she wanted to lose—that she wanted to be under him as badly as he wanted to sheathe himself within her.

Before ten seconds had passed, she'd had him laid out on the marble pavers with blood filling his mouth and his vision floating in and out of focus.

Until she'd straddled his waist and kissed him—then everything had become sharp and pointed, and devastatingly clear.

He'd still been reeling when she lifted her head and said, "When I am satisfied that your training is complete, I will take your body as I have just taken your mouth. Until that time, young Olek, there is only this. Only the fight."

Then she'd driven her dagger into his side, and chided him for letting his guard down.

It was fitting, Alejandro thought, that their only kiss had been flavored by blood and followed by pain.

Too much pain, because she'd been wrong: there hadn't just been the fight. There had been her laugh and her temper. Her unrelenting schedule, her unexpected moments of tenderness.

And there had been the days spent in her forge, where he discovered his Gift of fire complemented her affinity with metal. Where they'd created weapons, where firelight had danced across her pale skin. Where he'd pretended to study manuscripts, but watched over the pages as Irena shaped her intricate sculptures—where he'd posed for her more than once. And he'd trained tirelessly, waiting for the moment she was satisfied.

For months, there had only been swords and Irena—his heart, his life.

And with a single misstep and a demon's monstrous bargain, it had ended. Ended with the destruction of Alejandro's honor as she traded her body for his life. Ended with Irena holding the demon's head, his face a mirror image of Alejandro's. Ended with Alejandro walking into a bedroom whose iron walls had been decorated by blood, seeing what she'd done to the demon's body—and knowing how the demon must have used hers.

And he'd known that he'd failed her. Utterly failed her.

She'd cut off her braids one by one, tossed her hair and the demon's head onto the bed, and asked him to burn it all. Then she'd walked away without looking back.

Two centuries had passed before he'd seen her again.

In the two hundred years since, every infrequent encounter had been accompanied by his wish that he'd never laid eyes upon her. And with every encounter, it was an effort to tear his gaze away.

He made the effort now, turning to examine the memorial statue for a boy poet that stood beside a remnant of the ancient wall. Alejandro well remembered the gate that had once led into the city. It had already been falling to ruins in the late fifteenth century when, still a human, he'd journeyed to Rome. Now only a plaque marked the gate's former location, and it described how Roman slaves had opened the gate to the invaders who'd sacked the city. Irena, he knew, had been one of the slaves, serving in a senator's household.

In his human life, Alejandro hadn't been a senator, but almost the equivalent in the Spanish courts. Born into the position rather than elected—but still responsible for his people and his lands, even if it meant trying to protect them from the fanaticism of his king and queen. A politician, always maneuvering, staying a step ahead, making alliances with men he'd hated just to keep the long, dangerous fingers of the Inquisition from touching his people.

For years, he'd performed that subtle dance. Every movement was calculated. He'd married as one step, made alliances as another. And when a demon had outmaneuvered him, he'd died for it.

Irena's hatred for politicians almost burned as hot as her hatred for demons. Alejandro thought she had forgiven him for being one only because he'd died protecting his wife and children.

At the time, Alejandro's youngest son had almost been the same age as the poet memorialized here. All of his sons had grown into men, he prayed, but he only remembered them as boys. He had small statues of them in his cache— statues that Irena had made for him after he'd projected the image of his sons into her mind. She'd captured them perfectly, giving each figure details that were heartbreakingly realistic.

Even after five hundred years, he found it too painful to pull the statues out of his cache to look at them, but he took comfort knowing they were there.

Irena called out a loud greeting in Italian, and Alejandro's gaze returned to her as she threw her arms around the vampire's waist.

When in Rome, they all did as Romans do. Among the public, Guardians almost always spoke the local language. Unlike her French, Irena's Italian carried a Slavic accent, as it had when he'd heard her speak to the wastrel on the street.

And his body reacted in the same way as the wastrel's had.

In those months Alejandro had spent with Irena, she'd spoken Russian—but even then, her voice held the flavor of something older. And just as it was Guardian custom to speak the local tongue, so it was for a novice to speak the language of his mentor. Alejandro had defied custom, and answered her blunt commands in Spanish to signal that he'd had as much to show her, that he was her equal.

But after the demon's bargain, when they'd finally met again in Paris, she'd greeted him in French. But for his name, she'd spoken nothing but French to him since, and Alejandro had replied in no other language.

Four centuries had passed, yet he still responded to her husky accent. He listened for her every word and wished himself deaf. It was madness.

The vampire smiled as he returned Irena's embrace, but not enough to show his fangs. His broad hands splayed over the long muscles of her back, her pale skin bare but for the two leather ties that fastened her apron-like shirt. Over her head, Deacon's flat gaze targeted Alejandro.

The vampire didn't appear apprehensive. Perhaps Deacon didn't know Irena well enough to guess what was coming. Alejandro did, and he returned the vampire's stare until Deacon pulled back to look at Irena.

With a swift punch to Deacon's jaw, she laid the vampire out flat.

Yes. There was more than one reason Alejandro didn't often take his eyes off her.

SUNNY is a physician by training, and an author by lucky happenstance. A graduate of Vassar College and mother of two, this PRISM Award–winning author lives with her husband, author Da Chen, in New York's beautiful Hudson Valley. Please visit her website at www.sunnyauthor.com.

NOW AVAILABLE
from national bestselling author

SUNNY

Lucinda, Darkly

"The demon world has a new kick-ass heroine."
—*Fresh Fiction*

Lucinda, daughter of the High Lord of Hell, has endured centuries of eternal darkness with only the menial task of retrieving wayward demons and returning them to Hell. So when Stefan, a lone Monère warrior, offers himself to her, she finds herself desiring a new existence between the jealousy of the dead and the violence of the living.

penguin.com

M469T0509